Make Me Yours,
COWBOY

Dylann Crush

BERKLEY ROMANCE
New York

BERKLEY ROMANCE
Published by Berkley
An imprint of Penguin Random House LLC
penguinrandomhouse.com

Copyright © 2023 by Dylann Crush
Excerpt from *Kiss Me Now, Cowboy* copyright © 2022 by Dylann Crush
Penguin Random House supports copyright. Copyright fuels creativity, encourages
diverse voices, promotes free speech, and creates a vibrant culture. Thank you for buying
an authorized edition of this book and for complying with copyright laws by not
reproducing, scanning, or distributing any part of it in any form without permission.
You are supporting writers and allowing Penguin Random House to continue to
publish books for every reader.

BERKLEY and the BERKLEY and B colophon are registered
trademarks of Penguin Random House LLC.

ISBN: 9780593438756

First Edition: June 2023

Printed in the United States of America
1   3   5   7   9   10   8   6   4   2

Book design by Alison Cnockaert

To the country music artists who provide
much of the inspiration for the stories I write.
Thank you for sharing your talents.

1

Knox

Knox glanced at his phone as he headed into the glass-walled building that held his manager's office. Even though his publicist joked that he was a big enough star now that he didn't have to be on time, he still hated being late. The photo shoot his publicist had booked for him had run over, though, and he hadn't had time to head home and change before making the drive into downtown Austin for the meeting with Tripp.

The receptionist looked up when he passed through the entry. Her eyes widened in recognition, and she said something into the phone before hanging up.

"Mr. Shepler, it's nice to see you again."

Knox nodded. "Nice to see you again, Sienna."

"You know my name?" Her hand went to her chest, and Knox could almost see the heart clouds float from her eyes to hover over her head.

"Of course. I know the names of everyone on my team." He'd learned long ago that it was just as easy to be nice to people as it was to be a dick. And being nice got him a hell of a lot further in life, especially with people like Sienna, who didn't expect it.

"Come on back. Mr. Sanchez is expecting you." Sienna rounded the edge of her desk and led him through the closed double doors to the inner sanctuary of Sanchez Management.

Knox leaned forward to catch the door as she pushed through the doorway. He caught a whiff of something peppery as she passed. Her perfume made his nose itch, and he fought the urge to sneeze.

"There he is." Tripp Sanchez rose from his desk. "I'll take it from here, Sienna. Thank you."

She nodded and cast a longing glance toward Knox. Unfortunately, he was used to it. Even though the girls in high school wouldn't give him a second look, now he had more women throwing themselves at him than he'd ever imagined. Young ones, women old enough to be his mama or even his grandmother. Women of every shape and size propositioned him on a regular basis.

It's not like he wasn't ever tempted. He was a man, after all. Even though his heart had stopped working years ago, the rest of him still responded instinctively—sometimes embarrassingly—to a woman's advances.

He turned his attention away from the receptionist and focused on his manager. Tripp held out his hand and Knox took it.

"How's my favorite client doing today?" Tripp asked as he pumped Knox's hand up and down.

"I don't know. Tell me who he is, and I'll find out." Knox was joking, but there was a kernel of truth to it. Tripp was one of those guys who changed his mind faster than the weather in Texas could swing from one extreme to the other.

"Still cracking bad jokes, I see." Tripp gestured for Knox to take a seat at one of the chairs in front of his desk. "Tell me, how are the songs for the new album coming?"

Knox adjusted his cowboy hat as he leaned his back against the chair. "They're coming."

So what if he hadn't actually written a single, solitary word yet? He had some ideas about what he wanted to write. He just hadn't carved out the time to make it happen. Turns out people had missed him while he'd been on tour over the past year and a half. His mother expected him to catch up with everyone while at home.

Then there'd been Justin and Emmeline's wedding. It wasn't like he could have skipped that. He was just a little behind. With a little focus and some uninterrupted work time, he'd be able to come up with the material before the label needed it.

"I'm going to be honest with you here." Tripp eased into his chair. "The label's not sure about the direction you want to take the next album."

Knox had been waiting for this. He knew the label had a vision for his career. One that sounded a whole lot more like a sugar-coated rhinestone cowboy than the gritty, raw songs Knox wanted to hear on radio station playlists around the world.

"What do you mean?" Playing dumb might get him enough info to figure out the angle the label was working.

Tripp steepled his fingers under his chin. "I'm going to give it to you straight."

"By all means." Knox crossed his cowboy boots at the ankles.

"The label wants more of what you did on the last album." Tripp had broached the subject before, but Knox had avoided it.

The label wanted to turn him into the country-western version of a pop star. They'd even sent a stylist on tour with him who kept making gentle suggestions that he might want to cut his hair a certain way or wear a specific shirt that somehow found its way into his closet.

Halfway through his tour, they'd changed his opening act

from a guy with a voice like Hank Williams Jr. to a trio called the Strum Sisters. They sounded like a country-light version of Britney Spears and gyrated all over the stage in their matching glittered miniskirts. It took him two nights before he realized the women weren't really sisters. They just all wore the same long red wigs. It had fooled him from five feet away. He was pretty sure the public would never know the women weren't even related.

"What if I don't want to go in that direction?" Knox asked. He already knew the answer to that question as well. He'd used his first week at home to research attorneys.

"They can sue you for breach of contract." Tripp shrugged. "You get a bad rep for being a high-maintenance performer and possibly get blacklisted. I don't typically recommend that as a frontline strategy."

Knox figured as much. "So what do you recommend?"

"If you want to make music at the level you've been working at, you need to play by their rules."

"And that's your professional opinion?" Knox asked.

"You want to know what I think off the record?"

Knox nodded.

Tripp leaned forward. "Suck it up for another couple of years until you're so big even they can't touch you. Then you can do whatever the hell you want."

Another couple of years. Knox had heard the same refrain for most of his career. No matter where he was or who he was working with, everyone's advice seemed to be the same. Give it another couple of years. Don't quit now. You might only be one more gig away from being discovered.

Clearly the joke was on him. He'd been discovered, but the rules of the game hadn't changed with his success.

"What do you think?" Tripp's chair creaked as he leaned back and rested an alligator cowboy boot on his knee.

Knox could almost taste the greed in the air. Tripp had

stated his opinion. If Knox balked, he'd be on his own. Maybe there was room for a little bit of negotiation, though.

"If I give them more of what they want, can I have one single that's more in line with the direction I want to go in?" In the grand scheme of things, getting a say in one song was such a minor win. It probably didn't deserve to be classified as a victory at all. Surely the label wouldn't care as long as 99 percent of the album gave them their razzle-dazzle cowboy tunes.

Tripp took in a breath so deep that his shoulders lifted at least two inches. "I don't know what they'll say. They're behind you all the way, but I know they'll want to make sure whatever you put on this album is a solid fit with where they want to take this."

"Yeah, of course."

"It's that important to you?" Tripp asked. His eyes softened. But Knox wasn't about to mistake the look for Tripp having a moment of remorse. The man had suckered Knox in, probably knowing full well that he'd never be able to play the kind of music he wanted to once a label got ahold of him.

"You know it is." Knox cocked his head and ran his gaze over the gramophone-shaped awards lining the shelves. He'd hoped to have at least one of those on his mantel by now, but singing the watered-down crap he'd been forced to over the past couple of years would never earn him that kind of recognition.

"Let me see what I can do." Tripp rose from his chair, his lips spread into one of his wide got-you-exactly-where-I-want-you smiles.

"Thanks, man." Knox stood. Even without Tripp wearing his cowboy hat, Knox towered a good six inches over his manager. "I appreciate it."

"Though"—Tripp tapped his chin with his finger—"I bet they'd be a lot more willing to negotiate if they knew for a fact you were on the right track with the other songs."

Knox bet they would, too. "It's my top priority right now. I should have something to you soon."

"Great. You get me a song they'll go bananas over, and I'll make the ask." Tripp grinned like he'd just done Knox the biggest favor known to man.

Arguing any further would be a waste of time and energy. With a knot of defeat tightening deep in his chest, Knox clasped his manager's hand in a grip tight enough to make the man wince. "You'll have something soon."

"Fantastic." Tripp released his hand and headed to the door. "Sienna will show you out. I'll be looking forward to hearing what you come up with."

"You and me both," Knox muttered under his breath. When the office door closed behind him, he let out a huge exhale and adjusted the angle of his cowboy hat. It was time to get to work.

2

c⁓ ♡ ⁓ɔ

Claudia

Claudia wiped down the counter and tossed the rag in the sink. This time of year, they didn't get too many tourists at the beachside bar on Paradise Island. Except for the lack of tips, she didn't mind the off-season. It gave her a chance to slow down and try to relax. Nowadays, that meant losing herself in a good book or visiting the wild horse sanctuary where she'd been volunteering on her days off.

"I'm heading out," she yelled, loud enough for her boss to hear her, even through his closed office door.

The door creaked open. "Hey, hold up a minute. I want to talk to you about something," Chick said.

Claudia shoved her arms through the sleeves of her jacket while she waited for him to make his way down the stairs. "What's up?"

Chick pulled out a barstool and gestured for her to do the same. "What did we bring in today?"

Claudia angled the report she'd pulled from the register toward him, wishing there were at least another zero stacked before the decimal.

"Damn." Chick swiped his hand across his brow. "We need to figure out a way to pull people in."

She put her hand over his where it rested on the bar. "You say that every year. The winter months are hard, but come mid-March, this place will be busting at the seams with tourists."

"It feels different this year." Chick gazed up at her, worry reflected in his watery brown eyes. "I've been thinking about that offer the hotel chain made me for my stretch of sand—"

"Don't you dare." Claudia lifted her hand and slapped it back down on top of his.

"Wouldn't be my preference, but times have been a little tough lately."

"What about fixing up the bungalows and renting them out to tourists? We talked about doing that a while back. You'd make a killing."

"You mean besides the one you've been living in?" Chick eyed her over the top frame of his glasses.

"Well, naturally." When she'd shown up at Chick's bar four years ago, he'd offered her a job waiting tables that included room and board in one of the run-down beachside bungalows he'd bought along with the property. She'd fixed it up over the years, but there were several more just like it. Chick had never had the time to do much with them before, but if he needed to generate more income, that would be the best place to start.

"How much do you think it would take to get them ready for tourists?" he asked.

In her head, she ticked through a list of things that would need to be addressed. Besides the decorative touches, they all needed the plumbing and electricity checked out. "I don't know. Maybe a few grand each, plus the cost of new furniture."

"We could do the painting ourselves," Chick mumbled. "What's Antonio's bar bill sitting at right now?"

Claudia got up to check the ledger she kept under the bar "He's around three hundred as of last night." The handyman was a regular in the off-season. "Are you going to let him work it off in trade?"

Chick gave her a warm smile. "You know how this twisted old mind works."

"I'm pretty sure he'll go for it. Like you said, it's the slow season, so his business has been down, too." She flipped the ledger closed and studied Chick from across the bar. "You're not really thinking about selling, are you?"

A Cowboy in Paradise was legendary—at least to the several thousand tourists who flocked to Paradise Island each year. Not nearly as popular as South Padre Island, and not nearly as populated as Corpus Christi, Paradise was a well-kept secret and the perfect place for someone to leave the rest of the world behind and maybe even become someone new.

"I'd be lying if I told you the thought hasn't crossed my mind. Don't get me wrong, I love it here, but at some point, I might want to retire." Chick's bony shoulders rose and fell under the pearl-button western shirt.

"Running A Cowboy in Paradise *is* your retirement, remember?" Claudia joked.

Chick shook his head. "Just because I retired from bull riding half a lifetime ago doesn't mean I don't get to retire again."

She set her elbow down on the bar and cupped her chin in her palm. "So, you're like a cat with nine lives? Only you get to keep retiring as many times as you want?"

"Maybe. I kind of like that idea." The way his lips split and his eyes lit up was reward enough.

She'd always have a soft spot for Chick Darville. He'd saved her four years ago. No telling where she'd be if he hadn't taken her in, given her a job, and offered her a place to stay. When she'd arrived on Paradise Island, she'd been at the end of the line. Literally. She'd gotten in her shiny SUV and driven as far and as fast from Minneapolis as her all-weather tires could take her. She might have ended up in the Gulf if she hadn't stopped at a motel and heard someone talking about Paradise Island.

"Don't you dare sell to the hotel chain. If you decide it's time to move on, will you give me a chance to make you an offer first?" She glanced down at the bar as she softly said the words. There was no way she could afford it, not since she'd fled from her high-paying gig back in Minnesota. The thought of someone else taking over was almost terrifying enough for her to venture out of hiding and reconnect with a past colleague who might help her finance the place. A shiver rolled through her at the thought of asking for a favor. Only as a very last resort.

Chick tapped his gnarled fingers on the bar. "Don't worry. Nobody's making any big decisions tonight. Though I imagine if I decide to fix the bungalows, you'd be up for managing the project?"

"Of course." The tightness in her chest eased. Paradise had been her home for the past four years. It was a safe space where she didn't have to worry about anyone figuring out who she was, or more important, who her ex was. Four years ago, she dropped off the face of the earth. Deleted her social media accounts. Got a new phone number. Shut down her email.

She would have colored her hair, but her abuelita would roll over in her grave if Claudia touched the long, dark curls that came from her mama's side of the family.

"Let me think on it a spell, and we'll talk about it in a few days. How's that sound?" Chick nodded, his way of signaling the conversation had ended.

"Just let me know." She pushed off the bar, slung her bag over her shoulder, and rounded the bar.

"See you in the morning."

"Don't stay up too late," she said. Knowing Chick, he'd stay up past midnight watching reruns of *Bonanza* and be a bear in the morning.

"Don't worry about me. Have a good night."

She pulled the door shut behind her and turned into the salty mist blowing in from the ocean. Her bungalow was a short walk down the beach, but she headed in the opposite direction. Though she'd put in twelve hours behind the bar today, she still felt the need to stretch her legs. It wasn't like there was someone waiting on her to come home.

The sun had set, but the temperature, even in early February, was pretty mild. She shuddered when she thought about what the weather back home in Minnesota would be like right now. Her sister was the only person from her old life she kept in touch with, and she'd sent pictures of the recent snowstorm that had dumped fourteen inches on the Twin Cities.

Claudia fired back a photo of the sugar-sand beach along with an invitation for Andrea to come visit anytime. Though they talked on the phone at least once a day, Claudia hadn't seen her sister in person since the day she got onto I-35 and headed south. She wasn't about to go back to Minnesota under any circumstances, and Andrea wasn't inclined to travel with two kids and a third on the way.

Chick was pretty much her family now. He and the regulars who almost lived at the bar. The life she made for herself might not be the one she'd pictured, but it was enough. It had to be.

She leaned down to slip off her shoes, then picked them up and let them dangle from her fingers. The sand felt cold under her feet, but she didn't mind. This might be her favorite time of year on the island. The tourists were few and far between. Except for some snowbirds who migrated to the island to avoid the long winters in their northern home states, things were pretty quiet.

She stopped and faced the dark expanse of the ocean. Chick couldn't sell. Paradise Island was special. She'd seen it work its magic on everyone who needed it.

Everyone but her.

She might have found some sort of peace in Paradise, but she was still the broken woman who'd left an entire life behind. Not that she wanted that life anymore. She hadn't even recognized herself toward the end—before it all went to hell.

It might be nice to put down roots again, though. Find a place she wanted to call home for the rest of her life. Paradise Island might just be that place for her.

She'd have to do whatever it would take to keep Chick from selling.

3

Knox

Knox looked around the kitchen of the place Justin and Em had built right before their wedding. Even though he was happy for them, it was still weird thinking about two of his best friends marrying each other. Not so weird that it kept him from taking Em up on her invitation to come over for dinner. Tonight was the first night since the wedding that he, Justin, Em, and Decker had an opportunity to get together.

Emmeline shoved her hands into a pair of oven mitts and turned toward Knox. "Can you open the oven for me?"

"Sure." Knox lowered the door, then stepped back so she could reach in and pull out a casserole dish full of steaming hot enchiladas.

She blew a hunk of hair out of her eyes. "I hope these taste as good as they smell."

Knox waited until she'd moved away before closing the door. "You sure are looking very domestic."

Em laughed as she tossed an oven mitt at his head. "Hey, Justin does his fair share of cooking. You just happened to stop by on one of my nights to make dinner."

"What the hell does he cook?" Decker asked as he nursed a bottle of beer.

Knox knew his buddy was capable of feeding himself, but had never actually seen him prepare a meal. At least not one that didn't come in a can or could go from freezer to table via a few minutes in the microwave.

"He cooked burgers on the grill." Em lifted a shoulder. "They were really good."

"And hot dogs on the grill," Justin added.

"Hey, you're home." Em whirled around and launched herself at her husband.

Knox still wasn't used to seeing the two of them together. He was happy they'd found a partner in each other, but it was still weird to see them locking lips. He cleared his throat. When they didn't break apart, he did it again, louder this time.

"Are we making you uncomfortable?" Justin released his grip on his wife and gave Knox a half hug before turning to Decker to do the same.

"Not uncomfortable. It's still just a little weird," Knox said. Though Decker always had a woman on his arm, Knox had been able to count on Justin to hang out together when they were both in town. Now Justin had a wife.

And not just any wife. He'd married Emmeline, the fourth in their foursome of friends. Knox had only hung out with Em a few times without the other guys around, but he'd spent a ton of time with Justin. Now they were a package deal. So when he needed a friend to talk to, he'd ended up with an invite to come over for dinner with Decker instead of just going out for a couple of beers with the guys.

"Grab a seat. It's time to eat." Em nodded toward the table she'd set with the dishes they'd received as wedding presents.

Knox only knew that because he'd helped them move. If he'd known how much shit they had, he probably would have offered to pay for four guys and a truck instead of spending the better part of a weekend hauling furniture from Em's place to the house they'd bought out in the country

"How are the songs for the new album coming?" Justin popped the top off a bottle of beer and handed it to Knox.

"Slow." Knox took a swig, then wiped the back of his hand across his mouth. "Actually, I take that back. It's not even going slow. I've got nothing. I'm tapped out. My brain just can't spin the kind of tunes they want."

Em slid an enchilada onto his plate before handing it to him. "What did you do last time you needed to write?"

"He reworked the songs he's been writing since grade school and added a little bit more pop and sizzle to them, ain't that right?" Decker asked.

"Sounds accurate." When Tripp got him a deal with the label, Knox had notebooks full of ideas and whole playlists of songs he'd been performing for years. He'd handpicked the ones he could rework to meet the label's needs, but now he was out. If he wanted to make his deadline, he needed new material.

"Why can't you do that again?" Em asked.

Knox shook his head as he used the edge of his fork to separate a bite of enchilada. "I've used everything I can. The problem is they want something I'm not sure I can give them."

"So what happens if you don't?"

"They get to tell me what to sing." Knox let his fork clatter to his plate. "I'm already trying to be someone I'm not for them. I can't give them total control."

Justin closed his eyes and chewed for a long beat. "This is good, baby. Real good."

"Well, thank you. I'm glad to see someone's enjoying the dinner I made." She arched her brows and looked at Knox's plate. "You're not going to solve any of your problems on an empty stomach."

He shoved a bite into his mouth and swallowed without tasting it. "Delicious."

"You didn't even taste that." Em stared him down.

"I'm preoccupied. What the hell am I going to do?" He pushed back from the table and started to pace.

"Sounds to me like you need a break. Need to get out of your head and give yourself some room to think." Decker swiped his napkin across his mouth. "Have you thought about getting away somewhere?"

"Where am I going to go? I can't even leave my house without someone tailing me." Knox was used to the press while he was on the road, but now that he was home, it was more than a little annoying to be stalked by paparazzi day and night.

"We'll create a distraction like they did in, oh hell, what movie was it? The one where they had all the same vehicles leaving at the same time so people didn't know which one to follow." Em tilted her head back. "One of the Ocean's series, maybe?"

Justin rested his arm across the back of her chair. "I think that was the one with the Mini Coopers, wasn't it?"

"Y'all aren't listening. That might get me out of the house, but where the hell am I going to go?" If he bought a plane ticket, there would be press waiting for him when he landed. His only chance of getting away without being caught would be to make sure no one was tailing him and drive somewhere.

"Are you thinking what I'm thinking?" Em turned to Justin, then glanced over at Decker.

"Pretty sure I am," Justin said.

"It's perfect. Nobody's really there in the off-season." Decker shrugged. "He'd have the place to himself."

Justin nodded. "He could drive the whole way. Wouldn't even have to give his real name to anyone."

"Staying at a hotel isn't an option." Knox rolled his eyes. "As soon as I swipe my card, word gets out."

"No hotel. No credit card." A knowing smile spread across Justin's mouth.

"Want to fill me in?" Knox finally asked. He felt like he did when he sat in on the meetings between the label and Tripp. Like everyone else was figuring out his future without even letting him offer an opinion.

"You need to go to Paradise," Justin said.

Knox turned to Decker. "I thought your dad sold his place down there."

He couldn't keep the Wayne family collection of houses straight. Decker's dad had vacation homes on four different continents and was always buying and selling.

"He did, but Chick's got a few bungalows down there. I called the other day to check in on him, and he said he's going to fix them up to rent out," Justin said as he set down his fork and reached for his beer. "I bet he'd let you stay for cheap."

Knox digested that nugget of info. He'd heard great things about Paradise Island from Justin and Em. When Justin had been injured bull riding and needed to pull himself together, that's where Em took him. Sounded like it might just be the answer to his predicament. "Nobody could know who I am."

"So tell people you're staying in exchange for fixing the place up. You used to work construction in the summers. I don't think he needs major changes. You could work with your hands during the day and write songs at night." Justin turned toward Em. "I'd say the scenery is pretty inspiring, wouldn't you?"

"Mmm-hmm." Em leaned into Justin. "Remember that night on the beach?"

"Which one?" Justin nuzzled his nose into her hair.

Knox would have to have the emotional capacity of a rock

not to pick up on the flirty vibe the two of them were flinging around. "I guess I'll call down there and see what Chick says."

Justin lifted a hand, his attention completely focused on Em. "Yeah, tell him we said hi, will you?"

"I'll just take my enchilada to go, then." Knox pushed back from the table and grabbed his plate. Turns out there was a major downside to two of his best friends marrying each other.

Decker grabbed his plate and followed Knox through the front door to the swing on the wraparound front porch. "What do you think?"

"What do I think about what?" Knox sat down in the corner of the swing and balanced his plate on his lap.

"Justin and Em. It's just"—Decker glanced back at the doorway—"weird, isn't it?"

"No weirder than the idea of some woman falling hard enough for you to want to wake up to your ugly mug for the rest of her life." Knox got a little thrill from poking at his friend's ego. Decker had never lacked luck with the ladies. His good looks, charming personality, and last name guaranteed he always had a woman on his arm.

"I think I'm going to ask Cherice to marry me." Knox's eyes went wide as he sat down on the wooden bench on the porch.

"No shit?" he asked. The two of them hadn't even been dating very long. "So soon?"

"We've been seeing each other for four months."

That was longer than the last three relationships Decker'd had, combined.

"Do you think she'll say yes?" Decker asked. Hope shone in his eyes, past the careful shield he always seemed to have in place.

A kernel of doubt settled in Knox's gut. Cherice seemed like a nice woman. She'd never given him a reason to doubt her intentions or question her loyalty to his best friend. But there was something about her that gave him pause. He couldn't seem to shake the sense that she was more into Decker because of his last name than due to her heart.

"Yeah, but there's no rush, right? When are you thinking about popping the question?"

"Soon." Decker slid another bite of enchilada past his lips while Knox silenced the groan working its way up his throat. Decker's good ideas never seemed to turn out the way he envisioned them.

"How do you think you'll do it?"

"Would you be willing to play a short concert for two? If I set it up so we're having a private candlelit dinner somewhere and you play that song you wrote about growing old together. You know the one I mean, right?"

Knox's jaw ticked. "You mean the one I wrote for the chick who cheated on me with my sperm donor of a father?"

"Shit, man. I forgot." Decker shook his head. "Never mind."

"It's fine. Somebody should enjoy it." He'd played it so many times, he was numb. When he'd written that song, his own heart had been full of hope about happily ever after. Shortly after, he learned that some hearts just weren't made for love.

"Wow, you'll do it?" Decker's brows lifted.

It wasn't Decker's fault he didn't know just how deep the hurt behind that song had cut Knox. Some things were better left in the dark, even between best friends.

"Yeah." Knox nodded. "Just let me know what you need and how I can help."

"I'll do everything. If you'll just show up and strum a few bars, I'll pop the question and it'll all be good."

"I figured you for a huge romantic gesture when you got around to asking someone to marry you." Knox had grown up around Decker and his larger-than-life ideas. Thankfully, Decker also had the budget to make his dreams a reality. As the only son of a Texas oilman, Decker may as well have grown up with a silver spoon in his mouth. Though, knowing Decker's dad, it was probably more like a silver shot glass.

"Oh, I figured the proposal would be simple. I'm still working on the location. I was thinking of taking her out on the yacht somewhere. Maybe toodle around the Caribbean for a week or so and find the best place to watch a sunset. I can fly you in and out if we take the boat with the helipad."

Knox let out a laugh. Typical Decker. Any other guy who talked like that would be considered a self-entitled prick, but in addition to being the richest guy Knox knew, Decker was also the most generous.

"Yeah, I've got some time off before I have to head back out on tour. As long as you do it in the next three months, I'm happy to help you out."

"You think you'll ever get married?"

"Hell no." Knox had been on the edge of proposing to that same girl he'd fallen so hard for in high school. Thankfully, he'd never gone through with it. No telling where he'd be if he had. Since then, he'd kept a tight leash on his heart.

It's not like he didn't have plenty of opportunities. Women threw themselves at him all the time. Came with the territory of being one of country music's rising superstars. Knox steered clear of the limelight seekers. They were interested only in what they could get from him. In using him for the spotlight, like his ex had done. The easiest way to make sure he never got played again was to not give anyone the chance. He might get lonely out on the road, but at least he had his friends. Justin, Emmeline, and Decker had always been there for him. Through thick and thin, through sunshine and rain, through good times and bad, the four of them had always had one another's backs.

"Why not?" Decker asked.

Knox chuckled. "Where should I start? I find it difficult to believe you're so gung ho since your dad's on, what . . . his fourth wife?"

"Fifth." Decker shook his head while he scooped up a bite of beans on his fork. "When I get married, it's going to be forever. I don't subscribe to my dad's trade-them-in-for-a-newer-model philosophy. So, what do you think about taking some time off and heading to Paradise Island?"

"I think it might be just what I need." Working with his hands and letting his mind wander had worked for him before. He'd come up with most of his lyrics during the summers he spent working construction after high school. It had to be worth a shot. If that didn't work . . . He shook the idea away. It had to work.

He'd lost his family.

His friends were settling down.

His career was all he had left.

"Do you think we should take our dishes back inside or leave them here?" Decker looked up from his plate.

Knox finished the last bite of his dinner and set the plate on the swing. Though he was more than happy to clean up after himself or pitch in by doing dishes, he didn't want to risk walking in on something he wouldn't be able to unsee. He'd send Justin and Em a text later to thank them for dinner and let them know he'd left his plate on the porch. Maybe next time they decided to meet up on a Friday night, they could go somewhere in town.

"I say we bail. If they're in there doing what I think they are, I don't want to be close enough to hear anything."

Decker laughed and stacked his plate on top of Knox's. "Cherice is waiting for me, anyway. It was good to see you, man. Let me know what you decide about Paradise."

"I will." Hopeful that he had the answer to his creative

block, Knox got in his truck and pulled up Chick's cell phone number. The worst thing the man could do was say no. Knox had heard that word enough times in his life that the possibility of hearing it again didn't dissuade him from making the call.

The grizzly old bull rider's voice came through the phone. "Chick here."

"Mr. Darville." Knox cleared his throat, suddenly more nervous than he'd been the last time he'd taken the stage at Staples Center in LA. "Hey, it's Knox Shepler. We met through Justin and Emmeline. I know it's presumptuous of me, sir, but I was wondering if I could ask you for a favor."

Something had to start going his way. Statistically, it would be almost impossible for things to take a turn for the worse.

4

~⚬♡⚬~

Claudia

Claudia got up when her alarm went off and automatically went through her weekday morning routine. She stretched, then jogged a mile down the beach and back again. By the time she returned to the bungalow, the sun had already started to peek over the edge of the horizon. She grabbed her stuff to head for the shower, her mind already wandering to the long list of items on her to-do list.

First up, she'd see if she could figure out a way to add a small bathroom onto each of the bungalows. They each had a sink and a toilet, but the showers sat in a building in the middle of the complex. No one would be willing to pay big bucks for a rental without a private bathroom.

She hung her clothes on the hook outside one of the two stalls with running water and turned on the faucet to let the water warm up. Once Chick started renting out the bunga-lows, she'd probably need to find a new place to live. She valued her privacy too much to stay if there would be a bunch of strangers walking around.

The only problem with living on a small island was that real estate came at a premium. Most of the houses lining the beach were well outside her budget. Working with Chick didn't pay anything close to what she used to pull in when she ran her own business, but the benefits far outweighed the cons. On Paradise, everyone knew her as Claudia, the bartender with the curly hair who made a killer margarita. They didn't care about who Claudia Alvarez been before she arrived on the island. All they cared about was that she kept the alcohol flowing and the music playing.

She stepped into the stream of warm water and relaxed as it poured over her head. It would be nice to work on the bungalows . . . She'd always loved the design and staging part of her previous career in real estate. Though she hadn't let herself think about what she'd left behind, the idea of getting to work on a new project warmed her heart.

She'd just started to rinse the shampoo out of her hair when the door to the bathroom opened with a loud creak. Her heart skipped and jumped into her throat. The only other person who had a key was Chick. There was no way he would be up moving around this early.

Unnerved, she looked around for something she could use as a weapon. The only viable option was the bamboo stick attached to the loofah she used to scrub her back. It might be able to double as a club in a pinch.

Whoever had entered the shower room started to whistle. She couldn't place the song, though she had more important things to think about than playing a round of name that tune. Gripping the handle of the loofah tightly in her hand, she pressed her back against the cold tile wall and waited.

Footsteps came closer, and the whistling grew louder. Her lungs froze. She tried to take in a breath without making any noise.

The rings on the curtain in the stall next to hers rattled. Then the water turned on. Maybe the stranger hadn't come in looking for her.

"Hello?" Her voice came out like a strangled croak. "Who's there?"

"Oh, um, hey. I'm N N-Nolan. Sorry, didn't mean to scare you."

Claudia gripped the plastic curtain against her body and poked her head out of the stall. "What the hell are you doing in here?"

The guy stepped out of the stall next to hers. He held a T-shirt in his hands and her gaze stuck on his chest. His firm, cut, full-of-muscles chest that sat directly at her eye level.

"Chick's letting me stay in one of the bungalows while I help fix them up." Green eyes met hers. "If you want me to come back another time, I can."

She'd lost the ability to speak thanks to her mouth going as dry as the Sahara. Ducking back into her shower stall, she opened her mouth and rinsed it out with water from the shower. "Chick didn't say anything to me about having someone help out."

"Well, uh, I don't know what to tell you. I just drove down last night. Maybe you want to take it up with him?"

His voice . . . ugh. It was deep and almost musical. It pissed her off. How dare Chick hire someone to work on the project without telling her? And not just someone. A hot guy. With pecs. And abs. And a voice that sent a shiver racing up and down her spine.

"I will." She ducked her head under the faucet to finish rinsing her hair, then twisted the knob to end her shower. She'd left her things hanging in the first stall, since she hated when they caught the spray from her shower. This meant she had to walk past the shower stall he was using to get to her clothes. She tugged her towel around her chest and tucked the corner in between her breasts. The only thing that could make this morning any worse would be . . .

Her foot slipped out from under her, and she landed on the

hard tile floor. On her back. Half-in, half-out of the stall. The stall where the guy with the pecs and the abs and the voice stood under the spray of the shower.

Naked.

Knox

Knox was all about making a good first impression, but exposing himself in his birthday suit to the woman he assumed would be his new neighbor and coworker was taking things about a thousand steps too far.

Instinctively, he bent down to offer her a hand.

Her eyes widened, and she turned her head in the other direction as she scrambled like a crab on its back to get away from him.

Fuck. He may as well have just shoved his junk in her face. "Hold on a sec."

He reached for the towel he'd hung over the railing above. It barely stretched around his waist, but at least he wasn't hanging it all out there anymore.

"Here. Let me help you up." He thrust his hand at her.

Surprisingly, she took it. As her palm slid against his, a prickly sensation radiated up his arm.

"Are you okay?"

With one hand holding her towel closed and the other wrapped around his, she got her feet under her and stood. Knox took his first look at the woman he'd be working with for the next couple months. Huge brown eyes stared up at him. The pink stains on her cheeks grew darker by the second.

She tugged her hand away from his and readjusted her towel. "I'm fine. The floor can get slippery. I guess . . . I must have lost my footing."

Her gaze bounced from the wall to the floor and stayed there.

"At least we got the first impression out of the way, huh?" He was trying to make light of the situation, though he wasn't sure that was even possible.

She backed out of the shower stall, her gaze still glued to the ground. "We should work out some kind of schedule. For the showers. So something like this doesn't happen again."

"Yeah, of course." He couldn't keep his eyes off her. Though she'd wrapped the towel so tight around her torso that it could be cutting off circulation, Knox could still make out her shape. And hell, he liked what he saw. The towel on her head had fallen to the ground. Long, dark hair cascaded over her shoulders. Her skin looked like it had been permanently kissed by the sun.

Though she wouldn't make eye contact now, he had a picture of big brown eyes etched into his mind. Her hips flared out from her waist, and he could tell she had a whole lot of curves packed into her petite frame.

She shook her head, like she wanted to erase the entire encounter from her memory. Then she turned and walked away without another word.

Knox stared after her until she rounded the corner. Then he blew out the breath that had caught in his chest. A few minutes later, the door to the bathroom opened and closed with a heavy thud. What the hell was that? Chick didn't mention he had someone else working with him on the project. Knox tossed his towel over the rod and turned the water back on. He may as well confront Chick not smelling like he'd just wrestled with one of the bulls on Justin and Em's ranch.

Twenty minutes later, he sat across the bar while Claudia poured him a hot cup of coffee.

"Here you go." She slid the mug across the bar to him.

"Thank you." Cupping his hands around the warm mug,

he lifted it to his lips. "Any idea what time Chick usually rolls in?"

She spoke while she worked, not even pausing to look at him. "Unless he's opening, he typically comes in around ten."

Knox checked his phone. It was a little after nine. With no other plans beyond writing the songs for his next album and waiting to see what Chick needed, for the first time in a hell of a long time, Knox didn't have anything begging for his attention. The feeling was an odd combination of freeing and anxiety-inducing.

Claudia popped open a bottle of moscato and poured a couple of mimosas. He could tell by the confident way she moved around behind the bar that she'd been here for a while. She set the drinks on a tray and carried them over to a couple who'd sat down at a table overlooking the beach.

Knox hadn't gotten a good look at the place when he arrived last night. It had been after midnight and all he'd wanted was somewhere to crash. Chick had left the door to the bungalow unlocked, so Knox hadn't even made it inside the bar until this morning.

Now he took it all in. Cowboy and rodeo decor hung from the walls. Neon beer signs cast a colorful glow. The main attraction was the horseshoe-shaped bar that took up a huge portion of the space.

Thanks to Justin and Em's description of the place, Knox had an idea of what it would look like in person. But all the adjectives in the world wouldn't have been able to do justice to the floor-to-ceiling view of the beach.

Knox had spent the better part of the last eighteen months living out of a tour bus. He didn't mind, but he'd felt closed in. He'd grown up on a couple thousand acres of ranch land and missed being able to look out the window and not see another person or building for miles.

Staring out at the vast expanse of ocean gave him the same feeling.

"There he is." Chick's scratchy voice came from the main entrance. "How was the trip, son?"

Knox got up and turned in time for Chick to pull him into a gruff embrace. "Uneventful, just long."

"Yeah, it's a trek to get down here. Worth the view, though, don't you think?" Chick clapped him on the back, then turned to face the ocean.

"It's amazing."

"Think you'll find some inspiration here in Paradise?"

Knox's gaze drifted from the beach to Claudia as she stepped behind the bar. "Yeah, I think I might."

"I see you met Claudia?" Chick slid onto a stool and smiled as she set a mug of steaming coffee down in front of him.

"He walked in on me in the shower." She cocked her hip and planted a hand on her waist. "You didn't tell me you needed more help with the bungalows. We've already got Antonio working off his bar tab."

Chick took a sip of his coffee. "Yeah, but once Antonio clears his debt, he'll want to be paid. Knox here is working for room and board."

Her eyes flashed with annoyance, then she turned her gaze on Knox. "I thought you said your name was Nolan?"

"It is." He looked to Chick. He'd told him he wanted to fly under the radar. Wouldn't do him any good to go to the trouble of making arrangements for a private getaway if someone found out who he was.

"It's a nickname I came up with for him." Chick made a fist and rapped his knuckles on Knox's head. "He used to love knock-knock jokes when he was little."

Claudia rolled her eyes. "Great, so the two of you go way

back. Too bad you couldn't have warned me we'd be having a long-term visitor. How long do you think you're staying?"

Knox felt like he'd passed the first hurdle with her but still had a long way to go to gain her trust. "I'm not sure yet. Depends on how long Chick needs me."

"I'll print a copy of the list of things I've come up with so far."

Knox pulled out his phone. "Do you want to just text it to me?"

She blew out a breath. "I don't text."

"Email?" Knox narrowed his eyes.

She shook her head.

"I guess a paper copy will work just fine, then." He drained his coffee mug and got up to get a refill. Working with Claudia might be a little more challenging than he thought.

She blocked him from stepping behind the bar. "You need more coffee?"

"Yeah, I was just going to grab it myself."

"Let's get one thing straight. This area"—she gestured around the back of the bar—"is my space. That area out there is yours. You want something from behind the bar, I'll get it for you. Otherwise, you're on your own."

Knox held out his mug. "Okay, then. Could I please get a refill on my coffee?"

She set the carafe down on the bar. "Help yourself."

Clearly someone was feeling a little threatened by his presence. Knox would need to find a way to assure her he wasn't after her position at A Cowboy in Paradise. All he wanted was a place to hide out for a few weeks, work with his hands, and see if he could reconnect with the inspiration that had provided him with four number-one hits.

Chick might think the world of Claudia, but Knox didn't trust her enough to tell her the truth. And he didn't have enough time to find somewhere else to hide if she blew his cover.

"Look, I think we got off on the wrong foot this morning. Can we start over?" he asked.

She glanced up at him, her eyes slightly narrowed.

"I'm Nolan." He held out his hand. "It's nice to meet you."

After a few seconds of hesitation, she slid her palm against his. "Claudia. Nice to meet you, too."

The same prickle of awareness buzzed up his arm. She was an attractive woman. The dark eyes, thick curly hair, curvy hips, and full, pink lips attested to that. But Knox wasn't looking for a woman. Not even a one-night stand, though Claudia didn't seem like the type who'd be into that kind of thing, anyway. He needed to shut down any hint of attraction he might be feeling, and fast.

He loosened his grip, and she pulled her hand away. "That wasn't so hard, was it?"

The frostiness in her eyes thawed a little. "Not so bad."

"I'm between jobs right now. Chick offered to let me crash here for a couple months in return for helping him out. I'll try not to get in your way, and I'll be gone by the end of March at the latest. Does that work for you?"

She nodded.

"Great. Now, where's this list of projects? I need to start doing something or I'm going to get antsy."

5

Claudia

Hot guys came into the bar all the time. All. The. Time. So why was her body responding to Nolan in such a weird way? Maybe because of the run-in in the shower?

Claudia didn't typically fall for a pretty face, but Nolan had the body to go along with it. His chest looked like it had been carved out of granite. And his abs were so hard, someone could use them as a cutting board. When her gaze trailed down the rest of him . . . It made her blush, even now, to think about the full-frontal view she'd gotten in the shower, and that had been days ago.

She'd limited her interaction with the man to pouring his coffee in the mornings in hopes she'd get him out of her system before she embarrassed herself . . . again. Which was why she'd been going about her day with her guard down, totally avoiding the bungalows where he'd been working on demo.

"Hey, Claudia," Chick called to her from behind the bar.

"Yes?" The lunch rush had just ended, though they were still far enough away from spring break that the big rush consisted of a few regulars coming in for the fresh fish sandwich special.

"I was going to take this over to Nolan but my knee's bothering me again. Would you mind running it up to him?" Chick slid a canvas bag across the bar.

"What is it?" She eyed the bag between them.

"Just the lunch special. He's been working up a sweat so I threw in a few extra bottles of water. I appreciate it."

"Sure." She set her order pad and pen down on the counter, her stomach already tying itself into knots at the thought of seeing Nolan. With the canvas tote in hand, she followed the sounds of wood splitting to the farthest bungalow.

Classic country music floated through the open front door. She didn't want to go in and distract him, so she figured she would leave the bag sitting just inside the entrance.

"Hey, I brought you some lunch. I'll set it inside the door, okay?" Claudia called out, but he didn't answer. As tempting as it would be to leave the bag there, who knew how long it would take him to find it? The fish sandwich had a thick layer of homemade chipotle mayo on top, and all her food safety training stressed the importance of not letting mayo sit out for too long, especially since the days were starting to heat up.

She ventured into the bungalow, clutching the bag to her chest. He had his back to her. His shirtless, naked back. His shoulder muscles rolled as he lifted a sledgehammer. The way he hefted the tool, prepared to strike, made her feel like she was watching Thor handle his heavy, magical hammer. Her mouth watered, and she literally drooled over the sight of such a massive amount of manliness on display.

The sound of splintering wood knocked her out of her reverie. She jumped back and bumped into the small folding table holding a radio and a few other items. The table collapsed and crashed to the floor.

Nolan whipped around, his eyes wide. Even in her moment of panic, she couldn't help but appreciate the sight of his bare chest. All the blood in her body seemed to rush to her cheeks, and they burned like she'd touched them directly to the sun.

"I'm so sorry." She took a step forward and held out the bag like a peace offering. Her foot tangled in the power cord of the radio, sending her upper body sailing forward while her feet remained in place.

"What the hell?" Nolan's arms flew out to catch her.

She registered his tight grip on her hips, the way her cheek felt smashed against his sweaty, rock-hard pecs, and the unpleasant feeling of her blood turning to ice water and freezing her feet to the spot.

"Are you okay?" Nolan set her upright. His brow furrowed as he looked down at her.

"I'm f-f-f." Dammit. Now wasn't the time for her childhood stutter to reappear after all these years. She took in a deep breath. The scent of sweat and wood and something spicy and warm she didn't recognize filled her nose. "I'm fine."

Nolan ran his hands over her upper arms. "Sorry, I didn't hear you come in with the music so loud."

She glanced to where the radio had landed. A warbled country tune drifted out of the speaker.

"I ruined your radio." Claudia bent to pick it up. A piece of black plastic fell off the front, along with one of the dials. "I'm such a klutz. I'll get you a new one."

"That's okay. I'm surprised it's lasted this long." He let his hands fall to his sides like he'd just realized he'd been running his palms up and down her arms.

Immediately, she missed his touch, then chastised herself for being so weak that a run-in with a shirtless guy could knock her so off-center. "Chick asked me to bring over your lunch. His knee's been bothering him, so . . ."

"Thanks." Nolan reached down and pulled the plug for the radio out of the wall. An uncomfortable silence descended, thicker and heavier than the midday humidity.

Claudia tried to think of something flippant to say, something that would make them both laugh off the run in. But all she could do was stand there and stare at the slight sheen of sweat covering his well-defined pecs. Good grief, if the sight of a relative stranger's bare chest could send her into such a tailspin, she probably needed to spend some long overdue time with her battery-operated boyfriend.

She'd locked down her libido when she left Minnesota and hadn't had a reason to dust it off while she'd been in Paradise. One-night stands and physical flings had never appealed to her, since she could never seem to keep her heart out of the way. But something about Nolan made her wonder what it would feel like to have his hands roam over her skin or tangle her tongue with his.

"Do you want to join me?" Nolan glanced toward the front door. "I've ruined the kitchen, but we could find a spot out front to sit down and eat."

"Oh, no." She shook her head hard enough that the hoop earrings she had on bumped against her cheeks. "I mean, I'd love to, but I need to get back."

Liar, liar, pants on fire. She wouldn't "love to"; she was eager to get as far away as she could from the temptation of his heated gaze and sexy smirk.

"Okay then. Thanks for bringing me lunch. I guess I'll see you around." His lips split into a lopsided grin.

"Yeah." Wow, could she be any more awkward? It was time to remove herself from his proximity. If only she could remember how to walk. Tentatively, she put one foot in front of the other, careful to avoid the remains of the splintered cabinets spread all over the floor.

When she cleared the front door and stepped into the shaded path, she drew in a deep breath. The fresh air filled her lungs. What was it about Nolan that turned her into a blubbering mess? Avoiding him didn't seem to be working.

Maybe she needed to expose herself to him in small doses so she could build up a resistance. That had worked for her sister when she developed an allergy to dogs.

Only, her sister wanted to be able to get close to dogs and Claudia wanted to figure out a way to become immune to whatever hold Nolan seemed to possess over her. Too bad there wasn't something she could take to prevent herself from reacting to the charming contractor. But Claudia had never been one to give up easily. She'd figure out a way to protect herself against him. Giving in wasn't an option. She'd never let herself get sucked in by a man again.

Knox

With another day of demo under his belt, Knox was satisfied with the progress he'd been making on the bungalows. If he kept up his pace, he'd be done with demo within the next week. Working with his hands and letting his mind wander had been just what he needed to get in the right headspace to start writing music again. There was only one problem . . . Claudia.

Thoughts of the curvy bartender had taken up some serious real estate in his brain, especially when she showed up in shorts and a tank top that left little to his imagination. He'd been drawn to her from the moment he met her, though he'd never give in. He needed to focus on his goal. Write music. Impress the label. Earn the right to do his own thing. His priorities were crystal clear.

Only every time he let his mind wander, he found himself entertaining visions of Claudia instead of finding inspiration for his next single. Claudia leaning across the bar to pour his morning coffee. Claudia laughing at something one of the regulars said. Claudia gazing out at the ocean with a look of longing in her eyes.

There was something about her that tugged at his heart and made him wonder how she'd ended up second in command at a place like A Cowboy in Paradise. His mom always told him curiosity killed the cat, though he in turn always responded that satisfaction brought it back. She believed people had a right to their secrets and it didn't do any good to go poking around unless a person was ready to face a potentially unkind truth.

When he was younger, Knox didn't understand how she could overlook his dad's indiscretions, but she chose to ignore them. After he found out his dad slept with his girl friend, Knox couldn't let his mom live in denial any longer. She didn't blame him for telling the truth, but it still took her another year to leave his dad. Now they were closer than they'd ever been, since they'd both shut his father out of their lives. Maybe he'd ask his mom about Claudia.

He hung his head. She'd probably tell him to let sleeping dogs lie and not to go sticking his nose into someone else's business. In this case, she was probably right.

Knox shook the thoughts of Claudia out of his mind as he entered the bar. He'd washed the sweat and stink of a hard day's work away and planned to stop in for a bite to eat and to return the bag she'd brought over with his lunch.

There wasn't much of a dinner crowd, especially on a weeknight, so he had his pick of tables and selected one with an unobstructed view of the ocean. He'd just started heading that way when he caught a glimpse of Claudia leaning over the bar, her attention zeroed in on a dark-haired teen. Knox had seen the kid bussing tables, but now he sat on a stool with a notebook in front of him and a pen in his hand.

Knox edged closer, telling himself he was returning the

bag, that he had every reason to stop by the bar. But if he were being honest with himself, he'd admit he wanted to know what the two of them were so focused on that they had their heads bent together, their foreheads almost touching. Even though the kid couldn't be more than fifteen or sixteen, a twinge of jealousy pinched Knox's gut.

Clearly Claudia had let her guard down when talking to the kid. She twirled a strand of her long, dark curls around her finger and tossed her head back. Her laugh broke free—a deep, sexy rumble that sent flames licking along his skin. Did she have any idea what kind of an effect she had on him?

He slid onto a stood on the other side of the bar, hoping to observe their interaction for a little while without being spotted.

"Are you sure you like it better that way?" the kid asked.

Claudia spun the notebook around to face him. "I think so."

The kid hummed something too low for Knox to hear. Then he drummed his fingers on the bar and cocked his head. "Yeah, I think you're right."

"You've got this, Gabe. Just go with your gut. It won't let you down." Her hand landed on the kid's arm, and she gave it a squeeze. "I know how much you want this."

The warmth in her eyes and the relaxed set of her shoulders was a complete one-eighty from the tense awkwardness she'd shown toward Knox earlier. He was starting to see why the locals thought so highly of her and why Chick entrusted her with the day-to-day operations of his beloved bar.

"Hey, can I get you something?" One of the other bartenders stopped in front of Knox. He set a cardboard coaster down and waited for a reply.

"How about some iced tea?" Knox couldn't seem to stay hydrated. It had been years since he'd engaged in the type of manual labor he'd been performing over the past few days. His muscles ached from his efforts, but it was a good kind of pain. Reminded him of his past and the summers he'd spent working construction.

Those were the days when the music flowed and he couldn't write down the lyrics that filled his head fast enough. Decker and Justin said it was because he was too worn out to second-guess himself. They were probably right. But Knox suspected there was another reason the music wouldn't stop coming, and that's what scared him the most.

Back when he first started writing songs, he'd been deeply in love. Looking back, he recognized all the warning signs that she wasn't the one for him, but at the time he was a dumb kid who thought more with his cock than he did with his brain. He'd confused lust for love and spent hours pouring his heart out onto the pages of his notebook.

Those were the songs his agent had given to the label. Those were the songs that built his career. As he took his first sip of ice-cold tea from the glass the bartender set down in front of him, he tried to drown out the worry that bubbled up in his chest. He could swing a hammer for weeks, but what if his muse never showed up? What if all along his inspiration had been more about his misguided sense of love?

He wasn't willing to sacrifice his heart to find out. He'd barely pieced himself back together again after his dad's betrayal. His inspiration had to be here on Paradise Island. If he couldn't find his way back to the music, he'd rather give it up for good than become the shallow superstar his agent and label wanted him to be.

6

❦

Claudia

The next week passed in a flurry of prepping designs for the bungalows, finalizing the new seasonal menu, and trying to hold herself in check anytime Nolan came around. Since she'd walked in on him shirtless to deliver his lunch, he'd stayed out of her way. The only time they crossed paths was when he came into the bar for dinner. Sometimes he sat down and ate with Chick, but most of the time he ate alone. Then he'd disappear after dinner and she wouldn't see him again until the next morning when he stumbled in looking for coffee.

He seemed to know what he was doing on the bungalows, too, though so far all he'd been working on was demo. Ripping out old flooring and cabinets didn't seem that difficult. With that part of the project complete, Chick asked them to sit down and go over the next steps after lunch.

Claudia had finished her morning run down the beach and made sure she hit the shower during her allotted time slot. So what if she'd put in a little extra effort in front of the mirror this morning? It wasn't like she was trying to impress anyone. A woman had a right to focus on her appearance every once in a while. With the lunch crowd thinned out, she left the bar and kitchen under Tomas's control and went outside to look for Chick.

"There she is." Chick gestured to the chair next to him as she joined the two of them at an outdoor table.

"Hi." Nolan smiled up at her. His eyes crinkled at the edges from underneath the brim of his baseball cap. He hadn't shaved since he arrived, and his beard was coming in thick. She wondered if it would feel soft or scratchy if she reached out and ran her fingers over it.

Get a grip, Claudia. She pulled out the chair next to Chick and slipped into it. "Hey."

"Thanks for joining us." Chick pulled out a notebook with his chicken-scratch handwriting covering the page.

Nolan reached for the pitcher of water and filled a glass, then slid it across the table to her.

"Thanks," she mouthed. It was . . . nice . . . having someone do something for her for a change, even something so little as pouring her a glass of water.

"With demo done, we need to move onto the next steps. Claudia, I'd like you to head to the mainland to pick out the paint color for the interior walls and the cabinets you want to use for the kitchen areas."

Her chest squeezed. "Can't we just do that online?"

"Last time we tried that, my office ended up baby blue instead of light gray." Chick crossed his arms over his chest.

Claudia inhaled through her nose. She didn't like the idea of leaving the island and avoided it as much as possible. Paradise had been a safe haven for the past four years and every time she left, she felt like she was on the verge of a panic attack.

"Why doesn't Nolan bring back samples? That way, the three of us can make a decision together." It seemed like a viable solution. Let the new guy deal with it.

Nolan's brow furrowed as he studied her from across the table. She didn't want to appear weak, but Chick knew she didn't like leaving the island, even if he never questioned her reasoning behind it.

"Just so you know, I'm a little color-blind," Nolan admitted.

Seriously? "I'm sure someone at the store can help you with picking out colors if we give you some parameters."

"What's the big deal?" Chick leaned forward, resting his elbows on the table and leveling her with a no-bullshit stare.

"We've got that event this weekend that I need to get ready for, and Gabe asked if I'd help him finalize the song he wants to perform. Plus, I've been working with Tomas on the new menu for spring break season. There's just a lot to do." She'd been working with Gabe, one of the busboys, for the past few months on his performance techniques. He wanted to start performing his music during the amateur mic nights but hated getting up in front of a crowd, and she didn't want to let him down.

"What kind of event?" Nolan asked. "I thought y'all pretty much closed down during the slow season."

"It's just a couple of local guys playing a few songs for charity for open mic night." Chick reached out and squeezed her hand. "What's going on, Claudia? Anything you want to talk about?"

She shook her head, not wanting to show any sign of weakness in front of the two men. "No, it's fine. I'll reschedule with Gabe for tomorrow, and Tomas can wait. Can we go soon, though? I'd like to be back before the dinner rush."

Chick laughed. "The dinner rush this time of year is pretty much Tripod showing up for an extra bowl of veggies."

Claudia couldn't help but smile at the mention of the giant tortoise's name. He was a freeloader who'd shown up on the beach one day, and Chick had saved him. He'd lost one of his legs to a fishing net, but it didn't seem to bother him. Claudia looked forward to his visits and always kept an extra supply of romaine lettuce on hand, since that was his favorite.

"I'm ready when you are." Nolan finished his drink and set the glass back down on the table.

"Here." Chick slid a set of keys across the table to her. "Take the boat. That way, you don't have to wait on the ferry to come back when you're ready."

She picked up the keys and slipped them into the pocket of her jacket. Chick thought the world of his fishing pontoon, though she and the boat had a complicated relationship. "I'll think about it."

Nolan picked up the dirty dishes and took them into the bar area.

"Hey." Chick caught her eye. "Everything okay with you, hon?" The furrow between his brows let her know he was concerned.

"Yeah, I'll be fine. I just don't like change." That was an understatement. She hated change. Ever since she'd found Paradise, she'd fallen into a predictable routine. A safe routine.

There used to be a time in her life when she craved excitement. The anticipation of not knowing what might happen next had thrilled her to her core. She was different then. Younger. Naive.

Her impulsivity and tendency to throw caution to the wind had slapped her in the face. Now she was a lot more cautious, her decisions calculated. Since she'd arrived on Paradise Island, it had worked for her, and she didn't see any reason to switch things up.

"Change can be good." Chick patted her hand as he rose from the table.

Some change could be good. Changing the menu every few months was a good thing. Changing the paint color on the inside of the bungalows was fine. As for changing the way she'd been living her life for the past four years . . . no, thank you. There was a reason she'd left everyone and everything behind when she moved to Paradise. Any change that could rock her carefully constructed life needed to be avoided. She hadn't spent years building a safety net around herself only to lose it when some down-on-his-luck contractor came to visit for a few weeks.

She cleared her things from the table and headed to the door to meet up with Nolan.

"You ready?" he asked.

"Yeah." Claudia held up the keys to the boat. "Any chance you know how to drive a boat?"

Knox

The last boat he'd been on was one of Decker's dad's ski boats that practically drove itself. Knox turned the key in the ignition of the beat-up pontoon and listened for any sign that the engine might actually catch.

"I turned on the battery and pumped the gas line a few times. Any idea why it doesn't want to turn over?" Claudia asked. She wiped her hand on a rag she'd found in one of the compartments.

"Sorry, your guess is as good as mine." Knox wanted to give her an answer, but he had no idea. He'd fixed tractor engines on the ranch before and even rebuilt an entire ATV once. Excluding getting out on the lake with his friends, he'd never spent any time on a boat.

"Let's just take the ferry." Claudia flipped the cover to the battery closed. "It's either that or call Chick. By the time he gets out here, half the day will be gone."

Knox pulled the key from the ignition. Seemed like all

he'd done since he met Claudia was get in her way. He climbed off the boat and stopped next to her.

"I suppose we could take the party barge."

Knox followed her line of sight to a two-story pontoon boat painted in a rainbow of colors. "That's the party barge?"

"Yep." Claudia climbed aboard and headed to the captain's chair. "I haven't driven this one before, but he's got the key on the same ring."

Knox waited to see if it would start before he untied the ropes on the dock

The engine sputtered, and Claudia tried again. After a few long beats, it caught. She looked over at him, a huge smile stretched across her mouth.

Knox stood there. His gaze caught on her lips. He'd never seen a genuine smile from her directed his way before. This one had the power to knock him off his feet.

"Can you untie her?" Claudia called over the sound of the engine.

He bent down to unfasten the rope that had been looped over the cleat on the dock. After tossing the loose end onto the boat, he moved to the front and did the same. Claudia shifted into reverse and started to back out of the slip.

"Hop on."

He jumped from the dock to land on the lower level of the boat. The water churned behind them as they slowly backed up. Once she'd cleared the dock, Claudia shifted into gear and they pulled away.

"Nice job." He settled into a seat in front of the wheel.

"Thanks. I've never taken this one out before. After driving the pontoon, it feels like trying to maneuver a semitruck."

"You're doing a great job." He rested his arm along the back of the bench seat and turned to watch the island disappear behind them. There was something about having the wind whip past his ears and the salty spray from the ocean catch him in the chest that eased a bit of the heaviness he'd felt for the past couple of months.

Staring out at the endless horizon filled him with a kind of peace he'd been craving. For the first time in years, the pressure he'd been under eased. He relaxed against the back of the seat and closed his eyes. Thinking of how Claudia looked—the wind in her hair, a smile on her face—sparked something inside him. The first few bars of a tune played through his head.

Before he lost it, he pulled out his phone and jotted down a few words.

He was so focused on exploring the new idea in his head that he didn't notice they were approaching the dock until Claudia called out to him. Even though the barge was a beast, she maneuvered it into the slip like a pro. Knox hopped off the bow to secure the leads to the dock.

"Is that it? We can just leave it here?" He stood and wiped his hands on the side of his jeans.

She nodded. "Should be fine as long as we're not gone too long. Come on, we can catch a cab to the store."

"I've actually got my truck in long-term parking nearby, if you want to take that." The words were out of his mouth before he had a chance to think about it. What if he had left something in the truck that would give away his true identity? Chick knew, but he'd promised not to tell anyone. Knox couldn't afford to have his location compromised. Especially not since he'd just received his first flash of inspiration in too long to remember.

"That sounds great. How far is it?"

"Maybe we'd be better off in a cab. That way, we don't have to mess with getting it in and out of the long-term lot."

She squinted up at him, her hand pressed against her forehead to shield her eyes from the sun. "We might have to make two trips in a cab. I'm assuming your truck would be big enough to haul everything at once?"

"Yeah, of course." He cursed at himself for being such an idiot. He'd just have to check the front seat before he opened her door for her.

"Great. Lead the way."

Knox headed away from the dock and Claudia fell into step next to him. "Chick said you've been working with him for a few years now."

"Yep." She shoved her hands deep into her pockets and didn't break her stride.

Uneasy with the awkward silence, he pressed on. "How did you end up at A Cowboy in Paradise?"

"It's a long story. Let's just say I needed a break, and I found it here. Felt so good I decided to stay." She tossed him a tight grin.

"Where are you from then?"

"What is this, twenty questions?" Her nose wrinkled, and she forced a smile like she wanted to minimize the sting, but it was still a brush-off.

Knox shrugged. "Just trying to make conversation."

"Well, don't. You can save your breath."

He was tired of her sharp comebacks. Obviously she didn't want to talk about her past. That was fine with him. He wasn't too keen on talking about his own situation. But she didn't have to be so damn snippy about it.

"Look," he said, gently wrapping his hand around her arm and tugging her to a stop. "I get that you're not thrilled to have to put up with me, but I'm trying to get along."

The hardness in her eyes softened just enough to let him know she was putting up a front. "I'm sorry. I'm not used to working with someone. Not since . . ." Her voice trailed off.

"Not since what?" Knox asked.

"Nothing. It's not you, it's me."

Knox laughed. "If I had a quarter for every time I've heard that line . . ."

Her mouth tipped up at the corners. "Sorry, I didn't mean for that to sound the way it did. I'm not good with people."

"Especially people you're forced to work with?" he prodded.

Her shoulder lifted and fell in a slight shrug. "I guess so. Chick usually runs things past me. This time, he didn't."

"That's my fault." Knox didn't want to out himself, but he did want to establish some sort of peaceful coexistence with her. "I was in a bad spot and needed somewhere to cool off for a bit. I asked Chick if I could come down and hang out for a few weeks."

Her eyes narrowed, and she crossed her arms over her chest. "You're not in trouble, are you?"

Trouble? That depended on how one would define the term. Yes, he was in trouble. He was at risk of blowing his entire career if he couldn't come up with songs for his new album.

"I'm not in trouble with the law, if that's what you mean."

The tightness in her shoulders relaxed. "Good. The last thing Chick needs is to be caught hiding some fugitive on the run."

Knox bit back a grin. She was protective of the old man. Good to know. He had no intention of compromising Chick or the bar, which was why he had to make sure no one down here knew who he was. His new beard helped. He ran a hand over the hair on his cheeks and chin. The baseball cap didn't hurt, either. His fans had never seen him without a cowboy hat on his head and a pair of boots on his feet. He wiggled his toes in the steel-toe work boots he'd picked up on the drive down to Paradise.

With luck, he'd stay out of the limelight and find his muse.

7

❦

Claudia

They'd picked out paint, ordered cabinets, and had several cases of tile loaded into the back of Nolan's truck. Shopping had taken a lot longer than Claudia expected. The sheer number of paint choices alone had almost sent her over the edge. It had been a long time since she'd had to go to the mainland. Usually, she ordered supplies and had them delivered. Being around so many people had drained her. All she wanted was to get back to the island as soon as possible.

"Hey, are you hungry at all?" Nolan asked.

She hadn't had anything for breakfast that morning except coffee. But even though her stomach had been grumbling for the past hour, she didn't want to take the extra time. Being on the mainland made her antsy. Made her worry that someone would recognize her and the drama she thought she'd finally left behind her would start up again. "I'd really like to get back to the bar."

"Sure. You're in charge." He nodded, but by the way his hands gripped the steering wheel, she could tell he wasn't too happy with her response.

"If you want to drive through somewhere, we could do that." At least then she wouldn't have to get out of the truck. Even though it had been over a year since someone had confronted her in public, the anxiousness was always there.

"That's okay. I can wait until we get back." He tapped his fingers while they waited for the light to change.

Traffic roared by and the smell of exhaust hung in the air, reminding her of the life she left behind when she'd traded skyscrapers for a view of the ocean and a life of luxury for a run-down bungalow. It had been worth it, though. Her peace of mind was more valuable than anything else, and she'd do whatever she needed to do to protect it.

The light changed, and Nolan stepped on the gas. He pulled into the parking area by the dock and they started to unload their purchases from the truck to take down to the boat.

The light was fading from the sky when they finished. Now all Claudia had to do was wait for Nolan to return his truck to the lot and they could head out. She didn't like navigating a boat in the dark, especially something so big as the party barge. While she waited for Nolan to come back, she did as much as she could on the boat so they could take off as soon as he arrived.

"That's some watercraft you've got there." A guy who'd pulled up in the slip next to her nodded at the boat.

"Yeah, she's one of a kind," Claudia said.

"I'm sure you hear this all the time, but you look familiar. Have we met?" His gaze drilled into hers and she looked away.

"I don't think so."

He didn't look too threatening in a pair of khaki shorts, a collared polo, and a backward baseball hat, but her pulse ticked up as he continued to move closer. "Are you sure? I swear I've seen you somewhere."

With her nerves jangling a silent warning alarm, Claudia shook her head.

He flipped his baseball cap around and her heart stuttered to a stop. The Twin Cities Tigers logo sat in the center. She'd always hated that design.

"Your hair was shorter and not so curly." He squinted. "I'm sure of it."

Her lungs failed, and she struggled to take in a breath. He was going to figure it out. She just knew it.

"Hey, you ready to get going?" Nolan's voice cut through the white noise filling her ears. He stood on the dock a few feet away. "Fire up the engine, and I'll handle the lines."

The pressure in her chest eased enough for her to croak out a response. "Okay."

"I can't place it, but I've seen you somewhere before." The guy on the dock shook his head.

"She's the bartender over at A Cowboy in Paradise." Nolan probably thought he was being helpful, but now the stranger knew where she worked. That meant he'd know where to find her.

Her throat started to close. Darkness threatened the edges of her vision.

"Of course. I should have picked up on that from the boat." The guy laughed as he pointed at the colorful logo of the bar that covered the side of the party barge. "Thanks. That was going to drive me crazy all night."

"You're welcome." Nolan tossed the lines onto the boat, then hopped aboard.

Claudia pulled back the lever to back out of the slip. She needed to get away. That had been a close call, and she didn't want to stick around until the guy figured it out. He might have seen her at Chick's bar, but he also might remember seeing her a lot closer to Minneapolis. A chill raced through her as she wondered what kind of reaction the guy would have had if he'd been able to place her.

The engine faltered. Dammit. The last thing she needed right now was for the motor to fail. Easing up on the throttle, she slowly shifted into neutral and let it idle for a few seconds.

"Everything okay?" Nolan asked. He'd slipped his shades up to rest on top of his head. Concern was evident in the lines that creased his forehead.

"Why did you tell him where I work?"

"Sorry, I didn't know it was a secret." His gaze drilled into her like he was trying to figure out why it was such a big deal. "It's not like he couldn't tell where the boat was from."

She shook her head. That wasn't the point. Guys like Nolan didn't understand. He could go about his day, not worrying about catching someone's eye or becoming the target of a stranger's unwanted interest.

"What?" He rested a hand against the metal support running above her head.

"It's just . . . I bet you've never had to worry about some strange guy knowing where you work. Maybe he'll show up some night and hang out at the bar. Maybe he'll wait until I go to take the trash out or leave at the end of my shift. Meet me around back because he thinks the fact I smiled at him means I'm interested in him." She shut her mouth and bit down on the inside of her cheek. She'd already said too much.

"Hell, I was only trying to help." Any sign of teasing had disappeared from his expression. "I didn't think about any of that."

"Don't worry about it." Now he probably thought of her as a damsel in distress who needed to be protected from the big, bad world. She wasn't afraid of some guy hitting on her at the bar. What she was afraid of was much darker than that.

"I'm sorry." Nolan moved his hand like he was about to

touch her shoulder. He must have realized that wasn't a good move and rubbed at the back of his neck instead. "I didn't mean to make you feel uncomfortable."

"It's fine."

"No, it's not fine. You're right. Women have to think about things differently than guys do. I'll try to be more sensitive." The honesty reflected in his eyes made goose bumps pebble her skin.

"Okay." She held his gaze only for a brief moment, though it was long enough for heat to prickle her cheeks. There was more to the muscled handyman than met the eye. That was usually the case with Chick's friends. She'd learned over the years that her boss kept a wide variety of company. Nolan might say he was between jobs and just wanted a place to crash for a bit, but construction workers who were willing to work for room and board typically didn't drive decked-out F-350s or wear watches that cost more than the average person made in a month.

Though no one would know by looking at her now, she used to run in circles where people were judged by the brands they wore and the wealth they displayed. Nolan had a secret. She just didn't have any idea yet what it was.

She gently eased the throttle forward, and the engine caught. Thank goodness. With one hand gripping the wheel, she pushed the throttle down and tried to take in some calming breaths. What was it her therapist used to tell her to do? When she felt a panic attack coming on, she was supposed to pull herself out of it by focusing on her surroundings.

Three things she could see . . . a seagull overhead, the mainland disappearing behind them, a buoy floating in the water. Two things she could smell . . . salt in the air, the fabric softener she'd used on her shirt. One thing she could hear . . . Nolan's voice calling to her over the roar of the motor.

Feeling a little more grounded, she gestured to her ear and yelled, "I can't hear you."

He smiled and stepped next to her. The slight brush of his body against hers made her startle. Nolan put a hand behind her back, his fingers lightly splaying against the area just under her bra strap. "You sure you're okay?"

"I'm fine." She shifted, breaking contact.

"I was trying to ask if you wanted something to drink." He held up a bag with the home-improvement store logo on it. "I picked up a couple of Cokes for us."

Her pulse still beat erratically, but she forced a smile. That was sweet of him. "Thanks. I'd love one."

"Great. What kind? I've got lemonade, Dr Pepper, a Vitaminwater, or a root beer."

"I thought you said you bought Coke."

He let out a soft laugh. "You're not from Texas, are you?"

"What makes you ask that?" She was still shaking from her interaction with the stranger on the dock. Now Nolan seemed to be trying to figure out her secrets.

He pulled the lemonade out of the bag and set it in the cup holder. "Because every Texan knows that when someone offers you a Coke, they don't actually mean a Coca-Cola."

"You want to take the wheel for a bit?" She didn't wait for him to answer, just stood and took a step back, keeping her hand on the steering wheel until he slid into the seat.

"I guess I don't have much of a choice, do I?" He looked like a natural on the water. With his hair curling out from under the edge of his hat and his skin already tanned a golden bronze, he looked just like the guys who lived on the island all year long.

Claudia opened the screw top on the lemonade and took a swig. With Nolan behind the wheel, she could relax for a few minutes. They'd gotten a late start back. She'd hoped to be behind the bar before dinner, but the sun had already started to set. Pulling her sweatshirt around her shoulders, she tried to chase away the chill. Once the sun went down, it would be downright cold out on the water.

The ride back to the island only took about thirty minutes. Less than an hour from now, she'd be nice and toasty.

Then the engine sputtered, and the boat slowed. She stood and made her way toward Nolan. The only thing she could count on a boat to do was be unreliable.

"What happened?"

Nolan stepped away, and she jiggled the key in the ignition. "I don't know. We were cruising along and all of a sudden it died." He shrugged. "Sorry, I don't know a thing about boats. Could we have run out of gas?"

She glanced at the gauge that showed three-quarters of a tank left. In her limited time on the water, she'd been on a boat or two that lost the ability to keep accurate track of fuel levels. "Let me check."

Nolan followed her to the back, where the gas tank was stored. He held up the heavy cover while she opened the cap to the tank. The level sat right where the gauge said it did. They hadn't run out of gas. Something else had caused the engine to falter.

"Did you run over something?" She leaned over the back end of the boat and gazed into the dark water. "Go lift the trim so I can tell if something got wrapped around the prop."

Nolan moved back to the captain's chair, and the propeller slowly came into view. "Can you see anything?"

She saw something, all right. The propeller came up out of the water with a length of fishing net tightly wrapped around it. There was no way she'd be able to untangle it now. Not with the light almost gone.

"You ran over a net. We're going to have to call Chick and have someone tow us in."

Nolan pulled his phone out of his back pocket. "Damn, I don't have a signal. Do you?"

She slid her finger across her phone screen. It lit up, then dimmed. Before she even had a chance to bring up Chick's number, it died. Damn battery. She should have gone back for her charger before they left the island. Now she was stuck on a boat in the middle of the bay with no way to call for help.

"Hey, Nolan. How good a swimmer are you?"

8

Knox

Sharing a salted nut roll under the light of a crescent moon hadn't been an item on Knox's bucket list, but despite the chilly breeze, he was actually enjoying himself. Claudia had crawled all over the boat with his phone, trying to get a single bar of service, but had been unsuccessful. The only thing they could do now was try not to freeze and hope to flag down one of the ferries that crossed the bay.

"Hey, don't you think Chick will notice you're gone and head out to look for you?" he asked.

Claudia rolled her eyes. "You don't know Chick very well, do you?"

"He's an old friend of the family but we haven't seen each other in years." Knox didn't want to give himself up, so he decided to keep his association with Chick vague.

"Well, Monday night is poker night. He's probably three whiskeys deep into a heated game of Texas Hold'em by now. As long as someone keeps filling his glass, he won't notice I'm gone until he gets up tomorrow morning and no one's made coffee."

"You've been with him for a while now, huh?" Knox broke off another bite of nut roll and offered the rest of the bar to her.

She took it, and her fingers brushed his. Warmth rolled up the length of his arm. The more he talked to Claudia, the more he liked her. She put up a front. Based on how she'd reacted to the guy on the dock and Knox's own response, someone had done something to make her lose trust.

The way she looked out for Chick told him there was a whole other side to her once someone earned their way beyond her defensive wall. For the first time in a hell of a long while, he wondered what it would take to be in someone's inner circle. To be one of the few she let in.

She nibbled on a bite of the candy bar while a smile played over her lips. "Yeah, we've known each other for a while."

"Since I know you didn't grow up in Texas, how did you find your way here?" He might be pressing his luck by asking questions, but there wasn't much else to do. No doubt she'd shut him down if she started to feel threatened.

"I think folks who need Chick seem to find him. He's like a beacon for people who need help. I can't tell you how many lost souls have holed up in Paradise when they needed a break or had to get away from a bad situation. He collects people with a lot of baggage. I just haven't figured out what yours is yet."

"What makes you think I've got baggage?" He gave her an easy grin, but his chest tightened. Maybe she recognized him. It might not be the end of the world. If she'd been around Chick, there was a pretty good chance she knew how to keep things to herself. Based on what he knew about her so far, she didn't seem eager to be caught in the spotlight. He could probably tell her who he was and the real reason he'd come to Paradise.

"Everyone's got baggage." One of her shoulders lifted in a slight shrug. "Sometimes it just gets too heavy to carry by yourself and you have to set it down for a while."

"What's your baggage, Claudia? Did somebody hurt you?"

Pain flashed through her eyes, and she got up from the bench seat. "It's getting chilly. I'm going to see if there's a blanket on board."

Knox blew out a breath and took a sip of his drink. *Way to blow it, ace.* He knew better than to go poking around in someone's past. Even though he hated being in the limelight, working with a bunch of celebrities had taught him that everyone had something to hide.

She came back with a blanket and a bottle of something in her hands. "We're in luck. The blanket doesn't smell too bad, and after we have a few shots of this, neither one of us will care."

"What is it?"

"Tequila. Or as I like to call it, to-kill-ya. I haven't met many people who haven't had a bad experience with tequila shots." She arched a brow like she expected him to contradict her.

"You've got me there. I spent a very long night hugging a toilet thanks to my friend Don Julio."

"I'm impressed. Usually, it's my buddy Jose Cuervo who takes people down. You must have expensive tastes."

Knox chuckled. The only expensive taste he had was in guitars and the company his agent wanted him to keep.

"Sorry we don't have any shot glasses"—she held the bottle out to him—"or any glasses at all. I'm surprised Chick left this on board, since he usually clears everything out when he shuts down for the season."

Knox untwisted the cap and held the bottle up to his nose. Sure smelled like tequila, though he didn't recognize the brand. At least there wasn't a worm floating around inside. He took a swig and wiped the back of his hand across his mouth.

"Well?" Claudia had wrapped the blanket around her shoulders.

"As my uncle used to say, that shit'll put some hairs on your chest." He held the bottle out to her.

"I'd be happy to skip the hairy chest, but I could use some warming up." She took a sip of liquid. Her face scrunched up like she'd skipped the salt and shot and gone straight to sucking on a lime. "Ugh. It's been a long time since I've done a shot of cheap tequila."

It had been a long time since Knox had spent an evening alone with a woman, but he didn't want to share that nugget of info. "What time does the next ferry go by? I want to make sure we don't miss it."

"What time is it now?"

He checked his watch. Damn, he should have left it at home. It had been a gift from his manager when he signed his first record deal. He would have been happy with something a little less flashy, but he often pulled it out and put it on when he was planning on stopping in to visit Tripp. "Almost eight."

Claudia tilted her head back and stared up at the night sky. "It's Monday."

"Yeah." They'd already established that. "Does it operate on a different schedule during the week?"

"The last ferry on Mondays in the off-season runs at seven. There won't be another one until morning." She closed her eyes and returned her head to a normal position. "Unless someone happens to come along, we're going to be out here all night."

Knox nodded, though the words hadn't quite sunk in yet. All night. Floating around in the middle of the bay. With her.

"I knew this was a bad idea." She took another swig from the bottle, this one a much heartier swallow than the last one. Then she mumbled something in Spanish that he couldn't quite make out, though he did pick up a few choice curse words that his friends from school had taught him.

"It's okay." Knox was used to adapting on the fly. Though most of the time his shows appeared to go off without a hitch, he and his band dealt with major obstacles on a regular basis. The most recent crisis ended up with him playing solo to a crowd of forty thousand people for forty-five minutes while his stage crew tried to get the rest of the bands' mics turned on.

"I don't know how you think this is okay. We're probably going to float out into the Gulf of Mexico and wake up in the middle of the ocean." Claudia took another swig from the bottle. "I should have let you grab something to eat. One nut roll isn't going to tide us over until breakfast."

"Hey, I've got this." Knox looked around the boat. There was nothing on the upper level except for a few benches built along the railing, but the level where they stood now had a small cabin and plenty of storage tucked in under the seats. There had to be some sort of provisions on board.

"Why don't you seem worried?" She leaned forward and set her elbow on her knee.

"There are a lot worse places we could be right now. I figure we can anchor so we don't drift out into the gulf, then maybe I can catch us something with one of these fishing poles." He held a pole out to her that he'd found in the cabin.

"And what will we do if you catch something?"

"My friends would revoke my bro card if I didn't know how to fillet a fish. What do you say to a little moonlight fishing?"

"With an offer like that, how could I refuse?" She traded him the bottle for one of the fishing poles in his hands.

"All we need to do is figure out what to use for bait."

"Oh, Chick's got a huge tackle box in the cabin. Hold on a sec and I'll go get it." She got up and started for the door.

A wave rocked the boat, sending her crashing into his side instead. Knox wrapped his arm around her waist to keep her from falling. As he pulled her close, the scent of tequila, musty wool, and something that smelled a lot like coconut filled his nose. He could account for the tequila and the blanket, but the coconut . . . that had to be all Claudia.

"Sorry about that." He immediately let her go, but not before the scent imprinted on his brain. It had been so long since he'd held a woman in his arms. He doled out plenty of hugs to fans, but the last time he gave a woman a genuine hug had been too long ago to remember.

"Thanks." She put her hand on his arm. "I'm such a klutz. I'm surprised I haven't fallen overboard yet."

He could feel the heat from her hand, even through the thin layer of his shirt. "Please don't fall overboard. Not on my watch."

This close to her, even in the dark, he could make out the features of her face. A strong need to skim his palm over her cheek almost made him reach for her, but he stopped himself. He'd come to Paradise for one reason—to write the songs for his album. Letting himself get distracted by Claudia would almost guarantee he wouldn't make his deadline on time.

She nudged her chin up and met his gaze. The moonlight flickered in her eyes. The blanket slid when she lost her balance, and he reached out to resettle it on her shoulders.

"Can't have you getting cold. Especially if we're going to be out here all night."

"Thanks for looking out for me." Her eyes drifted closed, and she lowered her head. "It's been a long time since . . ."

"Since what?" He couldn't stop himself from touching

her. He put his finger under her chin and gently nudged her chin up so she'd be forced to meet his gaze.

"Since I found myself in a situation like this."

"What kind of situation are you in?" He knew exactly what kind of situation he was in, but he wanted to hear her admit to having the same kind of feelings. It couldn't be one-sided. The attraction was too strong. The need to kiss her was almost tangible.

She tilted her head and looked at him. The full force of her brown eyes hit him square in the face. He saw fear mingled with a hint of hope. Hesitation seemed to have control over the heat. "I think you know."

"If you're wondering if I want to kiss you right now, the answer is yes." His heart thudded like someone with a heavy foot had started a kick drum in his chest. It hadn't cost him anything to say it, but it felt like he'd just given up his entire soul.

"Then what are you waiting for?"

Claudia

Nolan leaned in, his lips not even a breath away. She should put her hand on his chest and push him back. Kissing him would open up a wound that hadn't properly healed. She didn't want to put herself out there again. Couldn't afford to go through what she'd experienced the last time she'd let someone get close.

She'd never been good at keeping her heart out of places it shouldn't go. She knew that when she started dating King. This was different, though. Nolan would be gone in six weeks. He'd said himself that he was between jobs and biding time in Paradise before he had to be somewhere else.

The risk was minimal, though the collateral could be

huge. All of that ran through her head in less time than it took for him to close the distance between them. As she considered all the reasons it would be a bad idea for her to let him kiss her, his lips touched hers.

Liquid fire raced through her veins at the contact. It wasn't the pressure of his mouth on hers, or even the way he cupped the back of her head in his palms. All of it combined made her knees knock together. The blanket fell off her shoulders, but she didn't care. With Nolan's mouth slanting over hers, she didn't feel cold. She didn't feel anything at all beyond the heat flowing through her body and pooling at her core.

He pulled away first and touched his nose to hers. "I hope that was okay."

Okay? She cleared her throat and tried to keep her voice steady. "It was fine."

"Just fine?" He let out a soft laugh. "Then we must have had two totally different experiences, because that was a hell of a lot better than fine for me."

She bit down on the laugh that threatened. "I meant it was fine that you kissed me."

"So the kiss itself wasn't fine?"

Her chest still heaved from him taking her breath away. "It was more than fine."

"Good." He skimmed his thumb along her jawline. "Maybe after I catch us some fish for dinner, you'll let me do that again."

Her knees went weak at the idea of him pressing his lips to hers once more. She had to be careful. Not wanting to seem too eager, even though every cell in her body silently screamed for her to smash her mouth against his, she took a step backward.

"The tackle box. I'll get it."

Nolan let his hands fall away. She felt the loss of his touch like she'd just hopped out of a nice hot shower and been plunged into ice water.

"Don't forget this." He reached down and picked up the blanket.

Claudia pulled it onto her shoulders. The smell of wet wool filled her nose, reminding her of what her dog used to smell like when he came in from playing in the rain. She'd rather bury her nose in Nolan's shoulder and inhale his warm, masculine scent, but she needed to pace herself.

First, the tackle box. Her brain was scrambled from not being able to think on an empty stomach. If he caught a fish, and if she filled her belly, then maybe she'd be able to think straight about whether kissing him again would be a good idea.

Her gut already knew the answer. Kissing Nolan would open up a treasure trove of past hurts she couldn't afford to face. Putting a firm halt to anything ever happening between them would be the wisest course of action. The safest.

She wrapped her fingers around the handle of the tackle box and carried it back out to the open deck. "Here you go. I have no idea what's what. Chick hires a guy from the mainland to take tourists out on this thing during the summer."

"Have you ever held a fishing pole?"

"I'm from Minnesota. Being able to fish is practically a requirement for high school graduation." She cocked a hip, then realized what kind of information she'd revealed. Maybe he didn't hear her. Maybe his head was just as scrambled as hers after the kiss they'd shared.

"Minnesota, huh? What part?" He'd unclasped the lid and crouched down to dig through the top layer of the tackle box.

"Oh, um, it's a tiny town up north. I doubt you've ever heard of it." Usually, the lies rolled off her tongue easily. Too easily. This time, a pang twinged through her stomach as she tried to make herself sound convincing.

"I went to northern Minnesota once. My dad and grand-dad took me and a friend camping up in the Boundary Waters. They say everything's bigger in Texas, but y'all have us beat when it comes to the size of the mosquitoes."

She forced a laugh. "I'm not sure I want to claim that honor, but I guess it is what it is."

"Here. Try this." He'd attached a neon lure to the line and handed her the fishing pole. "I don't know what will work this time of year down here, but we can give it a go."

"Thanks." She took the pole and walked to the edge of the boat. Staring into the dark water, she wondered how the hell she'd gotten herself into a situation like this and, even more important, how she was going to get herself out.

"Any chance you want to put a little wager on the fishing?" Nolan attached another one of the lures to his line and joined her at the railing.

"What kind of wager?"

"First one to catch a fish doesn't have to clean it." He arched a brow in a challenge. "Or we can each clean our own if you'd rather."

Claudia grimaced at the thought of scaling and filleting something for dinner. "You're on."

Nolan cast his line and slowly reeled in the slack. "What's it like in Minnesota?"

Of course he'd been paying attention. "Um, cold in the winter and nice in the short summers."

"So you know how to ski and snowboard and all that stuff?"

She didn't want to keep talking about her home state. If he put two and two together, he might figure out who she was. Or at least who she'd been. If she could change the subject, maybe she could get him talking about himself. Guys loved to do that. "How do you know Chick?"

"We met through a mutual friend. They were both into rodeo."

"But not you?" Talking about Chick would be safe.

"Oh, I tried a few times over the years. Never made it past mutton busting."

"That's riding sheep, right?" She tried to picture him as a kid, wrapping his arms around the neck of a fluffy sheep and trying to hold on for dear life.

"Yeah. I figured if I couldn't best a sheep, I had no business trying to ride a bronc or a bull. Chick, though, what a career he had, right?" His fingers rested on the knob on his reel.

Claudia nodded, pulling her attention away from watching his hands. Her skin still tingled from where he'd touched her earlier. "He's a legend."

Nolan reached for the bottle of tequila she'd set on the deck between them. "How long have you been tending bar?"

"Quite a while." She tried to settle back into her standard responses of noncommittal answers. No matter how detailed the question, she was usually able to evade a direct response. Being around Nolan had thrown her off. All she needed to do was a simple course correction and get herself back on track. Nolan handed her the bottle, but before she could take it, the line she'd cast vibrated slightly. "I think I've got a bite."

Nolan set the bottle down. "Go easy. You don't want it to spook before you hook it."

"I told you I know how to fish." She would have given him some major side eye, but she was too engrossed in watching the clear filament move.

"I'll keep my mouth shut, then. Show me how it's done." His tone teased—a surefire way to make sure she wouldn't let this one get away.

"Watch and learn." With a claim like that, hopefully she wouldn't botch landing whatever tugged at the end of her line. She let out some length, giving the fish a little extra space. When the hard tug came, she was ready. "I've got him."

"Reel it in, then." Nolan held his pole loosely in his hand and turned toward her.

She didn't look over but could feel his gaze. *Please let there be some sort of monster fish on the end of this line.* Not only was she so hungry that she could probably eat a two-hundred-pound tuna on her own, she wanted to impress Nolan. It was such an unfamiliar sensation—the desire for a man's approval—her palms started to sweat.

"You've got it, Claudia. That's it." He moved closer. "Is there a net anywhere on board?"

"Yeah, look under that seat over there." She nodded toward one of the bench seats.

Nolan set his pole in one of the holders Chick had attached to the railing and retrieved the net. "If you get it close enough, I can scoop it out of the water."

She continued to battle the fish, letting the line out, then reeling it back in while attempting to wear the creature out. It had to be a decent size based on the effort she was making. Her biceps burned from the constant pull, but there was no way she'd pass her pole off to Nolan. He wasn't going to get credit for reeling this baby in.

While she continued to work on landing the fish, Nolan's line wiggled. He grabbed for the pole right before it went sailing overboard.

"Nice save," Claudia said. Now it was even more important for her to be the first to catch a fish. She didn't want to be on the hook herself if he won their bet. The fish had to be getting close to giving up. Though she hadn't done much fishing in the ocean, she had plenty of experience pulling walleye and trout and muskie out of the lake where her grandparents had a cabin. She'd also gone along with King on several fishing tournaments. Although he'd grown up in

Arizona, he embraced the lake life and never passed up an opportunity to get out on the water,

"It's a big one." Nolan reeled in the slack in his line. "Looks like you might be in some trouble now."

She tucked her chin and pulled on the pole. This wasn't a battle or a bet she was going to lose.

9

◦──◦ ♡ ◦──◦

Knox

Claudia was beautiful no matter what she was doing, but standing a few feet away, all riled up at the idea of losing their bet and battling some sort of monster under the sea, she was stunning. Sweat beaded along her brow and she'd shrugged off the blanket. Though she had on a long-sleeve shirt, he could imagine what her muscles looked like underneath as she struggled with the pole.

"Need to take a break?" Knox asked.

"Of course not." She doubled down on her efforts.

He could have told her to be careful and not rush the process, but this was one time he wouldn't mind pushing his gentlemanly tendencies aside and beating her at her own game. She didn't have to agree to the bet.

Claudia leaned over the railing. "You might want to get that net ready."

Water splashed against the sides of the boat as the fish struggled against the line. A few more inches and she'd have it close enough to haul over the side. He held tight to his own pole while he reached for the net. There was still time for the fish to make a break for it.

"What is it? Can you tell what I caught?" she asked. "I hope it's a redfish. They taste just like red snapper. I'm so hungry, I'd eat just about anything. After you fillet it, of course."

Knox was about to admit defeat and cut his line so he could focus on helping her get her fish onto the boat. Then a fin popped out of the water. What the hell? "Uh, Claudia?"

"Yes?"

"I think you caught a shark."

"Are you kidding me?" She leaned over the edge, the pole still gripped tightly in her hands.

The fish tossed its head back and forth, fighting the line. Then it jumped. All Knox saw was a row of sharp white teeth. He slammed into Claudia, knocking her pole out of her hands and pushing her away from the railing. They fell to the deck, and he dropped his own pole. It slid across the deck and he pushed himself up to lunge for it. They couldn't afford to lose both fishing poles. It was their only chance at dinner.

His fingers closed around the base right before it sailed over the railing. With his heart thundering in his chest, he turned back to Claudia. She laid flat on her back, looking up at the stars while her chest heaved.

"You okay?"

She struggled to sit up. "That was a shark."

"Yeah, it was." Thankfully, they both still had all their fingers intact.

"Like, a real shark."

"As real as they get," he agreed.

"Well, looks like we're not having shark for dinner. I guess you win, seeing as how I don't even have a fishing pole." She bit down on her lip like she was trying to keep from laughing.

Knox's hands still shook from the close encounter. "Sorry for making you drop your pole. What if we call it a tie? You actually caught the first fish, but we wouldn't have been able to get it on board."

"A tie, huh? Does that mean you're going to do the dirty work?"

"Excuse me?" Knox's mind immediately went to a place he was pretty sure she didn't intend to send it.

"The gutting and stuff. I'll figure out how to fire up the grill if you handle the rest."

He slowly reeled in the line that had been let out while they'd been messing with the shark. "Sounds fair to me."

"Good. Now bring it in so we can get something in our bellies. Wrestling that shark wore me out."

It took another fifteen minutes, but between the two of them, the fish didn't stand a chance. Claudia disappeared to the back of the boat to mess with the grill and left him to deal with prepping the fish. It had been years since he'd had to fend for himself like this.

Granted, at worst he and Claudia would be stuck overnight, so it wasn't like they were really roughing it. When he'd been up in the Boundary Waters of Minnesota, he'd had to depend on the skills his dad and granddad had taught him. Skills like how to find the best place to set up camp, which berries he could eat and which ones he should avoid. Though he'd never inhabit the same space as the man he used to call his father ever again, he missed the time they'd spent out in the wilderness.

When he'd been on the road, he had a chef, a manager, a publicist, a driver, a road crew, bandmates, and more. Everyone had tried to make things easier on him, off-loading the things he didn't need to do so he'd be rested enough to perform. They didn't want him going anywhere alone. It was like having a babysitter watching his every move. Here with Claudia, he felt more free than he had in a long time.

"The grill's ready. How's the fish coming along?" she called out from the other side of the boat.

"Just about done." He set the fillets on a piece of foil she'd found inside and tossed the rest overboard. "Do we have anything to season it with?"

Claudia held up the bottle of tequila. "There aren't a whole lot of options."

"Well, let's see what we can do with that." He stepped into the head to wash his hands, grateful that there was still a supply of fresh water on board.

When he came out, she'd already put the fish on the grill. It smelled delicious—just like the foil fish packets his granddad used to toss on the hot coals when they'd go camping. If only he had some salt and pepper and a few slices of lemon. His stomach rumbled just thinking about it

"Want another drink?" Claudia offered him the bottle.

"What would you make with tequila if you had a fully stocked bar at your disposal?" He took a swig and handed it back to her.

"That's a good question. Most people would go for a tequila sunrise, but I tend to like a paloma better."

"What's in a paloma?" He considered himself pretty well versed when it came to cocktails, but he'd never heard of that one.

"Built around grapefruit juice." She lifted her brows. "It's delicious."

"I'll have to try that sometime. What do you usually drink?"

"Oh, I don't." She glanced at the bottle of tequila in her hand. "I mean, I usually don't. But desperate times call for desperate measures."

"Are these desperate times?" Knox didn't miss the slight slur of her words. If she was telling the truth and didn't usually drink, the tequila was probably knocking her a little off-kilter.

"I don't know." She leaned against a post that supported the second story of the boat. "Do I look desperate?"

"No, of course not." He'd learned enough from his friendship with Em not to take the bait. When a woman asked a question like that, he'd be shooting himself in the foot if he said yes. The last thing he'd call Claudia was desperate. She was gorgeous, funny, independent, and sensitive. He'd seen the way guys talked her up while she shot down advances at the bar. Desperate was definitely one thing she was not.

She slumped onto one of the bench seats. "Good."

"I'd never call you desperate."

"What would you call me, then?" She squinted up at him.

Several words came to mind. Kind. Hot. Caring. Beautiful. Driven. Desirable. Even though he knew he shouldn't be, deep down he'd been attracted to her from the moment her face appeared under the stall of his shower.

"Well?" she pressed.

"I'm thinking."

She patted the spot next to her. "You're not supposed to think about it. Just say the first thing that comes to mind."

His cheeks heated. He'd never admit the first word that came into his mind when he thought about her. It started with an *f* and ended with *uckable*. Even though he wanted her, she was so much more than that. "What about intriguing?"

Doubt creased her forehead. "Intriguing? What's so intriguing about me?"

"You've got secrets. There's something you're not telling me. Something that ruined your trust, I'm guessing." He held her gaze for a long beat. The tequila was starting to leach into her system. He could tell by the way her eyelids floated to half-mast.

"You're good, Nolan." She waggled her finger in front of him. "Maybe you should be a detective."

Hell to the no on that. All he'd ever wanted to do was make music. "I think we need to get something into your stomach. Let's go see if the fish is ready."

She lifted her shirt and rubbed her palm over her belly. "Can you hear it?"

Seeing her stomach sent a shot of heat straight to his crotch. "Nah, I can't, but I bet it's grumbling. Let's get you some dinner."

"Listen." She motioned for him to come closer. "It's talking."

Her fingers skimmed up and down her bare skin, skating over her belly button and making him wish he was touching her instead of gripping the railing of the boat.

"Put your ear right here." She patted her stomach.

"I don't think that's such a good idea." As much as he wanted her, he would never take advantage of her. She'd had too much tequila on an empty stomach. She didn't mean what she was saying, didn't really want what she was asking for. "Why don't you just tell me what it's saying?"

"It's saying 'feed me fish, please.'"

10

❦

Claudia

Dry cotton filled her mouth. She couldn't swallow past her tongue. It had multiplied in size overnight. Claudia cracked her eyelid open and immediately closed it again. The sun was too bright. Why hadn't she closed her shades last night? Last night . . . something poked at the back of her brain. Last night . . . a hazy memory of being on the boat drifted through her head.

She reached out to pull the covers over her head. Her hand patted the space next to her, searching for her lightweight bedspread. The one with the tiny, embroidered flowers on the edge.

Instead of a handful of organic cotton, her fingers wrapped around something warm. Something hard. Something male.

Her eyelids flew open. Nolan lay next to her. They were on the deck of the party barge, covered by a wrinkled blanket. In a flash, it all came back to her. Swigging tequila from the bottle . . . fishing off the side of the boat . . . nibbling on fresh grilled fish . . . then kissing. There had been lots and lots of kissing.

She held the blanket away from her chest. The sight of her bra and panties provided some level of comfort. Still, her breath caught while her heart rate spiked. They'd spent the night on the boat. Stranded in the middle of the bay. And Nolan . . . She glanced over at the man curled into her side. *Please don't let him be naked. Please.*

A quick peek under the blanket told her he was a boxer briefs man. His other clothes were scattered over the deck. A pair of jeans sat in a pile to her left and his shirt hung from the key sticking out of the ignition. A mangled moan worked its way past her engorged tongue. She needed water. She needed aspirin. She needed to get the heck out of there.

Nolan's eyelids parted. Any second he'd wake up and everything that had happened between them would become real. She wanted to close her eyes and fall back asleep. This was just a bad dream. A crazy, tequila-fueled nightmare that didn't actually happen. She shielded her eyes from the sun with her forearm and counted to ten in her head.

But when she opened her eyes again, nothing had changed. Nothing except that Nolan's eyes had opened, too. A deep furrow creased his brow.

"Claudia?" His voice came out soft. "You okay?"

How could she be okay when she couldn't remember much about the past several hours? "Um, maybe?"

He made a move to lift up the covers, but she clamped her arm down tight on the blanket. "Don't."

Gah, she needed a drink. The thought sent her stomach into a spin. Water. Just water. It was like a shop vac had sucked every bit of moisture out of her body and left her there to shrivel up like a raisin.

"It's all right. I just need to stand up and stretch for a minute."

"No." She shook her head so hard, she was afraid her eyeballs would keep spinning when she stopped, like in those old-time cartoons she and her sister used to watch.

"Let me get you some water."

The promise of water was tempting, but she wasn't ready to face what might have happened between them.

"We didn't do anything last night, did we?" They couldn't have. She hadn't had sex in over four years. At least not with a real person. Her battery-operated substitute didn't count. And Knox wasn't just any guy. Based on the size of his hands, if they'd done *it*, surely she'd remember.

Unless . . .

Unless it hadn't been good.

She closed her eyes and covered her face with her hands. Leave it to her to wait four years, then have sucky sex with a stranger. She should have let the shark drag her overboard last night and chew her into tiny pieces. That would be better than living through the absolute worst morning-after experience she could ever imagine.

"Is that what you're worried about?" Nolan rested his hand on her shoulder with the blanket between them. "We shared a few kisses. Then we got hot, so we both stripped down to our underwear and fell asleep. I woke up and saw you shivering so I pulled the blanket over us."

"That's it?" A sense of relief hovered around her, waiting for his confirmation.

"That's it. I could tell you were a little tipsy, and I would never take advantage of a woman."

She separated her fingers and peeked through the sliver of space between them. Nolan brushed her hair away from her forehead and held her gaze for a long beat. She was embarrassed for letting the tequila get the best of her but relieved she hadn't gotten too carried away.

"Thanks. I'm sorry for being such a hot mess last night."

His lips tipped up and his eyes crinkled at the corners. "You weren't a mess. You had a crappy day, including getting stranded on a boat and almost having your hand bit off by a shark. I'd say a little overindulgence in tequila was probably justified."

She smiled back, and despite the awkwardness of the situation and the headache pounding between her temples, her opinion of Nolan skyrocketed.

The sound of a horn blared. It was close. Too close. The Paradise Island Ferry was bearing down on them. She could see the captain sitting in the wheelhouse on the upper deck. He waved and picked up his radio.

"Ahoy there. Y'all look like you might be in need of some help."

Claudia mumbled to herself. This wasn't happening. Couldn't be happening.

Nolan stretched out, his long fingers reaching for his jeans a few feet away. "Stay here. I'll figure this out."

She pulled the blanket over her head and curled into the fetal position. She'd tried so hard to stay under the radar, and look where it got her. There were probably tourists aboard the ferry. Tourists with smartphones and cameras. Right now, they were probably snapping shots of her and Nolan. She'd left the spotlight behind in Minneapolis and now she'd end up a meme or, even worse, a GIF that kids would blast all over social media.

Nolan somehow wiggled into his jeans and got to his feet. She didn't dare peek out from under the blanket, but she saw him walk toward the bow of the barge.

"Hey, we could use a tow back to the island. We got stuck out here all night when a net got wrapped up in the motor." The calm and steadiness of his voice soothed her nerves. He was handling it. Maybe she could avoid having her face splashed all over the internet.

He leaned over and whispered to her, "I'm going to get us hooked up to be towed in. If you want to, you could hide out in the cabin until we get back to the dock."

"Okay." She gathered the few items of clothing she could reach and crouched into an awkward scramble toward the privacy of the small cabin at the back of the boat. When she got inside, she slammed the door behind her. The windows were covered in a layer of salt grime that would make it difficult for someone to see inside. Too bad it made it almost impossible to tell what was happening on the deck.

Muffled laughter reached her ears. She pulled on her jeans but had grabbed Nolan's shirt instead of her own. Desperate times called for desperate measures, so she shoved her arms through the sleeves of his shirt and buttoned it up the middle. Being surrounded by his scent lowered her pulse. She took in a few deep breaths as the boat began to move.

A few minutes later, Nolan knocked on the door to the cabin. "Hey, we're all tied up now. Should be back at the dock in about twenty minutes."

She cracked the door open. "Thank you."

"Of course. Are you feeling any better?"

Her stomach had settled and the painful throbbing under her skull had subsided. "Feeling better now. At least until I have to tell Chick what we did to his boat."

"It was my fault. I'll cover it."

"Don't be silly. I'm sure Chick's got insurance. I'll look into it when we get back." Nolan might have a nice truck and a pricey watch, but the man moved from job to job. She wouldn't let him pay for fixing the motor when she should have been the one navigating the boat.

"Well, if he doesn't, let me know."

"Okay."

"Okay." He nodded and was about to turn away when he stopped. "Hey, Claudia?"

"Yes?"

"I know you were worried about how far things went last night, but for what it's worth, if we'd been together you wouldn't be questioning whether or not it happened."

His cockiness caught her off guard, but she had a sneaking suspicion he was absolutely right. "How can you be so sure?"

"Because being with you would definitely be a night worth remembering." His lips curved into a smile, then he walked away.

She rested her forehead on the doorframe and let that sink in. Maybe she'd been wrong about Nolan. Maybe he wasn't too good to be true. Maybe he was exactly what she needed.

11

Knox

It had been three days since the night Knox spent in the middle of the bay with Claudia, and the music was still coming. He'd been scribbling down lines as fast as they hit him, jotting snippets of songs on scrap pieces of paper, napkins, and even a piece of a palm tree when he couldn't find the notebook he usually carried.

Every time he looked at her, inspiration struck. They weren't the same style of songs he'd had on his last album—they were better. More like the music he'd written when he first started out. The music that defined him. The music that came from deep down inside.

"We're about to install a toilet. What are you so happy about?" Claudia stood next to the big box holding the new toilet they'd ordered. A pair of well-worn overalls hugged her hips. His mouth went dry just looking at her.

"Can't a guy be in a good mood every once in a while?"

She frowned as he stepped past her. Chick had had a guy from the mainland frame out the bathroom and do the wiring and plumbing. Now they just needed to install the fixtures, and she'd have her very own en suite, including a steam shower.

"You're never in this good of a mood." Claudia followed him.

"Maybe the island is getting to me."

"Hmm." She looked him up and down, giving him an ex-aggerated once over. "You sure you didn't add a little extra something to your coffee this morning?"

Knox laughed. "You know it uses fewer muscles to smile than it does to frown?"

"Where did you hear that? Some inspirational podcast?" She crossed her arms over her chest and raised her brows.

"I saw it on TV this morning." He glanced around her cozy studio space. That's what was missing, a television set. "Hey, you don't have a TV in here. Why not?"

She took out a box cutter and sliced through the tape. "Too stressful. I'd rather listen to the sound of the waves when I'm trying to relax."

Fair enough. "Should we get your toilet installed?"

"That would be great." Claudia pulled apart the box, and he got the new toilet settled into place.

He could think of a million things he'd rather be doing than installing a toilet, but at least it gave him an excuse to spend time with her. Since they'd gotten back from their trip to the mainland, she'd been busy helping Chick set up for their upcoming event, and he'd hardly had a chance to see her.

Working together now, squeezing into the small space of the bathroom, tightening down the bolts while she crouched over him, he was reminded of all the things he'd enjoyed about her. Getting her to smile, even when she tried to hide it, made his chest swell. And she smelled amazing. Like a virgin piña colada . . . all coconut and pineapple with none of the rum.

Too bad he knew she tasted even better. He'd spent several hours lying awake in his bed, replaying every moment from that night on the boat.

"There. Should be good to go." He pressed the plastic caps onto the base to cover the bolts.

"Thank you. Now we only have seven more to do." She put her hands on her hips and looked around the small space. "This is amazing."

"It'll be nice not to have to hike to the shower house every day." Knox would miss having the chance to catch her on her way in or out, but he was glad that once he was gone, she wouldn't have to trek back and forth across the sand to shower. In the short time they'd known each other, he'd become a little possessive. It was unwarranted, and she'd be pissed if she found out, but ever since the night on the boat, he felt like they'd connected on a deeper level. The tough exterior she put in place was just that—an exterior. He'd seen behind the front she projected. Seen the vulnerability she wanted to keep hidden from the rest of the world.

"Yes, it will." She ran her hand over the newly set tile on the shower wall. "Now there won't be any risk of me accidentally exposing myself to a stranger."

"You say that like it was a bad thing," he joked.

Her jaw dropped. "It was a bad thing."

"I kind of enjoyed it." He lifted a shoulder in a slight shrug.

Her cheeks flushed. "I kind of enjoyed it, too."

His pulse raced. Had she just admitted she liked seeing him naked in the shower? Unless he was reading the signs wrong, he was 99 percent sure she'd just offered him an opening. Feeling empowered by her admission, he seized it.

"Hey, I was wondering if you might want to hang out sometime. I haven't seen much of the island since we've been working so hard."

Tossing a quick glance back at him, she gave him a cautious smile. "I volunteer at a wild horse sanctuary on Friday mornings. If you want to go with me tomorrow, I can show you that side of the Island."

"Yeah, I'd love that." He'd grown up on the back of a horse at his family's ranch, but he hadn't spent time there in years. Partly because his career had him on the road 75 percent of the time, but mainly due to the falling out he'd had with his dad. He missed being around horses. Missed a lot about ranch life.

"Great. Meet me in front of the bar at seven. We can take an ATV down the coast and I'll introduce you to some of my favorite four-legged beasts."

"Sounds good."

"Now, let's focus on getting the rest of the toilets installed. Chick and I are meeting with the guys from the local radio station in a couple of hours, and Gabe is coming in before his shift starts for some help with his song. I'd like to have the chance to try out my new shower before that."

Visions of Claudia in the shower raced through his head. He could have offered to join her. If she needed someone to soap up her back or help her rinse her hair, he'd be happy to volunteer. But they'd just reached a checkpoint in their nontraditional relationship. He didn't want to rush things and scare her away. Hell, he wasn't sure he should even be pursuing her. He'd be gone in a month or so. He didn't have time for a relationship. Not to mention he had serious trust issues when it came to dating again.

Then she bent over to pick up the wrench he'd been using. Her ass stuck up in the air and he wanted to run his hands along her hips, pull her against him, and forget all about pretending to be a construction worker between jobs. He wanted to hum against her throat and work out the chords for a new melody to go with the lyrics she'd inspired as he stroked her soft skin.

"Nolan?" She stood in front of him, arms crossed over her middle, a stern look on her face. "Did you hear what I said?"

"Sorry, I've had something on my mind."

The edges of her eyes softened. "Do you want to talk about it?"

"No, that's okay. I'll handle it myself." He couldn't tell her that he couldn't get her out of his head. That he fell asleep every night wondering what it would feel like to wrap his long limbs around her curves and bury his nose in her hair. That he woke up every morning hoping to see her face. That the only songs coming to him right now revolved around her.

She'd become his muse. She'd become his inspiration. She was also unavailable. No matter how he tried to work it out, there was no situation in which the two of them would end up together. It didn't make sense. She freaked out when she left the island, and he spent 75 percent of his time on the road.

The best he could do was gratefully take the inspiration she was unintentionally providing and be on his way. That's what would be best for Claudia, even if he wasn't sure anymore that it would be best for him.

Claudia

She didn't expect Nolan to be waiting for her on the empty strand of beach outside the bar at six fifty-five the next morning, but there he was. He must have gotten up extra early since he greeted her with a thermal mug of coffee. Two sugars and a splash of skim milk . . . just the way she liked it.

"Thanks. You didn't have to get up early to make coffee."

"Actually, I did." He nodded toward the mug she'd just lifted to her lips. "Chick told me what you're like before you get your coffee and I've caught a couple of glimpses myself."

"Really? What am I like?" She wasn't a morning person and knew she could be a bit of a grouch before the caffeine kicked in, but she wanted to hear it from Nolan.

His eyes widened and his brows shot up. "Not bad."

"Anyone ever tell you you're an awful liar?" She pulled the key to the bar's ATV out of her pocket and headed toward the storage shed where Chick kept it. Cars weren't allowed on the island at all, but a few people had ATVs and golf carts to get around.

Nolan let out a soft laugh. "I suppose there are worse things to be bad at."

"I can think of a few."

"Such as?" he asked.

"Well, there's the obvious one. Sex."

"Hey, I'm not bad at sex," he fired back.

She unlocked the storage-shed door and pulled it open. "How do you know?"

"I haven't had any complaints."

Men—they were all the same. "You think just because someone doesn't take the time to tell you you're bad at it, that means you're automatically good? Most of the women I know have faked it with more than one guy on more than one occasion."

Nolan sputtered, almost spitting out the sip of coffee he'd just swallowed. "I don't believe you."

"Why would I lie?" She pulled the tarp off the ATV.

"I'd be able to tell if a woman was faking." He nodded, like he needed to convince himself.

"You want me to go all *When Harry Met Sally* on you to make my point?" After she shoved the tarp onto one of the metal shelves, she climbed onto the ATV.

"That's not necessary."

"I don't want you to think I'm lying about it." She took

another sip of her coffee, then set it in the cup holder. Rolling her neck, she tried to work the kinks from her shoulders.

"I guess we'll agree to disagree about it."

She shook her head. It didn't work that way. She knew for a fact that she was telling him the truth. If he didn't want to believe her, that was on him. Unless she could prove it. A little early-morning embarrassment would be worth making her point. She sucked in a breath and let out a low moan. "Mmmmm."

He glanced over from where he stood at the entrance to the shed. "You okay, Claudia?"

"Ohhhhh." The word floated out on a long, breathy exhale. Even though it had been years since she'd had halfway decent sex, she could still remember the techniques she used to guarantee she wouldn't miss her favorite show on TV. Sometimes a guy didn't want to let up unless he knew he'd satisfied his partner. And sometimes no matter how awesome a guy's aim was when throwing a football, he couldn't find a G-spot without a map, custom GPS, and automatic targeting. Yeah, she remembered how to fake it. And shaking Nolan's confidence would be worth dusting off her acting skills and undermining the air of confidence he had floating around him.

"That's not funny, Claudia." He leaned on the shelving unit, nonchalantly sipping from his thermal mug.

"Yeah, right there, baby." She narrowed her eyes and let her head roll back. "Just like that."

Nolan's feet shuffled like he'd shifted his weight from one foot to the other, like he wasn't as comfortable as he might want to pretend.

"Mmm"—she lowered her voice into more of a moan— "mmm-hmm, just a little, oh! Yes!" She gripped the handlebars of the ATV and tossed her head to one side.

"Cut it out. You've made your point."

"Oh, Nolan, yes. Give it to me, sugar. More. Now. I'm close . . . so close. I need you. There. Right there. Oh . . ." She opened her eyes. The smirk on her lips faded as she met his gaze.

Fire burned in his eyes. The kind of heat she could feel from half a room away. He stared at her, pinning her in place with just his eyes.

He left his coffee on the shelf and took even strides toward her. She couldn't move. Like an insect caught in a dangerous spider's web, all she could do was wait and see what he'd do when he reached her.

Stopping in front of her, he crouched down until they could stare into each other's eyes. "It's too bad you're so good at that. Obviously, you've been missing out on some really good sex if you've gotten that good at faking it."

The comment landed where he intended. A jolt of heat surged to her core. She held tight to the handlebars of the ATV to keep herself from reaching for him.

"We ready to head out? I can't wait to see these horses."

She'd gotten a little turned on during her Oscar-worthy performance, but now . . . now her panties felt like she'd pulled them off the laundry line too soon. She shifted, uncomfortable with how her body reacted to him.

"Did you want me to drive, or should I sit behind you?" He gestured toward the elongated, narrow seat where her ass currently perched.

She considered the question. Would it be less of a turn-on to have his big hands splayed across her rib cage and have his muscular thighs sandwiched around her or have to press her cheek against his back and listen to the *thump thump* of his heartbeat the whole way down the beach?

"Well?" Nolan asked again. The way he arched a single brow let her know he'd taken control of the situation. She'd made her point, but now she was the one who couldn't get a picture of the two of them tangled in each other's arms out of her head.

"I'll drive down. If you want to take over on the way back, we can trade." She shrugged like it was no big deal. Like her entire body wouldn't be on high alert the entire ride down the beach.

He flung a leg over the seat and nestled his chest against her back. His thighs encased hers, his crotch pressing up against her ass. The only thing that prevented her from being embarrassed was the feel of something hard and thick against her backside. Unless he was packing something in the front of his pants, he was just as turned on as she was.

She turned the key and gave the ATV some gas. The trip down the beach to the horse sanctuary had the potential to be the longest ride of her life.

Nolan wrapped an arm around her middle. Though she knew he was only doing it so he didn't fall off the back end, the gesture felt possessive and casual at the same time. He had an easy way about him. Unlike King, who needed constant reassurance, Nolan exuded an air of confidence. Like he was comfortable in his own skin and didn't give a rat's ass about what anyone else thought. It was sexy. She'd never been around anyone like him before. Except for Chick. Her boss had the same air of confidence about him.

Claudia assumed that's what happened when a person was exactly where they were supposed to be and doing exactly what they were meant to do. She'd never felt that way. All her life, she had felt like she was trying to catch up. Trying to be the person other people wanted her to be. Since she'd been in Paradise, the feeling had faded, but it was still there. The only time she felt sure of what she was doing was when she was helping Gabe.

Sharing her knowledge with him made her feel like everything she had gone through with King, all the good and the bad, hadn't been for nothing. If she could save Gabe from getting burned by the spotlight, it would be worth it.

The beach was deserted this early in the morning. Except for a few boats anchored offshore, there wasn't another person or vehicle around. This was the time of day she loved the most. When it felt like the world belonged to her. Her gaze scanned the endless miles of ocean. Off in the distance, a pod of dolphins played.

She cut the gas and slowed down. Then she turned her head so Nolan could hear her. "Look out there. See the dolphins?"

His arm tightened around her middle. "Wow. What are they doing out there?"

"Swimming. Playing. Enjoying life?" He was close enough that she could feel the warmth of his breath brush her cheek.

"Looks like they've got it all figured out."

She swiveled her head to look at him. "What do you mean?"

"Enjoying life. Seems like things would be a whole lot easier if we took a few lessons from dolphins, don't you think?" His lips spread into a smile that sent warmth all the way down to the tips of her toes.

"Sure. Until a shark comes along."

He chuckled. "You're definitely a glass-half-empty woman, aren't you?"

She ignored the question and asked one of her own. "You ever wonder why the ocean isn't overrun with dolphins?"

"Because they get caught in fishing nets?" he offered.

That wasn't the point she was trying to make. "Maybe they're so busy playing they don't see the sharks coming until it's too late."

"Or"—Nolan moved his thumb, just a slight skimming over her ribs—"maybe if they played more, the sharks would leave them alone."

At that moment, one of the dolphins breached, jumping all the way out of the water and twisting its body around in a spiral before it disappeared back into the ocean.

"Sure looks like those dolphins are having a good time. Maybe your outlook would change if you had a little bit more fun, too."

She stepped on the gas, leaving the dolphins behind and putting an end to the conversation. Nolan might think he had her figured out, but he was way off base, and she had no intention of letting him get close enough to change her mind.

12

❦

Knox

Knox wasn't sure what was more mesmerizing . . . watching the wild horses as their hooves pounded over the beach, or watching Claudia's reaction to them. She'd checked in at the small office at the entrance to the sanctuary, then driven them both past the locked gate that marked the boundary to the sealed-off area.

He had no idea such a place existed, especially on such a small island. She filled him in on the history of the sanctuary as they made their way to the first station.

"Historians think the first wild horses ended up on the island when a ship crashed offshore. The horses swam to the island and have been living here ever since." She navigated the ATV over the scrubby trail. They'd headed inland from the beach to reach one of several feeding stations.

"I've heard of the wild horses in the Outer Banks, but didn't realize they had them down here as well."

"Yeah. There are other herds scattered up and down the East Coast. About twenty years ago, the population here had dwindled to only about a dozen. That's when the nonprofit formed and forced the island to donate the northern third as a sanctuary."

"They're beautiful." He'd only seen a few of the wild horses from far away. They'd been running along the surf when Claudia drove past the gate. The combination of muscular grace had him in awe. He'd always loved working with the horses on the ranch, but seeing them in their natural habitat, so wild and powerful and free, made him wonder what his own mount at home would be like if he'd never been broken.

"First stop is right here." She cut the engine and got off the back of the ATV. They'd loaded some supplemental hay onto the back when they'd checked in.

"Let me help you with that." He grabbed hold of the bale and carried it over to where Claudia stood. "Do you have to supplement their feed year-round?"

"Just in the winter months. They'd probably be fine without it, but we like to make sure none of them goes without."

"How long have you been helping out here?" The more he got to know Claudia, the more she surprised him. She hadn't told him yet what she did before she moved to Paradise. It didn't matter, but he wanted to know. He wanted to know everything about her. Where had she gotten the idea that she needed to protect herself? Who had hurt her so badly she felt like she couldn't be herself?

"Chick used to do it, but I took over for him about two years ago. He won't admit it, but all those years of being knocked around by the world's toughest bulls are getting to him."

"I can imagine." Knox thought of his buddy Justin, who came from a long line of professional bull riders. Thankfully, he'd gotten out before he'd suffered a permanent injury. Justin's brother hadn't been so fortunate. Jake would always walk with a limp.

"They might be wild, but they know a good thing when

they see one." Claudia nudged her chin toward the top of a short hill. "If you hold real still, they might come over and say hi."

Knox held his breath as a few of the wild horses cautiously approached. The sun glinted off the chestnut-colored stallion that seemed to be in charge. Knox gathered a handful of hay and held it out. The stallion moved closer, the muscles along his neck rolling under his gorgeous coat.

He nickered and nibbled a little bit of the hay from Knox's hand. Tempted to reach up and run his palm along the smooth coat of the horse's side, Knox resisted. This wasn't a tame ranch horse. He glanced up to see Claudia watching him. A hint of a smile danced over her lips.

Once Knox ran out of hay, the stallion shifted his attention to the bale instead. Claudia had spread some out, so the other horses didn't have to come as close. Knox moved to where she stood by the ATV.

"Isn't it a gorgeous sight?" she whispered.

"Yeah, it really is," he replied. He knew she'd been referring to the horses, but he couldn't take his eyes off her. She looked so relaxed, like she didn't have a care in the world beyond taking care of these beautiful creatures. Watching her was intoxicating. The sun had burned through the early-morning fog and now brought out the highlights of light brown in her dark hair.

She glanced over and caught him staring at her. Immediately, her cheeks flushed, and she shifted her gaze to the ATV. "We have a few more stops before we have to check the water troughs. You ready?"

"Lead the way." He slipped back onto the seat behind her, eager to feel her sandwiched between his thighs again. Maybe he'd tell her he didn't want to drive on the way back. If he sat in front, he wouldn't have the chance to nudge his nose into her hair or clamp his arm around her middle.

Too soon, they'd made the rounds with the hay and finished checking the water troughs. The sun sat directly overhead and his stomach growled, both indications that it must be around noon.

"I wish I could stay out here forever." Claudia rested her forearms on top of the gate they'd just passed through. A few of the horses stood in the distance. "When I'm out here, I forget about the rest of the world. All that matters is the horses."

"They're lucky to have you as a volunteer," Knox said.

She turned to face him. "I'm the lucky one. Most people will never even know this place exists, but I get to come out here as often as I want."

"Then you're both lucky." He let his gaze linger on the big chestnut stallion. What would it be like to feel so free? A knot tightened in the pit of his stomach. Between his obligation to his label and the fans who'd supported him all along, Knox would never know. He'd dreamed of being able to play his music for a living, but he'd never thought about what that might cost him. Sure, he was making money hand over fist. His last album had gone platinum. But there was more to life than money. He knew that; it was just nice to be reminded of it from time to time. Like today.

"Ready to head back?" Claudia elbowed him gently in the arm.

"Yeah." With a heavy sigh, he turned back to the ATV. "I think you should drive on the way back, though."

"Really? What made you change your mind?"

"You'll make fun of me if I tell you why."

She faked innocence. "Who, me? I'd never do such a thing."

At that point, he didn't care if she did. He was ready to admit the feelings he had for her. Ready to see if she had any interest in taking things to the next level for the short time he had left on the island. "You sure about that?"

"I promise."

"All right, then. The reason I want you to drive back is because I like holding on to you." He took a step toward her, closing the distance between them. "And I like feeling your ass between my legs."

Her cheeks flushed. "And why's that?"

He stepped so close that the toes of his boots tapped the toes of her sneakers. "Because it turns me on."

Her gaze flicked to the growing ridge behind his zipper. "I can see that."

"I think it turns you on, too." He was pushing it now, crossing a line he had never intended to cross. "You need a break, Claudia. Sunday afternoon, you and me. I'm taking you out."

"Yeah, right." Her lips split into a wide grin, but she shook her head. "Where would we go? There's no way I'm leaving the island again so soon, and there's literally nothing to do around here."

"You let me worry about that." He leaned in, his lips just millimeters from her ear. "Just say yes."

She got onto the ATV and he climbed on behind her.

"I didn't hear you say it." His arm tightened around her waist.

She nodded. Just a slight forward movement of her head. In one movement, she agreed to whatever he had planned. He only hoped she wouldn't regret it.

13

❧

Claudia

Claudia had been practicing how to back out of her date with Nolan for almost twenty-four hours. She couldn't decide whether to go for the "I'm not ready to date again" or the "It's not you, it's me" routine. It didn't really matter which route she chose. The bottom line was, she couldn't go out on a date. Making out on the boat after sharing a bottle of tequila was one thing, but letting him take her out on a real date was going too far.

She'd hung around the bar this afternoon, hoping Nolan would stop by before the open mic night, but he'd either slept the day away or gotten up and gone out while she was on her jog this morning. Gabe had just taken a tub of dirty dishes to the back and would be clocking out any minute to get some last-minute help on his performance.

The poor kid was so nervous. All he needed was a little encouragement, and he'd be fine. They'd been practicing for weeks and he had his song down pat. She wiped a rag over the bar and turned toward the door.

Gabe came out of the kitchen and Nolan walked in the front door at the same time. Great. Now she wouldn't have a chance to politely break her date with him before the event started.

Seeing Nolan walk through the door, his hair blown by the wind, his eyes crinkling at the edges with a smile, she wasn't sure she wanted to. It had been years since she'd enjoyed the company of a man. Four long years. Almost fifteen hundred days of relying on a battery-operated, handheld device to give her any sort of pleasure.

She took in a deep breath, filled her lungs, and steeled her resolve. It was for the best. Encouraging Nolan would only cause trouble for them both.

She'd enjoyed his attention over the past several days, but it couldn't go any further. He seemed like a nice guy, but so had her ex when they first met. Claudia wanted to get involved in another relationship about as much as she wanted to pound a nail into her own foot with a sledgehammer. In her experience, the nail would be a whole lot less painful.

"Hey." Nolan walked with Gabe back to the bar.

"Hey, yourself." She couldn't help but match the grin he gave her. Why did his smile seem to warm her from the inside out? Her belly lit up first, but it took only a few seconds for the burn to race through her veins and bloom on her cheeks.

"Miss Claudia, I don't know if I'm going to be able to do it tonight." Gabe put his hand over his stomach. "I feel like I might throw up."

"Let me get you some ice water. Sit down right here." She rounded the bar to pull out a stool for him, then reached for a glass and filled it with ice. This wasn't the first time Gabe had come down with a massive case of stage fright.

"Thank you." He wrapped his fingers around the glass and took a small sip.

"You know what I heard works?" Nolan slid onto the barstool next to Gabe.

Gabe glanced over at him. "If you tell me to picture the whole audience in their underwear, I really am going to be sick."

"I don't doubt it." Nolan shot her a grin. "That's never worked for me, either. The first time I had to get up in front of a big audience, my legs went numb. I thought they were going to have to carry me off the stage because I couldn't walk at all."

Claudia wondered why a construction worker would have had to talk to a huge audience from a stage, but she didn't want to interrupt the conversation. If he had a piece of advice that would settle Gabe's nerves, she wanted him to share it.

"What did you do?" A crease furrowed the spot between Gabe's eyebrows. He was probably worrying about being paralyzed onstage now, thanks to Nolan.

"They cut the lights and somebody came out to rescue me." Nolan chuckled. "Not one of my finer moments."

"I don't know about this. Maybe I'm not ready." Gabe grabbed onto the bar and started to push his stool back.

Claudia put her hand on his arm. So much for hoping for words of wisdom from Nolan. He should have just kept his mouth closed. "Wait, Gabe. You've got this. It's just going to be a few regulars watching. No big deal, right?"

"The next time I had to get out on a stage, I was prepared." Nolan clapped Gabe on the back. "Wanna know what I did?"

"Yes, sir." Gabe's thick black hair fell into his face as he nodded.

"Couple of things. Number one, visualize yourself nailing it. No mistakes, a perfect performance."

Gabe stared at him. "What, like now?"

"Yeah, close your eyes. Tell me what you see."

Claudia crossed her arms over her chest and waited to see how the visualization exercise would go. If Nolan said something to increase Gabe's already-close-to-debilitating anxiety, he'd have to deal with her.

"Um"—Gabe shifted on his stool—"I see the lights in my eyes."

"Start to sing," Nolan said. "Perfect pitch, precise timing. You feel it?"

Gabe scrunched up his nose. "Not really."

Nolan leaned closer. His voice dropped a few notches. "You're standing onstage with the lights shining down on you. The music starts and you get that feeling in your chest, that swell of emotion that's going to carry through the song. Do you feel it?"

Claudia stood by as Nolan put a hand on each one of Gabe's shoulders. He was focused, his intent serious as he continued to coach Gabe through the visualization exercise. Sounded like he'd done this or something similar a bazillion times before.

Gabe's chest rose and fell with each breath. "I feel nervous."

"Focus on the song. You start to sing. Your voice comes out strong. You've got the audience in the palm of your hand. They're hanging on every word. You hit the high notes and nail the low notes. Everything in between is pure magic."

The line between Gabe's brows disappeared. He nodded like he was keeping time to the music playing through his head.

"You're singing your heart out and the audience is caught up in the experience. Can you see them swaying in their seats and clapping along with the beat?" Nolan asked.

"Yeah." Gabe let out a breathy exhale.

"Good." Nolan squeezed the younger man's shoulders. "Now take that feeling onto the stage with you. I think you're ready."

Claudia tilted her head, contemplating the advice. She

was used to talking to people, had presented at conferences and team meetings for years, but she'd never gotten up on a stage to sing. The way Nolan described it—it was like he'd done it a million times before. Like he was speaking from personal experience.

"Thanks, Nolan." Gabe opened his eyes. The wild panic had disappeared. He didn't look like he'd fully embodied the confidence Nolan talked about, but at least his face had lost the greenish tinge. "I'm going to go practice a few more times."

"Let me know if you need a shot of encouragement before you take the stage." Nolan patted Gabe on the back as the kid turned to walk away.

"A shot of encouragement? He's fifteen. You can't give him a shot." Claudia clamped her hands to her hips. She might have bought into the mind game stuff, but there was no way Nolan was going to start passing out alcohol to a minor.

"Relax. I meant a few last-minute words of encouragement, not an actual shot." His mouth quirked up on one side. "You really think I'd give him an actual shot?"

Now she was the one feeling out of sorts. She shook off the uncomfortable tingles working their way up her neck. "Whatever. Listen, about tomorrow . . ."

"It's going to be great. I've got a fun evening planned. You might want to wear something casual."

Her eyebrows knit together. She'd been trying to find a nice way to cancel, but now he had her intrigued. "How casual?"

"Don't worry. I'm not planning on painting walls in the bungalows or anything. I just want you to be comfortable."

"What kind of plans did you make?" There wasn't a whole lot to do on Paradise in the off-season. Most of the businesses that relied on tourists were closed, along with a high percentage of the restaurants. She figured they'd grab dinner at one of the places that stayed open year-round and call it good.

"If I told you, it wouldn't be a surprise, would it?" He gave her another smile. One that hit her right below her belly button. A low burn spread from the bottom of her gut outward.

"I have a lot to do, and I don't think it's a good idea for us to get involved."

"We're just two friends hanging out, that's all. You shared the horse sanctuary with me, and I want to do something nice for you. That's all this is."

His words said one thing, but her body knew otherwise. Since the night on the boat, she'd stopped seeing him as a coworker and had started seeing him as a man. A hot-as-hell man who made her insides turn to molten lava and could render her senseless just thinking about his kiss.

"Yeah. Friends. Hanging out. Still, maybe I can get a rain check—"

"Too late. I have something booked." Nolan shrugged, shoved his hands in his pockets, and started backing away. "I'm going to put in a couple of hours on bungalow three before things get started tonight. See you in a little bit."

Claudia could have tried to stop him, could have insisted that she couldn't make it tomorrow. But she didn't. Instead, she stood there, thinking about whether or not she could be just friends with a guy like Nolan.

Tomas pushed through the doors leading out from the kitchen. "Hey, we just got a call for a group wanting to make a reservation for twenty tonight. Some kind of singles outing. Can we take it?"

"Yes, of course." Taking on a group like that in the middle of a Saturday night would mean shifting tables around and reassigning a few of the servers. With her attention pulled back to the job at hand, she put her date with Nolan on the back burner. No, not a date. Just two friends hanging out. Wearing something casual. Doing something that required a booking.

A sense of foreboding seeped into her stomach, but she forced it away. They could hang out once. She'd just put a stop to it after that. No big deal.

14

❦

Knox

Knox hadn't planned on working that night, but he'd needed an excuse to get away from Claudia. He'd almost blown it by helping Gabe with his stage fright. He could tell she was trying to figure out why a guy who worked construction would have experience on a stage. Not just a little experience, but enough that he admitted he had stage fright and knew enough to talk Gabe through it.

He walked out onto the beach and took in a gulp of the fresh ocean air. That made a few times he'd almost blown his own cover. He'd have to be more careful moving forward if he wanted to stay in Paradise. The way the words were flowing meant he didn't have a choice. If he wanted to be able to deliver an album's worth of songs, he needed to stay inspired.

Something nudged his thigh. He jumped back and looked down. The giant tortoise that hung around the bar stretched his neck toward Knox. Chick told him the animal craved attention, so Knox leaned over and ran his hand over Tripod's head.

"You like that, buddy?" Knox had been around turtles before, but nothing the size of the giant tortoise in front of him. Tripod's shell stretched at least three feet across. While Knox rubbed his hand over the tortoise's head, Tripod craned his neck to soak up the attention.

Justin and Emmeline had liked hanging out with Tripod so much they'd rescued a giant tortoise of their own. Knox tried to picture a creature like Tripod living on his family's ranch. He'd seen ranchers raise all kinds of animals, from emus to bison to alpacas. Maybe one day, when he got his own land, he could make sure he had room for a tortoise.

"I'm gonna go grab my guitar and try out some of the stuff I've been working on. Do you like music?" He gave Tripod a final pat on the head and stood. Damn, he must be losing it if he could hold an entire one-sided conversation with a tortoise. He left Tripod standing on the beach and headed back to his bungalow to grab his guitar.

He hadn't had much downtime over the past few days thanks to all the work they'd been doing, but having that time during the day when he could let his mind wander while he completed mundane tasks had been paying off. That wasn't the only thing that had been helping. Spending time around Claudia had provided some much-needed inspiration.

Knox found a lounger someone had dragged away from the bar area and sat down on the edge. He pulled his guitar out of the case and looped the strap over his head. Talking to Gabe about performing had made him itch to sing something. No matter how nervous he got before he went out onstage, he missed performing. It wasn't the applause of thousands of fans, it was the chance to lose himself in the music. With his band backing him and the sound system cranked up, he thrived on the energy that flowed through those giant arenas.

His fingers danced over the strings, and he made a few adjustments. While he messed around with tuning the guitar, Tripod wandered over. Knox had never played for a tortoise before, but there was a first time for everything.

With Tripod lazily blinking his giant eyelids, Knox closed his eyes and started playing the melody he'd been working on in his head. After a few minutes of tweaking, he added the lyrics he'd come up with.

I'm just a man trying to figure out who I am . . .
In a world turned upside down with a guitar in my hand . . .
But you . . . you make me believe in more . . .

He stopped, adjusted a few notes, and started again. For the next hour, he lost himself in creating music. It wasn't until he became acutely aware of someone standing behind him that he lowered his guitar to his lap. He should have been more careful. If someone found out who he was, he'd have to leave. With an icy-cold grip squeezing his heart, he slowly turned around.

Gabe stood there, his jaw slack. At least it wasn't Claudia. Or even worse, a tourist with a cell phone who could out him to the whole wide world in a matter of seconds.

"Hey, Gabe. What's up?" Maybe the kid didn't recognize him. The song he was working on wasn't like anything he currently had playing on the radio. With luck, Gabe was just impressed by his guitar-playing ability and had no idea the guy who'd given him advice for his stage fright was actually an award-winning musician.

"Where did you learn how to play the guitar like that?" Gabe's gaze darted to the custom acoustic in Knox's hands.

"Hell, I've been playing most of my life. My granddad taught me when I was two or three years old." A memory of sitting on his granddad's lap while the older man placed his fingers on the strings flashed into his head. Then a pang of regret sliced through his gut. He wished the old man had lived long enough to see where Knox's dreams had carried him.

"Can you teach me?" Gabe's eyes lit up with excitement. "I've always wanted to learn, but mom says we can't afford a guitar. Maybe I could practice on yours."

Knox cradled Bessie against his chest. Yes, he named his guitars. Each one had its own personality, but Bessie had been with him the longest. She was the first custom guitar he'd ever bought. Since then, companies had gifted him special editions, hoping he'd use them onstage. He had dozens in his studio back at home, but Bessie was special.

"I don't know. This one's kind of an heirloom."

Gabe let out a sigh containing all the drama a fifteen-year-old could be capable of. "Yeah, I get it. Anyone tell you that you sound a lot like Knox Shepler when you sing?"

Knox's ears perked. "Say what?"

"Yeah. My dad used to like his music. Until he became a sellout."

Knox's chest squeezed tight. At least the kid didn't recognize him. Not that it made up for his dad's views. Truth was, Knox knew exactly what Gabe's dad meant. Back in the early days, before Tripp discovered him and he got caught up in record deals and worldwide tours, Knox had played the songs he liked to sing. Once the label got ahold of him, they changed his sound. Instead of allowing him to play songs with heart and grit like he'd listened to at his granddad's feet, they tweaked his original tunes. Added more bass. Brought in some drums. Basically, they pop-ized him. Took the best parts of what he'd been building and merged them with their vision of what modern-day country music fans wanted.

Knox gave in at first. The money was good; the fame was addicting. But that only lasted for so long. Now, eight years in, he felt like a sellout. It was too bad to hear that his original fans thought so, too. He had to get back to his roots, back to the kind of music he enjoyed playing. The kind packed full of meaning and emotion. Sure, the kids wanted something they could dance to or party all night long with, but maybe it was time for someone younger to start wearing that mantle.

"Tell you what. You go in there tonight and do a good job, and I'll think about letting you handle my guitar, okay?"

Gabe's eyebrows shot up. "Really?"

Hell, if Knox could bottle that enthusiasm, he could give himself an infusion. "Yeah."

"Thanks, Nolan. I'm going to give it my all. If you teach me, I promise I'll be careful with it."

No doubt he would. But how could Knox explain to the kid that sharing your guitar was like sharing your woman? It was like sharing a piece of yourself. Even though he wanted Gabe to do a good job, he wasn't sure if he'd be able to hold up his end of the bargain.

"Hey, one more thing?" Knox caught Gabe's arm before he turned to go.

"What?"

"I don't really want anyone to know I've been messing around on my guitar. Do you think you can keep this just between us?"

"Really?" Gabe's brow furrowed. "But you're good. If I played as well as you, I'd want everyone to know."

"I'm just not ready. Do we have a deal?" He held out his hand, hoping he wouldn't regret putting his trust in the hands of a fifteen-year-old kid.

"Yeah, of course." Gabe pumped his hand up and down with a little too much enthusiasm. "Oh, and they're about to start inside. I came out to let you know."

"Thanks." Knox let Gabe's hand drop and pulled the guitar strap over his head. "I'm going to take this back, then I'll be in to cheer you on." He followed Gabe's progress all the way to the bar. That was a close call. He'd have to be more careful, especially if he started teaching Gabe how to play.

He'd finally found a way back to the music. He couldn't afford to do anything to fuck it up.

Claudia

Gabe knocked it out of the park. Claudia didn't know what Nolan said to him right before he went onstage, but whatever it was had worked. Gabe's voice came out strong and clear, with no trace of the shakiness she'd heard multiple times during practice. The song came to an end, and the small crowd erupted into applause.

Nolan put his fingers in his mouth and let out a loud wolf whistle. The pride in his eyes made her breath catch in her throat.

"He was great, wasn't he?" Nolan asked.

"Yeah, he was." She glanced down at the order tab one of the servers had slid onto the bar. Another piña colada. One of these days, maybe someone would challenge her to come up with a drink that didn't smell like suntan oil.

Gabe left the riser set up against the back wall and rushed over to where Nolan sat at the bar. "I did it. Just like you said."

"You were awesome." Nolan clapped him on the back. "A rising star, that's for sure."

"You mean it?" The hope in his eyes pulled at Claudia's heartstrings.

"Heck yeah, I mean it. How are you feeling?"

"Kind of like I want to do it again." Gabe took the glass of water Claudia slid over to him and chugged it down.

Nolan shook his head. "Careful. Looks like you just got bit by the bug."

"What bug?" Gabe asked.

"The music biz bug. Once you've been bitten, it's hard to go back."

"And you would know that how, exactly?" Claudia set the drinks she'd just made down at the edge of the bar for the server to pick up. Nolan kept spouting off advice like he knew what he was talking about.

He lifted a shoulder. "That's what I hear. I went to high school with a guy who headed to Nashville after graduation. He used to sing at school dances and talent shows and stuff."

"That's what I want to do," Gabe admitted. "Can you imagine what it would feel like to sing on a stage in front of a hundred people instead of a couple dozen?"

"You get really good and you'll be singing in front of thousands of fans, not hundreds." Nolan leaned forward and rested his arms on the bar.

He'd pushed up the sleeves of his button-down and the sight of his tan forearms did something funny to her insides. She could see the vein on the underside of his arm and she wanted to run her tongue along it, all the way down to suck one of his long, thick fingers into her mouth.

"Miss Claudia?" Gabe asked.

She startled, nearly knocking over the container of garnishes sitting on the bar. "What's that?"

"I asked if you think I'm good enough to go to Nashville?" He looked so hopeful, so naive, so young. How dare Nolan seed his mind with unrealistic expectations?

"Nashville's a world away from a high school talent show." She didn't want to come off as dismissive, but she also didn't want to encourage him too much. He was the oldest kid of nine and his parents barely made ends meet. The best thing he could do, in her opinion, was get through college and start on a stable career.

"Yeah." The light in his eyes dimmed a little. "I'd better get home. Mom doesn't like it when I leave my sister in charge, and I promised I'd only be here long enough to sing my song."

"Hey." Claudia didn't want him to leave on a down note, even if she didn't think he had a snowball's chance in hell of making it to Nashville. "You did really well tonight. I hope you're proud of yourself."

He nodded, but his shoulders dipped, and the excitement had faded.

"See you tomorrow." Nolan held out his hand for one of those complicated handshakes guys did with each other. Then he turned on his stool to watch Gabe cross the restaurant area and exit through the back door.

"You didn't have to fill his head with big dreams like Nashville. Do you know what percentage of people head there with stars in their eyes and never make it?"

Nolan mumbled something under his breath as he fiddled with one of the paper coasters.

"What's that?" She leaned in, assuming he was cursing at her.

"He's good, Claudia. Real good." He looked up at her. "Better than the guy I'm talking about from my high school."

"Well, maybe you can make an introduction, then. See if your buddy can take him around and introduce him to all the major players on the Nashville music scene." She pinned him with her glare, waiting for the inevitable apology.

"Maybe I will."

That wasn't the response she expected. "So you're still in touch with this guy?"

"Kind of." Nolan rubbed his hand against the back of his neck. "I can make a few calls."

Her heart jammed against the walls of her chest. She was only trying to call his bluff. She didn't mean for him to take her seriously. "No, don't."

"Why not? First you tell me to, now you're telling me not to? I don't get it."

She put both hands flat on the bar in front of her. How could she explain without giving her whole story away? "I don't want him to get hurt. He's just a kid."

"A kid with a million-dollar voice," Nolan said. "If that's his dream, doesn't he deserve the chance to make it come true?"

His gaze drilled into her like he was trying to figure her out. She didn't want to suffer his scrutiny. She'd been the one with stars in her eyes once upon a time, and look where that had gotten her . . . hiding out in the last place anyone would think to look for her, hoping the hate that chased her away from her hometown wouldn't catch up with her. Gabe couldn't handle that kind of pressure. She was only trying to protect him, to keep him safe.

Instead of answering, she gestured to the order slips a server had just set down at the edge of the bar. "I need to get back to work. About tomorrow—"

"I'll meet you around three." Nolan got up from his stool and walked away before she had a chance to tell him she didn't want to go. It had seemed like a good idea the other day when he'd had his big body wrapped around her and her hormones had been firing like the freaking Fourth of July. But now that she'd gathered her scattered wits and taped them back together again, she realized letting herself get attached to him would just delay the inevitable.

He wouldn't stay in Paradise. Neither would Gabe. Whether he went to Nashville to try to break into the music industry or managed to get into college, he'd be leaving Paradise. Even Chick seemed to be looking for a way out. She needed to keep a closer guard on her heart.

Vowing she'd start that very second, she turned her attention to the drink orders waiting to be filled. The rest of the night passed in one big blur of pouring cocktails and listening to one off-key performer after another. By the time she closed down the bar and made it to her bungalow, she was wiped.

She shoved the key into the door, and her foot bumped something on the stoop. Bending down, she used the light from her phone to try to see what was there. Someone had left a basket wrapped in cellophane in front of her door. It wasn't her birthday, and she didn't know anyone who'd have a reason to give her a gift. Maybe someone had dropped it.

She scooped it into her arms and carried it into her bungalow. Once she flipped on the lights, she could see a tiny envelope tied to the top with a ribbon. Her name was scrawled in cursive on the outside of the envelope, so whatever it was, it was obviously intended for her.

The card slid out of the envelope, and she held it up.

> *Looking forward to seeing you tomorrow. I figured you might need these.*

> *Nolan*

Her stomach rolled. This was too much. He was getting too close, too personal. They hadn't even been on a date and he was giving her gifts? Still, her curiosity won out, and she untied the ribbon holding all the cellophane closed. A collection of paintbrushes sat inside the basket along with a pair of hot pink coveralls. Where the heck was he taking her?

Even though it was after three in the morning, she pulled out her laptop and opened up a browser. What could they possibly be doing that would require that kind of assortment? After scrolling for several minutes, she gave up. Fine, he had her on the hook. She needed to find out what he had planned.

15

⟋⟍ ♡ ⟋⟍

Knox

Getting Claudia to agree to go out had been a challenge. Knox couldn't remember a time he'd fought so hard not to be turned down. Even back in high school, before he'd grown into his lanky limbs and outgrown his stutter, girls hadn't resisted him as much as she did.

He'd stopped by the bar to check in with Chick before he had to meet up with her.

"You're all set for tonight?" Chick asked.

"Yeah."

"Thanks for doing this." Chick leaned over the bar and clamped a hand on his shoulder. "I appreciate it."

"Any idea why she's so scared to leave the island?" Knox asked. He'd planned on taking Claudia to dinner at one of the restaurants down the beach—one with a few more stars than the burgers and wraps at A Cowboy in Paradise rated. But when Chick found out they were spending an evening together—and Knox hadn't told him, so he had no idea how the older man had come across that tidbit—he asked Knox to take her somewhere on the mainland. Said he was worried about her and she needed to get out more.

"You could ask her, but I doubt she'd tell you. Whatever the reason, I think a woman her age needs to be out and about, not hunkered down in a beachside bar with a grizzly old cowboy like me." Chick turned to pull clean glasses out of the plastic rack and slide them onto the shelves behind the bar.

Claudia didn't seem like the kind of woman who'd take kindly to someone interfering in her life, so Knox tried to figure out how to word the question he really wanted to ask. Too forward and Chick would shut him down. Too vague and he wouldn't get the answer he was looking for.

"What?" Chick asked, his salt-and-pepper eyebrows pulling down over his eyes.

"Before she came here . . . I know Claudia used to live in Minneapolis . . ."

"Then you know a hell of a lot more about her than most people." Chick leaned forward and lowered his voice. "It's not my story to tell, but I guarantee you, the version of Claudia you know is a hollow shell of the woman she once was. She likes you. Maybe you'll be the one who can coax her back to life. She's still got a lot of living to do, son. She's just forgotten how."

Knox blinked, a long, slow blink that did nothing to calm the pounding of his heart. What the hell was that supposed to mean? Chick reminded him of his granddad. Both men talked in riddles, and if you weren't smart enough to figure out what they were saying, they didn't take the time to bring you up to speed. It was like they were both members of the same fucked-up club.

"You're doing a good thing." Chick nodded, then moved down the bar.

Knox rolled his head from side to side and took in a deep breath. He liked Claudia. Really liked her. Not only was she gorgeous, but she also had a great sense of humor and a huge heart. He'd seen the extra meals she sent home with Gabe, heard about the long hours she spent volunteering at the horse sanctuary, and watched her give her all to revamping the bungalows. If the version of Claudia he knew was a shell of the woman she'd once been, well, hell, then she must have been a firecracker.

He shook off the feeling that he was manipulating her by getting her off the island and headed toward her door. Before he could lift his hand to knock, she pulled it open.

His breath caught at the sight of her. She had on a denim skirt and a pair of beaded leather flip-flops. Her top fell off one shoulder and the bright colors accentuated her bronze skin.

"Hey, you look . . . amazing," he said.

"Thanks. You said casual, but then I got the basket and I wasn't sure what kind of casual. If I'm too dressed up, I can change." Her gaze darted from his eyes to his chest, then off to the side. She was nervous.

"What you have on is perfect." He meant it, too. The denim encased her hips and showed off toned, tanned legs.

"Where are we going?" She pulled the door closed behind her and locked it before slipping her key into the small purse hanging over her shoulder.

"I've got transportation lined up, but we have to get there first. Do you want to walk, or should I get the golf cart out of the shed?"

"I can walk. Just lead the way." She slung the strap of her bag over her shoulder. "I'm assuming I need to bring the paintbrushes and coveralls?"

"Yep." Knox held out his hand. "Want me to carry that for you?"

"I've got it."

They started down the walkway toward the main road. When Chick had talked to him about taking Claudia out,

Knox knew she wouldn't be too eager to get back on a boat. Thanks to one of Chick's connections, Knox was able to arrange for a helicopter ride. All he had to do was get her to the private helipad halfway down the island. Once she saw where they were headed, he wasn't sure he'd be able to convince her to get on. The woman's fear of leaving the island was almost palpable.

"So, where are we going this afternoon?" She fell into step next to him, and he adjusted his stride to match hers.

"You don't want to be surprised?"

"Surprises are way overrated." Claudia shook her head. "I hate them."

"Even good surprises?" Knox asked. He'd never been a big fan of surprises, either, at least not when they were directed at him. He never minded pulling off a prank on someone else, especially Decker or Justin.

She looked up at him, a hint of a smile playing across her lips. "Even the good ones. So, are you going to tell me where we're going?"

"I've got a helicopter waiting—"

"A helicopter?" She came to an abrupt stop. "No, that's not a good idea."

Knox turned back. "I thought it would be fun to see the island from the air. You said you haven't done much of the touristy stuff since you moved here."

The smile faded. "I thought we were going to stay on the island. After last time . . ."

"Hey." Knox reached for her hand and gave it a squeeze. "I've got tickets to an event on the mainland. Something I think you'll really like. We'll fly over the island for a few minutes, then the pilot will drop us off on the mainland."

"Tickets to what?"

Knox took it as a good sign that she hadn't turned around to run back to her bungalow. Though he hadn't shared the truth about who he was, he wasn't going to flat-out lie to her about where they were going. "I got us tickets to the Grand Home Tour."

Her forehead crinkled. "You want to tour houses together?"

Damn, based on the way she'd talked about the houses the last time they'd been on the mainland, he thought she'd be all about touring some of the mansions on the beach. "We don't have to if you don't want to. I thought you might get some ideas about how to make the bungalows more appealing."

She took in a deep breath and gripped his hand. "I've always wanted to go, but it never seemed like a fun thing to do by myself. I can't imagine Chick would be interested in walking through a bunch of huge houses."

"Not unless he could sit by the pool with a beer and wait for you." Knox's shoulders relaxed. She wasn't mad. She actually looked excited at the idea.

"What about the paintbrushes? And the coveralls? We don't have to paint, do we?"

He laughed. "No. That's a surprise for after the tour. Do you want me to tell you what it is?"

Her eyes narrowed for a moment, then she shook her head. "I think I want to keep it a surprise. You're sure about the helicopter?"

"We can take the ferry instead, but waiting will probably make us late."

She got a glimmer in her eye—a spark of excitement. "Let's do it."

"All right. Let's do it."

Knox tucked her arm in the crook of his elbow and led her toward the helipad. Chick had been worried about nothing. Getting Claudia off the island hadn't been so hard. Or maybe she'd agreed for another reason. His pulse ticked up, sending blood whooshing through his veins.

Maybe, just maybe, she liked him.

Claudia

She didn't want Nolan to know exactly how nervous she was as the pilot flipped a switch and the big blades began to whirl. Nolan picked up his headset and slipped it over his ears, then gestured for her to do the same.

"You okay?" His voice crackled through the headphones. She nodded.

"Have you ever been on a helicopter before?" he asked.

She nodded again. "It's been years, though."

"Where did you go?"

He looked genuinely curious, but she wasn't about to tell him the last time she'd been in a helicopter was when King had taken her to New Zealand and they'd gone on a helicopter tour of one of the glaciers. She didn't owe Nolan anything, especially details about her life prior to when they met, but she still felt like she was hiding things from him. Like she was lying to him by omission.

That was a term she'd learned from her real estate business. When a seller knows something is wrong with a house and doesn't divulge it, they can be in violation of lying by omission. This wasn't the same, though. Contracts couldn't be broken for her not divulging the truth to Nolan.

"Just a touristy thing." The half-truth sailed off her tongue too easily. She'd been bending the truth for so long now, trying so hard not to let on about her previous life, that she wondered how long it would be until she'd rewritten her whole history. "How about you?"

"Oh, I used to take a helicopter all the time when I, uh, worked on a special job site out east." He turned to look out the window as they lifted off the ground.

She gripped the side of her seat so hard her fingers ached. The run-in with the Tigers fan had thrown her last week.

She'd gotten too comfortable in Paradise. The way her stomach clenched, the way her entire world got flipped upside down in an instant, was like a cold bucket of water to the face . . . a reminder that she wasn't safe no matter how long it had been.

As the helipad grew smaller, a pang of regret hit her. She'd given up so much when she left Minnesota. If there'd been a way to stay and fight for her business, she would have seized the opportunity. At the time, it didn't seem possible. With Nolan taking her on the home tour, it all came rushing back.

He reached over and wrapped his hand around hers. When she looked up, he was smiling at her. "Heights used to get to me, too."

Claudia didn't mind heights, but she did mind leaving the island. It was easier to let him think she was scared to let her feet leave the ground. She couldn't tell him the real reason her jaw was clenched so tight she'd probably have a migraine later.

The pilot's voice filled their ears. "Welcome aboard. I know y'all need to get to the mainland for an event, but as long as I've got you, I figured I'd give you a quick tour of Paradise. If you'll look out the left window, you'll see some of the most beautiful beaches in North America."

She was on the left side of the helicopter, so Nolan leaned close to peer out her window. The fresh scent of his cologne drifted to her nose. It must have been laced with pheromones, because her palms immediately went damp and her pulse jumped.

"Look at that." Nolan nodded to a secluded strand of beach framed by a thick border of scrubby trees on both sides. "Think we could find that stretch of beach on the ATV?"

"Probably." She pointed to a spot a little farther inward. "See that?"

"The waterfall?" He was so close his breath tickled her ear. Shivers raced down her spine.

"Yeah. It's one of my favorite places to go."

"Will you take me there?" He brushed her hair over her shoulder, a gesture that was so basic, but so intimate at the same time.

She turned her cheek in an attempt to meet his gaze, but he was too close. Her nose bumped his, and they ended up inches apart.

"On your right, you can see one of the cruise ships. Paradise is too small for them to stop, but they cruise from Galveston down to Mexico and back again all year long." The pilot was oblivious to the sizzling fireworks going on in the back seat of his helicopter.

Claudia stared into Nolan's eyes, wondering if he was going to kiss her. Parts of her wanted him to. The long-neglected parts of her that had gone without a man's touch for way too long.

She broke eye contact first, tipping her chin up to indicate the window behind him. "Want to see the cruise ship?"

His tongue darted out to run along his lower lip. She fought the strong urge to lean into him, to tilt her head to the side to better fit her mouth against his.

"The cruise ship. Yeah, of course." He shifted, slipping his arm around her shoulders and turning his head to look out the window on his side. "Have you ever been on a cruise?"

Finally, something she could tell the truth about. "Nope. You?"

"Yeah." His thumb skimmed over her shoulder. There was no way her pulse would ever return to normal if he kept touching her.

"Where did you cruise?"

"Oh, um, I've done an Alaska cruise, one that went through the Panama Canal, and my favorite, a super casual giant sailboat that just sailed from island to island in the Caribbean for a couple of weeks."

"That sounds like fun,"

"It was. You should try it sometime. The rum punch never stops flowing and the music never stops playing." His eyes took on a dreamy haze as he talked about it.

"Reggae music?" she asked. It seemed to be the genre of choice for the people who visited Paradise.

Nolan shook his head. "Nah, country."

"A country music cruise to the Caribbean?" She got her fill of country at the bar. When she first started, the vintage jukebox held only country music, but Chick had let her bring in some other tunes that people requested. She didn't mind country, just hadn't ever listened to it. King had been all about hard rock, so that was all she listened to with him. He said it helped him get pumped up for a game. Music had never been that important to her.

"Come on, you can't tell me you've never sung along to the chorus of 'Margaritaville' or listened to Kenny Chesney on repeat for hours at a time."

Claudia just smiled.

"Hell, I'm going to make it my personal mission to make sure I expose you."

"What exactly are you planning on exposing me to?" She arched a brow. "Don't you think you've exposed enough of yourself to me already?"

A wave of pink rolled up his neck from the collar of his shirt, over his chin, and onto his cheeks. "That was an unintentional exposition. This would be a calculated, carefully constructed, intentional exposing."

Claudia clamped her lips together to keep from laughing. "A calculated exposure. I see."

"Back on the left, you'll see the oldest home on the island." The pilot continued his commentary. "Local lore says it was built by a wealthy Mexican general for his lover. He planned on moving there when the Mexican–American War ended, but then Texas became part of the United States and he lost his property and his lover. Local women believe that if you visit the property on the night of a full moon, the general's lover will take your wish and make it come true."

Claudia had heard the nonsense local women talked about. Every once in a while, a lovesick woman came into the bar looking for information on the deserted property, but Claudia had never believed it.

"Maybe you can show me that, too." Nolan leaned over her again to see out her side of the helicopter.

"I stay away from legends like that," she said. The closest she'd ever come to believing in all that hocus-pocus was the time she'd wished on a falling star for King to propose. After a few months of her gazing up at the sky every night and straining her eyes to spot a shooting star so she could make her wish, he'd popped the question. The universe should have left that wish alone. Since then, she'd learned the only thing she could rely on was herself.

The helicopter turned and Claudia tensed as the nose dipped, then leveled off.

She pointed out the window at the old lighthouse. "I've always wanted to tour the lighthouse."

"We should do it." Nolan's chin rested on her shoulder.

Instead of pulling away, she leaned into him. It was nice to have someone to make plans with, even if they probably wouldn't happen. He'd be leaving in a few weeks, and there was no way they'd be able to fit in all the sightseeing he wanted to do and still stick to their timeline for the bungalows.

She'd already added a section to the website that mentioned the rentals they'd have coming soon. Chick didn't want to deal with all the email inquiries, so he'd asked her to handle it. She had no doubt they'd be booked at 100 percent occupancy as soon as they made the reservation system go live.

That also meant she needed to find a new place to live.

The pilot pointed out a few more sights, like the turtle sanctuary, the docks, and the boardwalk, before he turned toward the mainland.

"Ready for the tour?" Nolan asked.

"It's too late to turn back now, isn't it?"

His eyes softened. "I don't know why this is hard for you, and you don't have to tell me. You don't seem like the type of woman who'd be comfortable living with restrictions. I'll be with you the whole time, Claudia. If it gets to be too much, just let me know and we'll go, okay?"

She searched his eyes, wondering if Chick put him up to that. Didn't matter. The only thing that did matter was that he was right. She'd been living inside a box she'd constructed for herself. It was time to venture outside, time to stop restricting herself.

With Nolan by her side, she could see herself walking down the sidewalk like a normal woman out on a date . . . touring the mansions along the beach like a regular tourist . . . enjoying things she used to without constantly looking over her shoulder.

She nodded. "Okay."

16

❧

Knox

Knox couldn't get over the change in Claudia as they walked through some of the biggest homes he'd ever seen. She noticed everything and pointed it out to him, from the crown molding on the ceilings to the recessed lighting and tile treatments in the bathrooms. The way her eyes lit up, her smile widened, her gestures became more animated, let him know she was in her element.

Chick hadn't told him what kind of life she'd led before showing up on Paradise, but after seeing her reaction to touring the first home, Knox had no doubt she'd done something in the housing market. Maybe she'd worked for a builder. Whatever she'd done, she knew a hell of a lot about all the details that went into a home.

"Did you see the solar panels on the roof of that last one?" She ducked into the second row of the shuttle that took people from one house to another. Most of the homes were tucked away in gated communities along the shore, so the only way to get to them was by typing in a key code at the gate.

"Yeah, pretty cool." He'd never paid attention to stuff like that. He had a condo in Nashville where he stayed between tours, but he was there so rarely that it didn't feel like home. One day, he'd build a huge ranch home on some land in Texas, hopefully close to his mom. Then he'd have to think about things like solar power and carpet-pad thickness and high-tech security systems. The thought of so many details made his head hurt.

"And the windows," Claudia continued. "Did you see the blinds in between the panes?"

"No, I didn't notice."

"I'll point it out if the next house has them, too. I loved the way they did the stone facade on the chimney."

"You're really into this, aren't you?" He bumped his shoulder against hers as the shuttle pulled away from the house.

She shrugged like it wasn't a big deal to obsess over wallpaper textures and the benefits of luxury vinyl over real hardwood floors. "I've always been interested in home projects."

He wanted to see if she'd open up about her past, but he didn't want to pry. And the very last thing he wanted to do was scare her off. "Living in the bungalow at Chick's doesn't give you much of an opportunity to do many home projects, does it?"

Her shoulder lifted in a half shrug. "I've been enjoying working on revamping the bungalows. Once that's done, I'll probably look for a place of my own."

"Don't you like living by the bar?" In the time he'd been on Paradise Island, he'd already grown used to waking up with the ocean right outside his door and falling asleep to the sound of the waves crashing on the shore. The idea of going back to Nashville or heading back to Texas to stay at his mom's place for a little while made his chest squeeze tight.

"It's convenient, but once Chick starts renting out the bungalows, I think I'll want more privacy."

Knox smiled as he remembered the incident in the shower house. "With your own bathroom, right?"

"Riiiiiight." She turned to look at him as she drew out the word.

He leaned against the back of the tall seat and took in a deep breath. "What's your ideal place look like?"

"What do you mean? My ideal house?"

"Yeah. You seem to know a lot about them. Is it a two-story Cape Cod? A Tuscan-inspired colonial? I don't know, if you could build the house of your dreams, what would it look like?"

She let her head fall back against the headrest. "First off, a Tuscan-inspired colonial would be painful on multiple levels. That should never be a thing, okay?"

"Got it."

"As for the house of my dreams, I don't know. I love places that look like they belong in their surroundings, you know what I mean?"

"Like the thatched-roof beach huts Chick's got for bungalows?"

"Kind of. The thatched roofs definitely fit the look of the beach, but if I'd been involved in designing those, I'd make sure each one of them had floor-to-ceiling windows that faced the ocean to take advantage of the view. I'd also set them a little farther apart, so people felt like they had their own little slice of island paradise."

The way her gaze focused on nothing but a spot off in the distance made him think she'd disappeared into her own thoughts.

"It's not too late to add more windows if you want to." He'd missed working with his hands. Having the chance to help with the bungalows reminded him of how much he'd enjoyed it. Working with a piece of raw wood was similar to putting together a song. He could get inspiration from the piece itself, almost like it would tell him what shape it wanted to be. All he had to do was bring out the natural beauty just waiting within.

"That's an interesting idea. We could even knock out the wall from the living room and put in a huge slider. All they'd have to do is slide the glass doors open, and they'd double their living space."

"Wait, where's the patio coming from?" The bungalows currently had a small pad by the front door made out of a few pavers. Chick hadn't said anything about adding on a patio for each bungalow.

"Think about it." Claudia turned toward him, her cheeks flushed with excitement. "We can add a small patio to each place and replace the living room window with an extra wide slider. I think it would be a huge draw to have a private outdoor area with a grill and some chairs. Don't you?"

How could he say no to something she was clearly so excited about? The project had been moving quickly so far. He would have time to incorporate her ideas before he had to head home. "I think it's a great idea. We just need Chick to adjust the budget, now, don't we?"

Her palm landed on his thigh. Heat radiated out from where she touched him. "If we gang up on him, he won't be able to say no."

Knox wasn't about to say anything that might make her move her hand. "Sounds good to me."

They rode the rest of the way to the next house, lost in their own thoughts, with a comfortable silence between them. He was glad he'd asked her out, even happier that she seemed to be enjoying herself so much. The way she'd come out of her shell during their tour made him curious about what her life had been like before she'd shown up on Paradise. He wanted to respect her need for privacy, but he was also desperate to know more about this woman who'd gotten under his skin.

As they passed houses that were big enough to fit A Cowboy in Paradise along with all the bungalows inside, he pieced together what he knew about Claudia so far. She was from Minneapolis. At some point in her past, she worked in some profession that gave her the opportunity to learn a lot about houses. She might have been an interior designer or a custom builder, or even a real estate agent. His heart skipped over a beat at that thought. Real estate. Based on the comments she'd made about the price per square foot and resale value as they walked through some of the houses, she had to have a background in residential real estate.

His stomach twisted in on itself with guilt. While she'd been enjoying herself and jotting down ideas for how to decorate the inside of the bungalows, he'd been cataloging all her actions and words to try to figure out more about her. What did it matter to him if she'd been in real estate?

He sat with that thought while the shuttle entered another exclusive community. This one had fountains sitting atop brick columns on either side of the gate. Two huge molded concrete fish spouted water from one side of the road to the other. Knox felt like he was pulling into a Vegas resort instead of entering a housing development.

"Did you see that?" Claudia turned in her seat as they passed through the gates.

"Yeah. I feel like we're in Miami or something with the nod to the fish."

"Oh, you should see the fish decor up north. My grandparents had a cabin on Leech Lake that we used to go to in the summers, and you couldn't go a few feet without running into a giant statue of a walleye or muskie."

He waited to see if she'd say more. She'd been so hesitant to share any details about her life before, and now she seemed to be willing to give him more info than he'd asked for.

"You said you liked to fish that night we were out on the boat."

"You mean the night we got stranded on the boat?" Her eyelids closed in a long blink. "I don't mind fishing so much in fresh water, but I don't think I'll be eager to fish down here again anytime soon. Almost getting my arm bitten off by a shark can turn me off a potential hobby real quick."

Knox laughed. "Got it. I'll axe the fishing part of the evening, then."

"There was a fishing part to the evening?"

"No. But I was planning on taking you to a painting class."

"Ah, that's the reason for the paintbrushes and coveralls."

"It's one of those paint-and-pour places. They set it up on the beach and ply us with wine until we create something that might resemble the sample artwork. If you're not up for it—"

Her palm slid against his thigh again. "It sounds wonderful."

With warmth coursing through his veins, Knox set his hand on hers and threaded their fingers together. Tonight was turning out to be better than he could have imagined.

Claudia

Claudia squinted at the painting taking shape on the canvas in front of her. She'd tried to follow the technique the instructor demonstrated to capture the layered colors of the gorgeous sunset going on right in front of them. Whatever she had happening on her canvas looked quite a bit different from the instructor's. Wondering how Nolan was doing, she leaned over to sneak a look at his canvas.

"No peeking." Nolan blocked her view of his painting.

"Come on, my sky looks like a toddler got into the finger paints." Claudia tried to move his arm so she could see how his looked.

"Not until I'm done." Nolan angled his easel away from her.

"Fine." She huffed out a breath and reached for her glass of wine.

"Once you've got the sky how you like it, you can start working on the water." The instructor held up one of her brushes. "I'd suggest starting with the darkest color."

Claudia tuned her out and looked out over the water. This was her second favorite time of day. When the sun hovered at the edge of the horizon and the sky turned every shade of orange and pink. Since she usually worked evenings at the bar, she rarely got to indulge in sitting still and watching the sunset. She took her wine and stepped closer to the waterline.

A line of lounge chairs sat in the sand and she lowered herself onto one. A brisk breeze blew in from the ocean. Her skin pebbled with goose bumps and she pulled her wrap around her shoulders to protect them from the wind.

"Are you giving up on painting?" Nolan sat down on the lounge chair next to her.

"Just taking a break to enjoy the sunset." She gave him a genuine smile and held out her hand. "Thanks for bringing me here today. I've really enjoyed it."

"Good." His fingers twined with hers.

She refocused her attention on the sun. The feel of his hand in hers made butterflies beat their gossamer wings against the walls of her chest. She hadn't felt that way in such a long time, she'd forgotten what it was like to be in the company of someone she liked. It was so easy being with Nolan. Even though she felt guilty about not telling him about her past, she felt like she could be herself with him, or as much of herself as she felt comfortable being.

"Are you hungry at all? I've got a reservation for dinner here, or if you'd rather get back to the island, we can grab something at one of the resorts on the beach."

She took in a deep breath. "I think I'm okay. I usually don't like being off the island, but it's going all right."

Nolan deserved the credit for that. With him next to her, she felt like she could handle the mainland. That he'd keep her safe and shield her from anyone or anything that came her way.

"All right. I'm going to go finish my painting, and when we're done, we can grab a bite to eat before we head back."

"Thanks." Claudia squeezed his hand and watched as he turned to head back to the painting class. He had on a pair of khakis tonight. She preferred him in his worn-out jeans, but he looked just as hot in either. With a final glance at the sun, she picked up her now empty glass and resumed her spot at her easel.

She did her best to add water to her painting and by the time she was done; it didn't look nearly as bad as she thought it would.

"Let me see." Nolan turned his easel away from her. "Show me yours first, then I'll show you mine."

Claudia let out a laugh. "Is that how this is going to work?"

"Seems fair, don't you think?"

She took one last look at her original art, wishing she'd been able to capture the way the light danced across the water and the peace that filled her heart when she looked out over the shore. "Here goes nothing."

Nolan sucked in a breath as she turned her picture around. Instead of following his gaze, she kept her eyes trained on him, evaluating his reaction. He didn't say anything, just stared at the canvas.

"Well?" she asked.

"It's amazing." He lifted his hand and pointed at the spot where the sea met the sky. "It's almost like you took a picture. The way you've got the ocean blending into the horizon, it's exactly like it looks in person."

"Stop." Clearly he was trying to patronize her. Heat marched over her cheeks and she pressed her fingertips to her face, wondering if he'd notice.

"Hey." He reached up and caught her hands in his. "It's true. You've got talent, Claudia."

The way her name drifted off his lips—in a mix of wonder and awe—made her lower lids swell with unshed tears. It had been so long since she'd poured her heart into creating something beyond a cocktail. She forced her voice to come out steady.

"Thanks. If I'd had more time, I could have blended more of the sky into the water, and—"

Nolan put his finger to her lips. "It's beautiful just the way it is."

She couldn't hold his gaze, not without letting the tears that threatened spill down her cheeks, so she shifted her focus to the ground.

"I mean it." Nolan's finger under her chin nudged her head back up. "And at the risk of sounding way too cheesy, I'm going to say it."

"Say what?" He had a way of lightening the mood.

"Say it's beautiful the way it is, just like you." His lips spread into a huge grin.

"Yeah, that was way too cheesy." It might have been cheesy, but he'd chased off her tears. "Show me yours now."

"Mmm, I thought you'd never ask." He let go of her hands long enough to flip his canvas around.

Claudia's eyes went wide. He'd been working so long and the image he'd created looked like some impressionistic version of what it was supposed to. "I see you took some creative license," she said.

"Just a smidge." He held up his hand, his pointer finger and thumb almost touching to demonstrate how much creative license he'd taken.

"What are we going to do with them now?" The class had wrapped up, and the instructor had almost finished packing away all her supplies.

"We could hide them in the restaurant and see if anyone notices."

"You don't think these would stick out? They don't exactly look like they match the ambience of the decor." Claudia hadn't gotten too good of a look at the inside of the restaurant as she'd walked through on her way to the patio, but it felt like an old-time supper club, not like a bright, beach-themed place to grab a bite.

"Here, you keep mine. I'll find a place to put yours where it will fit right in. Then we can come back, what, six months from now to see if it's still here?"

"Sure." Claudia held out her painting. Six months from now, she'd still be slinging drinks behind the bar at A Cowboy in Paradise.

They went inside and checked in at the hostess stand. The woman led them to a table with a view of the beach. As soon as they were seated, Nolan disappeared with her painting. Claudia stifled her giggles in the linen napkin as she watched him walk toward the bathrooms.

When he came back, he didn't have the painting in his hands. "That was easier than I thought it would be."

"Where did you put it?" She leaned across the table and lowered her voice.

"I can't tell you that. We'll do a walk-through after and you can see if you can find it. How does that sound?" He rested his arm along the back of the booth. How could he be so calm and cool at a time like this? They were lucky no one had caught him.

"What do you think would happen if you got caught?"

"Don't you mean 'we'?" he asked. "After all, it's your painting."

"Oh no you don't. I might have painted it, but you're the one who hung it somewhere it shouldn't be." She was having fun. The realization washed over her, catching her by surprise. She hadn't thought about King or being recognized on the mainland for several hours. This—the feeling she had when she was with Nolan—was what she needed more of in her life.

He made her forget about the worries that had been plaguing her for the past four years. She hadn't been looking for a guy like him, hadn't been looking for a guy at all, but now that he was here, she realized she didn't want him to go.

Nolan sat up straight when the server came over to take their order. Though the woman gave him every opportunity to respond to her flirtatious overtures, he didn't take her up on it. He made Claudia feel special, like she was the most important woman in the world to him, at least for the night.

The conversation flowed throughout dinner and she found herself giving up more personal info than she had since she left Minnesota. She talked about her sister and how they'd lost both their parents in a tragic accident eight years ago that summer.

If her parents had still been alive when everything went down with King, no doubt they would have propped her up and encouraged her to stand her ground.

She missed them terribly and went so far as to tell Nolan a few of her favorite stories about times she and her sister went fishing with her dad.

He twined their fingers together, his calloused thumb skimming over the back of her hand.

"What about you?" she asked. "Tell me more about growing up in the country."

"What do you want to know?" he asked.

"You were on a ranch? Does that mean with cows?"

"I was raised on an eight-thousand-acre cattle ranch deep in the heart of Texas. The land's been in my family for generations."

"Do you still live there now?"

"That's a story for another time." He slid his wallet out of his pocket as the server headed their way with the check. "We don't want to miss the ferry and get stranded on the mainland for the night, do we?"

Claudia might have imagined the challenge in his eyes. At that moment, missing the ferry and being stuck somewhere overnight with Nolan didn't sound like the worst thing that could happen. In fact, it sounded like just the opposite. She wanted to spend more time with him, wouldn't mind spending another night with him.

The server brought back his change, and Nolan nodded toward Claudia. "Ready?"

"Yes, but you still need to show me where you hung my painting." She got to her feet and glanced around the interior of the restaurant.

"Don't worry, you'll see it on the way out." He put his hand on the small of her back and guided her toward the entrance.

Her gaze flitted from one wall to another with no sign of the painting. She'd almost given up trying to find it when Nolan leaned over her shoulder, his beard brushing against her cheek as he whispered against her ear.

"Look up."

Claudia angled her head to glance up at a spot over the entrance. Centered over the doorway, her painting looked like it had been there for years. It almost blended into the dark blue background.

"You put it over the door? How did you get away with that?" she asked.

"If I told you my secrets, that might make you my accomplice," he mumbled against her ear.

Her nerve endings stood at attention at the hint of contact. With a final look at her painting, she passed through the doorway, nowhere near ready to be heading home.

17

❧

Knox

The ferry skimmed across the bay, carrying them back to the island much sooner than Knox would have preferred. He'd felt a shift between him and Claudia earlier, like a piece of the armor she held so close to protect her had loosened, leaving him a sliver of space where he might slip through.

He didn't want to push her, but the more open she became, the more inspiration he felt. Even now, with her sitting by his side, his arm looped over her shoulders, he couldn't wait to get back to work on the song he'd been struggling with for the past two days. She'd become his muse. As much as he wished he could change it, he didn't want to risk shutting down the words.

The way she talked about her family, the way her eyes lit up and the edges of her lips curled, told him more about her values and what she held dear than asking her outright would have. Being by her side while she toured the houses, he felt like someone had flipped a switch. She'd always been beautiful, but when her eyes lit up in excitement, she looked like she wasn't of this world.

He'd pulled the small notebook he always carried with

him out of his pocket to jot down phrases and snippets for lyrics as they filled his head. If luck was on his side, he ought to have the first version of a new song ready to share with Tripp before the week was over.

"Thanks for coming out with me tonight." He snugged her against him as the ferry slowed in its approach to the dock.

"Thanks for not taking no for an answer." She picked up the painting he'd made from where she'd set it on the bench seat next to her. "I can't wait to find a spot to hang this up in the bungalow."

"I'd be happy to drop it in the dumpster for you when we walk by," Knox offered.

"Are you kidding? This is priceless." Her grip on the canvas tightened.

Thankfully, she didn't know who he was. Otherwise, she might be tempted to post his poor excuse for a painting on social media. No doubt some overzealous fan would spend big bucks to get their hands on his amateur artwork.

The ferry docked, and the few other passengers filed toward the exit. Knox stood and waited for Claudia to gather her items together. The clock hanging on the wall showed that it was only eight o'clock. He'd been keeping a close eye on the time so they didn't miss the ferry. As much as Claudia tried to pretend she was okay with being on the mainland, he didn't want their first date to end with her in a panic attack.

They made their way down the dock and onto the main road. Knox tugged her to a stop next to him. She faced the mainland across the bay. A few of the houses they'd toured sat close enough to the water that they could see the lights dotting the shoreline.

"You asked me about my dream house while we were on the tour." Claudia stared across the bay, her gaze locked onto something he couldn't see in the distant darkness.

"Yeah, what about it?"

"As much as I love the beach, I think I'd want a place in the country. A big old log cabin kind of lodge out in the middle of nowhere."

Her answer surprised him. He had a difficult time picturing her anywhere but the beach with the breeze blowing through her hair and the kiss of the sun warming her skin. "Would you have animals?"

"Maybe. But for sure, kids. At least two, but no more than four. You?" She looked up at him with such curiosity in her eyes, he wondered if she was asking to try to find out if they were compatible.

"Are you asking if I'd want animals at my place or kids?"

"Both."

He'd thought about what he wanted to do once his star fizzled from the music scene. The house in the country near his mom was a given. But did he want to follow in his dad's footsteps and work on the land every day, or be a weekend cowboy like some of his friends? If it were up to him, and in some ways he supposed it was, he'd play music until people got tired of listening to him. That had always been his dream, though his dream had changed over the years.

Now he'd give anything to have a do-over at breaking into the music business. He'd hold his ground and not let a bunch of executives dictate the kind of country artist he could be.

Claudia squeezed his hand, pulling his attention back to the present. "You don't have to answer."

"I want to." He took in a breath, drawing the fresh ocean air into his nose. "My dad's a cattle rancher, so I grew up around animals. Everyone in the family helped out however they could."

She flipped her hair over her shoulder and looked up at him with wide eyes. "Oooh, like on *Yellowstone*? Did you have ranch hands and take people to the train station when they didn't toe the line?"

"Not exactly." He didn't even try to stop from chuckling. "Not everything's like they make it out to be in the media."

She blew out a breath. "That's for sure."

"We did have cattle, but we used ATVs more than horses to keep them in line. I miss being around animals, but I'm not sure I'd want to run an operation like that." Too much red tape. Too much bullshit.

"So, some animals, but not a lot?"

"Yeah." He could see it. A hobby farm of sorts. Half a dozen horses, maybe a few goats and a pig or two. And chickens. He missed having fresh eggs in the mornings. If he had a hobby farm, he'd have to carve out a place for some hens.

"And the kids?"

After what his dad did to him, he couldn't imagine wanting to pass on those genes. "I don't know."

"It's a big decision."

Knox nodded. "Yeah. Raising kids . . . it's a big responsibility. I'd be afraid I'd totally fuck them up."

Her laugh rang out. "I think everyone's scared of that. My sister has kids. A two-year-old, a four-year-old, and another one on the way. I didn't used to think I wanted a family, but after seeing her with her kids, I changed my mind."

"Well, maybe someday I'll change mine." His mom would be over the moon if he had kids. She didn't even care if he was married. She'd been asking when he thought he might give her a grandkid for years. His younger brother had already told her he wasn't going to reproduce, so it was all up to Knox. Maybe someday . . . maybe if he had someone like Claudia to help him navigate the tricky waters of parenting.

They'd entered unchartered waters in their topic of conversation. Ready to change the subject, he swung their hands between them. "Did you get any good ideas for decorating the bungalows today?"

"I sure did." Her face glowed as she ticked off all the ideas she'd taken away after their tour. "I'm thinking we do a mix of bohemian beach with a modern feel."

Whatever the hell that meant. Knox nodded along as she talked about ways they could incorporate the current features and, with minimal effort, update the overall look.

"What did you do before you came to Paradise?" he asked. "I mean, with the way you talk about the houses we toured and changes to make to the bungalow designs, you had to have been involved in design or something."

The soft laugh lines at the corners of her eyes faded. It was like shutters snapped closed and cut off any light from her eyes. He didn't mean to make her feel threatened, but clearly his comment had shaken her.

"It's an area I've always been interested in. My parents used to flip houses when I was a kid and I helped out with lots of projects." Almost as soon as the fear appeared in the depths of her eyes, it was gone.

"Oh, that sounds like fun. So you've been at it for quite a while." He nodded, trying to pretend that he hadn't noticed the way her spine stiffened and her jaw clenched when he mentioned it.

"Yeah. A family business. Not too different from yours, I guess." Her nose crinkled as she glanced over at him. "Except you were working with cows and we were scraping wallpaper off walls."

"You probably didn't smell as bad as I did." He bumped her with his shoulder.

"I like the way you smell." Her teeth captured her bottom lip like she hadn't meant to make the admission.

"Thanks." He stopped when they reached the path through the scrubby bushes to get to the beach. The moon sat high in the sky overhead and the sound of the waves hitting the shore played in the background. "I like the way you smell, too."

She glanced at her feet. "I probably smell like paint. Enough of it ended up on my hands."

"You have beautiful hands." He took the painting from her and set it on the ground between them. Then he clasped both of her hands in both of his.

Her eyes sparkled, the reflection of the moon shining in their depths.

"You have beautiful everything," he muttered under his breath. He couldn't keep his gaze from bouncing from her cheeks to her eyes, to the rapid beating of her pulse he could see on her neck. Beautiful everything? Hell, he wrote songs for a living. What kind of dumbass compliment was "You have beautiful everything"?

She rose to her tiptoes and pressed her chest against his. "You have beautiful everything, too."

His lips stretched into a smile right before he touched his mouth to hers.

He'd just found the title to his song.

18

Claudia

Her feet barely touched the ground as she went about her Monday. Nolan's kiss had given her wings, and she felt like she was literally flying between chores. Once she got things set for the lunch crowd, she claimed a table at the back of the restaurant and pulled up the new list of features she hoped to incorporate into the bungalow designs.

Chick would flip a gasket when she told him what she wanted to do, but going on the home tour with Nolan yesterday reminded her how much she loved taking a halfway decent property and turning it into something amazing.

When she ran her own real estate office in Minneapolis, her favorite part of the business had been staging a property right before putting it on the market. Most agents hired a professional stager, but Claudia never gave up the opportunity to do it herself. There was something so satisfying about taking an empty house and choosing the perfect elements. Like taking a blank slate and turning it into something amazing.

Chick finally walked in a few minutes before they officially opened for lunch. By that time she'd sketched out the floor plan she wanted to propose and put together an estimate of the cost. Once he saw the income potential, she couldn't imagine he'd say no. They'd just need to get moving soon if they wanted to finish up before Nolan had to get to his next job.

Thinking about him leaving put a damper on her good mood. Though she didn't want to get attached, she'd miss him. It had been a long time since she'd felt the kind of feelings he stirred up inside her. Without knowing it, he'd reminded her of how much she enjoyed working in real estate. She didn't think she'd ever go back to being an agent. Not with the need to avoid being in the public eye. She couldn't risk having anything similar to what she went through in Minnesota happen again.

But she could work in the background. She could flip houses or maybe even buy a few properties of her own and operate them as long-term or short-term rentals. For the first time in a long while, she felt like she had a purpose again. Beyond just existing, she had something to focus on, something that would get her excited to wake up every day.

"How was the home tour?" Chick eased himself onto the chair across from her.

"It was fantastic. I got several new ideas for the bungalows."

He stared into his coffee cup and rubbed at his temple. "How much is this going to cost me?"

"Don't you want to see my ideas?" She turned around the paper she'd been sketching on. "Look. If we add a Murphy bed in a few of the units, we can accommodate more people. And the one farthest down the beach is big enough to do a separate living room and bedroom. Adding solar panels to the roofs would make them energy efficient. It would cost more up front, but you'd come out way ahead in the long run."

His gaze skimmed over the page. "You're enjoying this, aren't you?"

"You mean costing you money?" She laughed.

He lifted his head and met her gaze. His brown eyes seemed like they could see right through her. "The planning. Feels good to be using your brain for something more than memorizing orders, for a change, doesn't it?"

Her breath caught. Chick knew why she'd left her business behind. He'd never pushed her to do more than she was comfortable doing since she'd arrived in Paradise. "Maybe."

The chair creaked underneath him as he relaxed against the back. "Maybe it's time for you to think about what you want to do when you leave here, Claudia."

Her chest tightened. "Leave here? Are you trying to kick me out?"

"Not yet. But you can't hide down here forever, hon. You're made for more than this, and you know it."

"I'm not hiding . . . I'm just taking a break." The lie sounded pathetic, even to her. Hiding had been exactly what she'd been doing.

He pushed the paper across the table to her. "I trust you to do what you think is best. Oh, by the way, you might want to find something to do tomorrow afternoon. They're putting in a new breaker box, so the whole place will be shut down."

"I'm sure we can find something to work on in the bungalows, even with no power." She didn't want to waste an entire day. They'd been talking about replacing the breaker box for months. Odds were no one would show up again and it would be business as usual.

"Take the afternoon. I bet Nolan wouldn't mind seeing more of the island. Or you could always head back to the mainland for supplies if there's anything you need."

"We won't need anything else for a while." She eyed Chick through narrowed lids. The old man might think he was being sly, but she was on to him and his obvious attempt at matchmaking. "I'm sure Nolan has other things he wants to get done."

"Y'all talking about me behind my back again?" Nolan appeared at her side. He must have walked in while she was giving Chick the evil eye.

"I was just telling Claudia that we'll be shut down during the day tomorrow. Power will be out, so there's no use trying to get anything done. The two of you should take some time off."

"Really?" Nolan's brow furrowed, like he couldn't understand what Chick was trying to do, either. "I can work on the expanded patios Claudia wants, or—"

"Take the day off, will ya, dammit?" Chick glared at both of them, then pushed back from the table, grabbed his coffee mug, and stomped toward the bar.

"What the hell was that?" Nolan asked.

"His attempt at getting us to spend time together," Claudia said. The idea of spending a day with Nolan sent a shiver through her, even if it was Chick trying to manipulate the two of them to get together.

"Well, that's . . ." Nolan seemed to search for the right word. "Advantageous?"

She bit back her laugh. "You treated me to the home tour and a painting class. How would you feel about me treating you to a tour of some of my favorite places on the island?"

"I'd say yes." Nolan held out his hand to shake and make it official.

She slid her palm against his. The same kickback she'd felt before sent a jolt through her nervous system. It didn't matter how they touched, her reaction was the same. Whether he wrapped his arm over her shoulders or barely brushed her hand with his, her body reacted to his touch like she'd been jump-started.

"Okay then. Meet me at nine tomorrow morning. I'll pack a picnic and we'll hike out to the waterfall we saw from the

helicopter." She hadn't been to that spot in months. Hope
fully the path wasn't too overgrown.

"You've got a deal. I'm going to head over to the bungalows to do some work this afternoon. What did Chick say
to your ideas?" He set his hand on the table between them,
though he didn't let go of hers.

"He said to go for it. Looks like we have some more supplies to order. Are you sure you're up for the changes? Do
you have time to get everything done before you have to head
to your next job?"

"Yeah." A tiny crease appeared between his brows, making her wonder if there was something he wasn't being 100
percent up front about. "I can be a little flexible on the start
date."

"That's great. I can't wait to see these come together."
Reluctantly, she pulled her hand from his. "I need to make
sure everything's ready for lunch. If I don't catch you before
tomorrow, I'll see you in the morning."

"See you in the morning." The heat in his eyes could have
set fire to the paper napkin under her palm. She was probably
reading into the look, but to her it promised more of the same
sizzle she'd felt last night when he'd touched his lips to hers.

She told herself she was imagining things as she pushed
back from the table. Every part of her begged her to stay in
the seat across from him, to spend the afternoon watching
his lips move as he talked, to just exist within the orbit of his
presence. That's what had gotten her into her current predicament. She was done losing herself over a man, even one
who smelled as good as Nolan.

"Have a good afternoon."

"It would be better if I were spending it with you."

The admission slammed into her like he'd just tossed a
bowling ball at her gut and she'd caught it with her abs. Her

fingertips tingled. White noise filled her ears. She lowered her voice and leaned across the table. "You can't say things like that."

"Why not? I'm not lying. It's true." He stared at her, the truth stamped across his face like a tattoo on his forehead.

"Because we're not supposed to like each other."

"Says who?" His lips tipped up in the lopsided grin of his that made her heart beat in triple time.

"I've got to get to work. Nine o'clock tomorrow morning. Be there."

"Oh, I'll be there, all right." He pushed back from the table and stood. "Wouldn't miss it for the world."

Claudia waited until he'd strolled out of the restaurant before she trusted herself to stand. What was happening to her? Nolan had gotten under her skin. It wasn't that he was the only guy who'd shown her attention over the past few years, either. It was how he made her feel inside. Like she could do anything.

It was addictive, that feeling that she could shed her fear and put herself out there again. She'd learned her lesson about trusting a man, though. No matter how different Nolan seemed from the man who'd violated her trust, she had to be careful.

19

Knox

For the first time in years, Knox hadn't slept well the previous night. Usually, he was so worn out from traveling or trying to squeeze the creative juices out of his brain that he dropped into bed and fell asleep before his head even hit the pillow. But after his conversation with Claudia, sleep wouldn't come.

He lay awake, his mind filled with images of Claudia. The way her eyes held a world of sadness but could still light up an entire room. The way her skin warmed under his touch. The way her entire face changed when she tipped her lips up at the corners into a smile.

And today he'd get to spend the whole day with her. He hadn't been this excited since the Christmas Eve before Decker told him Santa Claus didn't exist. His nerves tingled, his mouth had gone dry, and he couldn't seem to stand still for longer than a few seconds at a time.

Finally, a few minutes after nine, Claudia drove toward him on the ATV. He pulled his baseball cap lower to shield his eyes from the sun as he followed her progress down the beach.

She cut the engine when she stopped in front of him. "It was either this or riding horses. I figured you'd be okay on either, but I do much better on wheels."

"Maybe someday I'll teach you how to ride a horse."

"Maybe someday I'll let you." She slid off the seat and nodded for him to take her spot. "You can drive this time."

"You sure?" He'd been looking forward to sandwiching her between his thighs again.

"Oh, I'm sure." She took the backpack he'd packed and attached it to the back of the ATV, where she'd already stashed a tote. "Let's get going. We're burning daylight."

"Are you in a hurry?" He flung his leg over the seat and tried to get comfortable while he waited for her to climb on behind him.

"In a hurry to start having fun." She had on a pair of dark shades and he would have given just about anything to get a look at her eyes.

"Let's get moving, then." He turned the key, and the ATV hummed to life.

Claudia slid a leg over the seat and held on to his shoulders. He waited until she told him she was ready, then gunned it so she'd have to hold on tight. She moved her hands down to squeeze her arms around his middle and squealed.

"Hold on," he called out over his shoulder. Her breasts pressed against his back, and he could feel her thighs next to his. He didn't care about anything at the moment except the thrill of racing along the beach with Claudia. All the details that had been crowding his head floated away on the salty sea breeze. He didn't care about his obligation to the label, the threats from his manager, or the countless number of people depending on him.

As the wind blew past his ears, he was just a guy speeding down the beach on a Tuesday morning with a gorgeous girl squeezing him tight. The freedom chiseled the heaviness away from his heart until he could feel it floating around in his chest, lighter than it had been in a long damn time.

"Over there." Claudia pointed to the tree line ahead on their left. When they'd been in the helicopter, flying high above the island, he hadn't paid too much attention to the waterfall. Now they entered the trailhead and started to climb.

After quite a while, Claudia yelled over the roar of the engine, "We'll have to walk the rest of the way."

Knox pulled to the side of the trail and killed the engine. "Wow, that was fun."

"I'm glad you liked it." She climbed off from behind him and he immediately missed the heat of her body against his.

He took his backpack when she untied it from the back and then silently offered to carry the tote bag she'd brought with her. "Lead the way."

Claudia started up the trail first. He followed, grateful for the training regimen he'd committed to while on tour. The trail climbed and twisted its way up the side of the hill, but Claudia barely seemed to break a sweat. After about twenty minutes of serious hiking, they stepped through the trees into a clearing.

They appeared to be halfway up the hill he'd seen from the helicopter. Water rushed down the wall of rocks in front of them, landing in a clear pool.

"Wow, it's beautiful." He pulled his water bottle out of his bag and offered it to Claudia first.

She took a sip. "Worth the hike?"

"Yeah." The break in the trees gave them an unobstructed view of the clear blue sky. Rocks and dense tree coverage surrounded the pool while in front of them a wall of rock stretched up to the sky.

"Come over here and take a seat." Claudia picked her way

over some large boulders until she came to one with a wide, flat top. Once there, she pulled a light blanket out of the bag.

Knox caught the other side and together they spread the blanket out over the boulder's surface. "This is great. How did you find this place?"

"They call it Lovers' Falls. Chick told me about it once. He said it was his thinking spot." She climbed onto the blanket and patted the spot next to her. "Lie back and look at the sky."

Knox joined her, threading his fingers with hers as he stretched out on the rock. The trees reached for the sky, providing a frame for the section of blue that was visible directly overhead. "So, do you come here to think?"

"I used to when I first came here. Then I got busy and couldn't find the time. Oh, I wanted to show you something." She sat up and reached into the tote bag he'd carried. She pulled out an old-style boom box, the kind his dad used to listen to in the barn.

"Where did you find that, an antiques store?" he joked.

"Hey, don't knock it. They don't make them like they used to." She searched through the bag until she found what she was looking for, then popped a CD into the tray and pressed a button. "Wait for it. This is going to be good."

Knox propped his head on his hand and rested his elbow on the rock so he could watch her. The music started to play, and she tugged him over so they were lying side by side. The first strains of an instrumental song came through the speakers. A flock of birds, startled by the music, took flight from the trees to their right.

Claudia reached over to adjust the volume, turning the music up until he could feel it vibrating through the rock underneath them. The rocks surrounding the area provided natural acoustics. The notes bounced off the rocks, amplifying the sound. It was similar to how it sounded when he'd played the Red Rocks Amphitheatre in Colorado last year.

He closed his eyes and stopped listening to the music. Instead, he felt it. From the tips of his toes to the top of his head, the music flowed through him. Beethoven's *Moonlight Sonata*. He'd come to love it while listening to his mom play piano when she thought no one else was around.

The song came to an end, and he opened his eyes to find Claudia beaming at him.

"What did you think?" Her grin was contagious, and he smiled back.

"That was incredible. It was like the music was . . ."

"Inside you?" she asked.

"Yeah." He squeezed her hand, grateful they'd shared the experience. "How did you know I'd like that?"

"Who wouldn't like that?" She let go of his hand and dug through the bag again. "Let me play something else for you. Oh, here, you're from Texas. You like country, don't you?"

"Hey, just because I'm from Texas doesn't mean I automatically like country mus—"

The opening notes to the first song on his very first album floated out of the speaker. He remembered the day he recorded that song like it had happened yesterday. He'd gone into the studio, a notebook full of songs in his backpack and stars in his eyes. That was when his manager had told him the label had tweaked the songs he'd come up with. "Gave them a little more commercial appeal" were the exact words Tripp used. "Ruined them" was a more accurate description of what they'd done.

Claudia stood on the rock and started to shake her hips. "This is more pop than country, isn't it?"

She didn't know it was his song. She couldn't, based on the way she held her hands over her head and laughed like she didn't have a care in the world. He bent over and rummaged through the bag.

"Do you care if I switch it up?"

"Sure. I don't really like this stuff, anyway. Put on something we can dance to."

He took his CD out of the player and replaced it with one full of country ballads. "Come here."

The slow strains of a steel guitar played while he reached for her hands. Wrapping one arm around her back, he twined his fingers with hers. The steady, slow rhythm of his favorite Buck Owens song brought his pulse back down to a normal level.

Claudia nestled against him, her hand in his and her other arm looped up around his neck. If he could have stopped time right then and there, he would have been tempted. The sun's rays reflected off the clear pool, the breeze rustled the leaves in the trees, and Claudia's heart beat in time with his.

He sang the words out of habit, his voice low and barely more than a whisper.

She pulled him closer, and he skimmed his hand over her back, taking his time covering the distance from the base of her neck to the spot just above the curve of her ass. The song ended, and they stood on top of the rock, their bodies swaying in time to the music he could still hear playing in his head.

"I guess not all country music is awful." She tilted her head up to look at him.

The unintentional insult against his own music made him bite back a grin. She was right, that first album of his was bad. Now he had a chance to change things. To become the kind of country music artist he'd always wanted to be.

"You're not such a bad singer, either." Claudia smiled. "Maybe you should sing at open mic night this weekend."

"Maybe I will." He held her there, his gaze locked with

hers. Then he leaned closer until the distance between them disappeared. His lips touched hers and he lost himself.

Claudia

She couldn't breathe. All the air had been sucked out of her lungs when Nolan's mouth connected with hers. Her chest heaved, and she pulled back, the need for air too difficult to ignore. Gasping in a breath, she put a hand to her heart. The rapid *badump-badump-badump* under her fingertips made it feel like her heart might beat right out of her chest.

"You okay?" Nolan asked.

"I'm fine." She moved her hand from her heart to his. The beat of his heart matched hers.

"Do you want to sit down for a minute? Maybe catch your breath?"

She shook her head. "There's too much I want to show you. Since we're down this far on the island, it's the perfect time to visit the lighthouse."

"The one we saw from the helicopter?"

"Yeah, you want to go check it out?" She could have spent the entire day lying on the rock and trading kisses with Nolan, but she was too nervous, too afraid. It would be so easy to let him in. She wanted to. She'd been trying to convince herself that she could have fun with him without baring her soul. That's what normal people did. They had one-night stands and hooked up with people they barely knew.

She'd never been able to do things like that. She always got attached, always gave so much more than she received in return. Based on what she knew about Nolan already, he wasn't the kind of man she could enjoy for a day or two and let go. He was considerate and kind. Protective and masculine. Just looking at him in the low-slung jeans he had riding on his hips had nearly made her cancel the whole day trip and invite him into her bungalow instead.

Her sister said life was too short not to enjoy every single second of it. Claudia thought those sounded like great words to live by, but she always got caught up in the actual living-of-them part.

"I'm game if you are." Nolan let his hands fall away from her. Was it wishful thinking, or did he look a little disappointed?

"Okay, we can hike up the rest of the hill or go back down to the beach and drive over to the trail that leads right to it." She waited for him to make the call.

"I could go for a little more hiking if you want." He shrugged, his big shoulders rolling under the thin T-shirt he had on.

She put the boom box back into the tote and slid the straps over her shoulder.

"Hey, I'll get that." He reached up and took the bag from her.

"I can carry my own bag, you know." She was used to hauling her own stuff around. Used to not depending on anyone else.

"I know you can, but I want to do it for you, if that's okay." Nolan picked up his backpack and tossed it over his other shoulder.

Claudia nodded. Yeah, it was okay. It was nice to have someone looking out for her for a change. She'd been handling things on her own for so long she'd forgotten what it was like to have someone want to help. Even if it was something so simple as carrying a bag for her.

"Sorry, I'm out of practice at accepting help." Her cheeks flushed with heat. He was going to think she was some kind of weirdo.

Instead, he put his hand on her back. "Don't worry, I'll be more than happy to help you practice."

Hearing him say things that like turned her insides to mush. Either he was playing her like a violin he'd practiced on all his life or he really was that nice a guy. Even though it would make everything more complicated, she hoped with all her heart it was the latter.

They continued on the trail, climbing up the side of the waterfall. The path switched from dirt to steep steps set into the rock before it leveled out at the top. Claudia had to stop several times on the climb to catch her breath. She hadn't been getting her morning runs in for the past couple of days and her muscles let her know it.

Finally, they reached the top. Claudia paused to look down at the face of the waterfall. She'd only climbed up this way once before and the effort had been worth the amazing view that greeted her. To their left, the waterfall crashed down the hill. To their right, the Gulf of Mexico sparkled. The turquoise water melded together so many shades of blue and green that she lost track of where one started and another began.

"What do you think? Is the view worth the climb?" She glanced over her shoulder at Nolan, who'd just come up behind her.

He looked at the waterfall and over at the ocean. Then his gaze rested on her. "Yeah, I'd say so."

Her stomach twisted tight at the look in his eyes. She wasn't sure he was talking about the waterfall or the Gulf. "The path to the lighthouse is just through the trees over there. We'll probably have the place to ourselves today. It's not open to the public and most people who come up for the view come on the weekends."

"Lead the way." Nolan nodded for her to go ahead.

She picked up the trail to the lighthouse, and they followed it through some trees until they reached the area that had been cleared out around the tall structure. Every time she stood that close to it, she tried to imagine what it was like on the island more than a hundred fifty years ago when a group of locals built the lighthouse to prevent ships from crashing into the rocky wall at this end of the island.

"It was built a little over a hundred fifty years ago by residents on the island," she told Nolan. "The original lighthouse keeper lived here for sixty years."

"All by himself?" Nolan asked.

"Herself," Claudia corrected him with a sassy grin. "There's a museum on the mainland that tells the history. They say she lived here all alone, and every night she climbed to the top to light the lantern and keep sailors from hitting the rocks below."

"Sounds like a brave woman to me."

"She was. There's a song the sailors used to sing about her. Something like the angel of light who kept them safe."

They reached the fence constructed around the perimeter to keep tourists out of the building. Claudia slipped the key Chick had given her out of her pocket. No one was around. They could head inside for a few minutes and maybe even climb the steps to the top and see the view. Chick was on the board for the nonprofit group that managed the property, so he had special privileges he didn't mind sharing. There was talk of selling the lighthouse, but so far they hadn't done anything about it.

"We get to go in?" Nolan asked.

"I know people who know people." The lock clicked open and she pushed through the gate. A cool breeze blew past her. They weren't that high up, but the temperature had definitely shifted a few degrees. She locked the gate behind him and wrapped her arms around her middle. "It's a little cool out here. Should we explore the inside?"

"I've got a long sleeve shirt in my backpack if you want it." He made a move to slide the pack off his shoulder.

"I'm fine. Though it looks like it might rain soon." She glanced toward the sky. It had been bright blue a half hour ago when they'd gazed up from the rock by the waterfall. Now dark clouds gathered over the ocean. It wasn't that unusual for a quick afternoon storm to blow through. It would probably pass them over while they were inside looking around.

"Let's get inside, then." Nolan waited for her to unlock the door to the lighthouse, then turned the knob. "Ladies first."

She squeezed past him, letting her eyes adjust to the dim interior. The group that owned the lighthouse wanted to keep it in original condition, so they'd only made repairs that were necessary for structural integrity. That didn't include updates to the electrical system, so when Claudia flipped the light switch, a lone bare bulb flickered to life from its spot on the wall.

Steps spiraled upward on their right. Claudia headed into the room to the left, where the original keeper's cottage connected to the base of the tall structure. She pulled a flashlight out of the tote bag Nolan set on the ground. A quick sweep of the room showed not much had been done to the place since the last keeper abandoned the post almost forty years ago.

They stood in what once was a very cozy living room and kitchen area. The curve of the outer wall followed the lines of the lighthouse. She moved toward the wall of windows that looked out over the cliff.

"What a view. Can you imagine sipping your morning coffee in a room like this?" she asked.

Nolan came up behind her and set his chin on her shoulder. "It's amazing."

She stood still, relishing his closeness. If she wasn't careful, she'd get too used to this. That wouldn't do either one of them any good.

"Want to go up to the top?" She stepped away, breaking contact.

"Yeah, that's what we came here to see, isn't it?" He had a look on his face that made her think he was giving up on her. That he'd tried making multiple passes and had been met with her rejection enough. As much as she hated being the reason for the tight set of his jaw, it was for the best.

She just needed to keep reminding herself of that.

20

Knox

He followed Claudia up the narrow, steep spiral staircase into the darkness above. It was barely noon, but the interior of the lighthouse structure didn't have very many windows. They passed the second-floor landing, then the third. The stairs ran up the inner wall of the structure. Each landing had an empty room that opened up to the side, though the dimensions grew smaller and smaller the higher they climbed.

His thighs burned with the effort. He couldn't imagine having to repeat the climb multiple times a day. Finally, they reached a hatch that opened into what Claudia told him was once the keeper's work room.

"They kept spare parts here, and it's where the lighthouse keeper wrote in the daily log. The log's on display in the historical society's museum if you ever want to check it out." She moved around the room with her flashlight in hand. The windows on this level provided more light. Or, at least, they would have if the sky hadn't turned dark as night with the promise of an incoming storm.

"Can you imagine what it was like to live out here a hundred years ago?" Knox asked. "No power, no running water, no phone?"

Claudia shivered. "I like my privacy, but I'm not sure I could handle being so isolated. Back when they used this lighthouse, the island wasn't developed at all. The keeper got a delivery every few weeks but had to be self-sufficient in between visits."

Knox moved to the table set against the exterior wall. "At least it doesn't get too cold here. I've read about lighthouses up in Maine and Canada, where it's isolated and freezing."

"The cold never used to bother me. I think now that I've been in Texas for so long, it would be hard to get used to the snow again." Claudia moved toward a ladder attached to the wall that led up to the lens room.

"Does that mean you plan on staying in Texas?" Knox had been receiving such mixed signals from Claudia that he didn't know how to read her. One minute she was leaning into him, eager for his kiss. The next she was pulling back, reinforcing the shields she'd welded into place.

"We should go all the way to the top." She grabbed on to the ladder and climbed the short distance to a door on the ceiling. Holding on to a rung with one hand, she tried to push the door open, but it wouldn't budge.

"Need some help?" He stood at the base of the ladder. They couldn't both be on it at the same time. There was barely room for one person, let alone two.

"Yeah, why don't you try it, Mr. Muscles?" She climbed down and stepped aside so he could take a crack at the door.

The hinges creaked and complained before they gave way. Knox pushed the door open and passed through the cutout in the ceiling. "Come on up."

She clambered up the ladder and joined him in the room, where the giant lamp sat in the center. A metal catwalk surrounded the huge lens, and floor-to-ceiling windows provided a 360-degree view.

Claudia took in a deep breath. "I feel like I'm on top of the world."

"We may as well be." Knox moved next to her and they both looked out at the ocean. "I bet it's gorgeous up here on a clear day."

"You can probably see all the way to Mexico." Claudia surely didn't mean to, but she slid her fingers along the rail and brushed the side of her hand against his.

A spark of heat passed between them. He didn't move. The warmth traveled up his arm and across his chest, then split to send a flush of heat to his cheeks while another surge headed straight toward his dick. How could she ignore it and pretend like it wasn't happening when she had to feel it, too? They stood in silence, lost in their own thoughts for several minutes.

Then they both spoke at once.

"Claudia, I—"

"I'm sorry, but—"

"You go first," Knox said.

She shook her head. "I can wait. What were you going to say?"

He swallowed his apprehension. This was it. He could understand why she might be reluctant to get involved, especially since she knew he'd be leaving in a few weeks. But he hadn't felt the kind of intense attraction he had with Claudia since high school. Back then, it consumed him and made him turn a blind eye to the red flags that had been waving in his face all along. Now there were no red flags. There was just Claudia.

Claudia with her big brown eyes, her plump pink lips, her miles of curves he couldn't wait to explore. She'd become his muse, and he didn't want to leave Paradise without making one last play for her. What they had between them couldn't last, but it could work for now. That's all he wanted, a chance to explore the feelings between them.

He turned his back to the ocean and reached for her hands. "I was going to say that I can't stop thinking about you. There's something between us. I know you can feel it, too."

She broke eye contact, shifting her gaze to the floor underneath them. "Nolan, I'm not going to lie to you. I know there's something there, I just . . . I just can't."

His breath caught in his chest. "Somebody did a real number on you, didn't he?"

She nudged her chin up so she could look him in the eye. He expected to see anger burning in the depths of her eyes, but instead her lower lids brimmed with unshed tears.

"Hey." He dropped her hands so he could pull her into a comforting hug. "It's okay. I shouldn't have pressed."

Her arms wrapped around his back, and she clung to him. Tears fell, drenching the front of his tee, but he didn't give a fuck. All that mattered was getting her through whatever was bothering her. He smoothed a hand over the back of her hair and whispered into her ear. "I've got you. Let it out, sweetheart. Just let it out."

After she ran out of tears, she pulled back and wiped at her eyes. "How embarrassing."

"Come here." He wiped her cheeks with the pad of his thumb. "There's nothing to be embarrassed about."

"Yeah right. You're not the one who just cried enough to fill the Gulf of Mexico." She tried to turn away, but he lightly gripped her upper arms, not wanting her to shut him out again.

"You want to talk about it?"

"No." She shook her head so hard her hair flew around her shoulders.

"Got it." He rubbed his hands up and down her arms. The storm that had been rolling in from the gulf had reached them. Rain splattered the windows and a cool breeze blew in through the poorly insulated space. "You want to head down a level so we can warm up a little?"

"Sure." She ducked down the ladder, then continued all the way to the bottom.

The wind howled outside, finding its way in through the cracks. Knox reached the ground level and searched for his backpack. "There's got to be a fireplace or stove in here somewhere."

"Even if there is, you think they've had the chimney cleaned out recently?" Claudia joked.

"Good point. We can't head back down the trail in this weather." He pulled out a blanket he'd tossed in his pack thinking they might end up spending some time on the beach. "Come here. I've got a long-sleeve tee and a blanket you can use to warm up."

Claudia didn't resist. She took the shirt he offered and pulled it over her head, then shoved her arms through the sleeves.

He took off his shirt that had been soaked through with her tears.

She glanced over and immediately looked away. "Hey, you should keep this shirt. I didn't mean to get your other one all wet."

"That's okay. Maybe we can share the blanket?" He held one end out to her.

She wrapped it around her shoulders and slid down to rest her back against the wall. "Come here. I don't want to be responsible for you catching cold and not being able to work on the bungalows."

He took a seat next to her, slinging his arm over her shoulder and settling the blanket around them both. "How's this?"

"Are you comfortable?" She turned her head and looked up at him. Even in the dim light, he could trace the outline of her cheeks with his gaze.

"More than comfortable."

"About earlier," she started.

He waited to see if she'd continue. When she didn't, he nudged her and asked, "Yeah?"

"I'm afraid." Her voice came out soft, barely more than a whisper.

His heart softened at her tone. He tightened his arm around her shoulders, every part of him wanting to protect her. "Afraid of what?"

"You."

Claudia

She cringed as she confessed her fears to Nolan. He was going to think she was pathetic. How could a grown-ass woman be afraid of letting a man get too close? A man who'd done nothing but show her kindness and concern? Who'd never given her any reason to doubt his intentions or cause her mistrust?

"I'm not going to hurt you, Claudia. I don't know what happened to you in the past, but I'd never do anything to intentionally hurt you, baby." His fingers skimmed her arm under the blanket he'd wrapped around them both.

Her chest rose and fell as she sucked in deep breaths. She didn't want to be afraid anymore. Didn't want to close herself up and lock away her heart. Nolan said he didn't want to hurt her, and she believed him. Though she wasn't naive enough to think he'd stick around. If she let this happen, she'd get hurt.

Maybe it was time to take another chance, to let herself feel again.

He pressed a kiss to her temple, his lips lingering for a long moment. She breathed in his scent. Even in the darkness of a summer storm, he smelled like sunshine. Like a world she used to live in where everything was possible. She wanted to be a part of that world again.

Wanted it more than anything.

Wanted it enough to turn her head.

Wanted it enough to graze his lips with hers.

Wanted it enough to wrap her arms around his neck and pull his head down to deepen their kiss.

Nolan shifted, pulling her onto his lap. He settled the blanket around her shoulders and slanted his mouth over hers.

His tongue pressed against the seam of her lips, and she opened for him. With that one move, she forced her doubt and fear down and let her need for him bubble up to the surface. She'd suppressed it for so long—her need for a man's touch—that it consumed her.

But Nolan wasn't just any man. He was the only one she trusted to handle her heart with care. He'd shown her time and again that he deserved it. Now she couldn't wait for him to take it. To take her.

Flames licked up her sides as he skimmed his hand over her ribs. She'd gone from chilled to burning with desire in a matter of moments. Tossing the blanket off her shoulders, she pressed her palm to his chest. His skin felt soft and smooth under her hand.

His pecs flexed as he laid her back, trying to spread out the blanket before her back touched the ground. She didn't care that the floor probably hadn't been swept in a decade. She couldn't feel anything except for his hands working their way under her shirt and the touch of his fingertips as they grazed the skin at her waist.

Hovering over her, he was in charge. Instead of feeling trapped, she welcomed him taking control. She'd been in charge of everything for so long. It was nice to have someone else take the lead. He slid his tongue against hers while his fingers explored her belly. Heat shot through her, settling at the apex of her thighs. She hadn't been turned on in so long, she'd almost forgotten how it felt . . . the delicious anticipation.

Every part of her ached for him, but she didn't want to rush it. She wanted to draw this out as long as she could. Wanted to refill that place inside she could draw on to remember how it felt to be desired.

"You feel so good, Claudia. Even better than I imagined." His voice brushed against her ear. Goose bumps pebbled her skin at the idea of him thinking about what it would be like to kiss her. To run his hands over her curves.

"How long have you been imagining it?" she whispered.

"Too damn long." The ridge of his erection slid against her thigh as he moved closer.

Knowing how turned on he was made her even more eager for his touch. Her fingers danced over his back. His muscles bunched and rolled underneath her hands. His whiskers scraped against her skin, and she loved it. Loved every single second of feeling his weight pressing down on her, his hands on her skin.

He slid the hem of both of her shirts up over her stomach, then shifted his mouth to her neck, working his way down her collarbone, then moving lower to trail soft kisses across her belly.

Her knee came up, catching him in the leg as she squirmed underneath him. "Cut that out, I'm ticklish."

"Careful, or you'll put me out of commission." His hand blocked her from accidentally catching him in the crotch.

"Sorry. I can't help it."

"It's nice to know you have a weakness." He grinned, then dipped down and went to work on the button of her jeans. "I'll file that info away for when I need it most."

Her skin still tingled from his touch, but she forced herself not to react. Then he tugged her zipper down. Her lungs seized and for a split second, she froze underneath him.

"Is this okay?" His breath landed on her belly. Heat uncoiled from her core, sending tendrils of need to every nerve ending she possessed.

She didn't trust herself to speak, so she nodded. Anticipation had stolen her voice. His baseball cap had fallen off at some point, so she ran her fingers through his hair. It was thick and dark, the perfect length to hold on to in a moment of—oh—in a moment just like this.

Nolan worked her panties and jeans over her hips and down her thighs. The cool air drifted over her skin, but she wasn't cold. There was no way she could be cold with him nestled between her legs. The heat from his exhale ghosted over her clit, and she closed her eyes.

She was doing this, really doing it. As he dipped his tongue to flick it against her most sensitive spot, she shed the last of her inhibitions. She stopped trying to outrun her past and decided to enjoy the present. Her muscles relaxed as warmth flowed through her veins. God, it had been so long. She'd forgotten what it felt like to have a man lavish attention on her.

And Nolan knew exactly where to touch her, exactly how much pressure to apply, exactly how far he could push her before she plummeted over the edge. He took her to that spot with his tongue—over and over again. Her nails dug into his shoulders as she held on for dear life.

Just when she thought she couldn't take any more, he slipped a finger inside her. It was just the tip of his finger, but he crooked it, somehow knowing exactly where to touch her.

Her world exploded into a mind-blowing release. Pieces of her scattered as she came undone. He didn't let up. Not when she grabbed a fistful of his hair. Not when she screamed his name at the top of her lungs. Not even when she arched into him, aching for him to fill her.

"Stop, god, Nolan, stop before you break me." Her chest heaved as she tried to catch the breath he'd sucked out of her.

His whiskers scraped the inside of her thighs as he finally relented. "We can't have that."

"No, we can't."

"If I broke you, I wouldn't be able to do what I want to do next." He wiped his palm across his chin, then got to his knees. "You sure you want to keep going, darlin'?"

"Yes. Please. So much, yes."

Nolan laughed, a low chuckle that tugged at that place deep down she'd kept locked up for so long. "I should probably warn you, it's been a while for me, so I'm not sure—"

"Shh." She pressed her finger to his lips. "It's been a while for me, too, and I'm committed to staying right here for as long as it takes for us to get it right."

He kissed her finger, then flipped her hand over and pressed a long kiss to the inside of her wrist. She would have melted if she hadn't already.

Then he reached for his backpack. "Don't get the wrong idea, but I usually keep a condom in my first aid kit."

"I don't care why you have one. Just please get it on as quickly as possible." Her legs still splayed wide open underneath him. She didn't have the strength—or the desire—to try to close them. Especially not when she planned to wrap them around his hips and dig her heels into the spot just above his gorgeous ass.

He didn't say another word, but she heard the rip of a foil packet, then felt him shift back to the spot between her legs. Her eyes adjusted to the darkness, and she watched him strip off his pants and take his cock into his hand. He was doubly blessed in the dick department, with the length and the girth to match. As he rolled the condom down his thick hardness, she braced herself for impact.

Instead of getting right to it, Nolan leaned over and gently lifted the two layers of shirts over her head. He even bunched them up and formed a makeshift pillow for her. Then he cupped her cheek with his hand. His gaze met hers. Even in the dark, she could see her own need reflected in the depths of his eyes.

His finger trailed down her neck, skimming over her shoulder and stopping to cup her breast. Her nipples immediately peaked while a hollow ache grew inside her. He skimmed his thumb over her nipple before bending to suck it into his mouth. Heat shot to her core, and she writhed underneath him.

He shifted to the other breast. Her need to feel his lips on every inch of her skin warred with the desire to have him bury himself inside her. He didn't seem to be in any hurry. Though she could feel the steel-hard rod of his cock lodged against her thigh, he acted like he had all the time in the world to pay homage to her right breast. Not that she minded, but yeah, she kind of minded. Because when a woman decides it's time to go all the way, she really wants to go all the way right fucking now.

She reached down to try to tug his big body up.

"You need something, sweetheart?" The cocky glint in his eye told her he knew exactly what he was doing. Not only that, he was taking great pleasure in making her wait. In driving her so wild with need that she was on the verge of begging him for it.

No matter how desperate she was to have him sink deep inside her, she wasn't going to beg.

He shifted his hips, and the tip of his dick grazed her clit.

Begging wasn't so bad, right? It didn't make her desperate.

He notched his cock at her entrance and let the tip slide through her slick heat. She was soaking wet thanks to the first round. All she needed to do was tilt her hips up a few degrees and he'd be inside her. She bit her lip. Hard. Wiggled her hips.

Nolan pulled back, his gaze locked onto hers. He knew how much she wanted him. She could tell by the way his lips tipped up on one side. The way the dimple on his cheek winked at her.

"Last chance to change your mind." The smile faded, and he lifted his brows.

As if she could turn back now. He might have started it, but she was going to make sure he finished it.

"No chance of that." She bridged her hips, taking in as much of him as she could.

The teasing glint disappeared, replaced by a hunger she knew way too well. He clamped an arm underneath her and drove into her. A feeling of complete and utter fullness filled her. She could have come right then, with just one thrust, but he pulled out.

Before she had a chance to miss him, he pumped into her again, this time sinking deeper. She wasn't going to let him go again. Wrapping her legs around his middle, she locked her ankles over his ass.

"Gotcha now, don't I?" Victory rushed through her.

"You want to take control, sugar? Be my guest." He flipped them both over, putting her on top.

Her thighs straddled his hips. At this angle, she could take him even deeper. She propped one hand on the wall over his head and searched for something to hold on to. Over and over, she lifted herself up and down, riding his cock until she lost track of everything except the feel of him underneath her. Around her. Inside her.

Then she came.

21

⚯

Knox

She looked incredible as she came on his cock. Her hair mussed, her lips swollen from his kisses, her breasts full and heavy in his hands. Once he knew she was satisfied, Knox took control. She didn't put up any resistance when he gently flipped her onto her back, nudged her legs apart with his knee, and eased into her.

The little moans she made as he pumped into her made his cock even harder. He tried to hold back as long as possible, not wanting the feeling to end, not wanting to have to pull away from her. His orgasm ripped through him, powerful and deep, wringing every last bit of pleasure from him.

Spent, he collapsed on top of her, being careful not to crush her under his weight. Their breaths rose and fell in tandem. Neither of them had the strength or the lung capacity to utter a single word.

Knox shifted to his side and pulled the blanket over her. He brushed her out-of-control hair away from her face and touched his lips to her cheek.

"How do you feel?" He didn't want to break the magical spell that had fallen over them, but he wanted to make sure she was still with him. That she hadn't sunk back into herself, filled with regret.

"I don't know." She cracked her eyelids open and gazed over at him. The afterglow of multiple toe-curling orgasms lingered around her. He could actually smell the sex in the air and his dick tried to rally.

"I-don't-know bad or I-don't-know good?" Knox asked, fairly sure he already knew the answer based on the way she curled into him.

"Definitely I-don't-know good." Her lashes fanned out over her cheeks and he wanted to freeze the moment in time. The moment when everything was perfect. The moment when they were still coming down from their high. The moment before she realized what they'd done and freaked the hell out.

He tied off the condom, then pulled her even closer.

"How do you feel?" she parroted back at him.

"Amazing." He kissed the top of her head. "You're amazing, Claudia."

Her soft laugh bounced off his chest. "You said it's been a while. Are you sure you weren't just glad to be back in the saddle again?"

He wasn't going to let her laugh off how awesome it had been by pretending it was just because his dick hadn't had a chance to engage for a long time. "Hey, that wasn't just wow-it's-been-a-long-time good sex."

"Oh yeah? What was it, then?" She propped her chin on her hand, a challenge in her eyes.

"It was holy-hell-I-want-to-spend-the-rest-of-my-life-buried-inside-this-woman kind of sex." He lifted his brows, proud of the compound adjective he'd come up with off the cuff, though it didn't begin to do justice to what had just happened between them.

"I think you need to get out more." She buried her face in the crook of his arm.

"I think I need to get into you more."

She nudged him in the ribs with her elbow.

He might be teasing, but he meant it. He'd never been so head over heels for a woman. Not like this. He loved the way her cheek felt pressed against his pec. Loved the smell of her shampoo right under his nose. Loved the smooth feel of her legs intertwined with his. And that was just what he loved about her in a split second. When he thought about adding up all the split seconds that made up a day, he realized he didn't just love things about her. He actually loved her. All of her.

He couldn't tell her that. She'd run out of the lighthouse with a blanket wrapped around her shoulders and not stop until she reached the Minnesota state line. He might not be able to tell her exactly how he felt, but he did need to tell her the truth about who he was. Not that it should make a difference when she found out, but he didn't want there to be any lies between them. Secrets had a way of revealing themselves at the worst possible moment, and he didn't want to risk her finding out before he had a chance to tell her.

"Hey, Claudia?" He ran his hand along her arm, afraid if he stopped touching her, she might disappear.

"Mmm-hmm?" Sleep laced her voice.

"There's something I want to tell you." It would be better to come right out with it. Rip the bandage off. Get it over and done with as quickly as possible.

She blinked her eyes open. A hint of apprehension met his gaze. "Okay. There's something I want to tell you, too."

Eager to delay his revelation, he nodded. "Why don't you go first?"

Propping herself up on an elbow, she stared down at his chest. "You asked me why I came to Paradise. The truth is, I was running."

"Did someone hurt you?" His fingers curled into fists. If

anyone had so much as touched a hair on her head, they'd have to deal with him.

"It's not what you're thinking." She tilted her head. "I was involved with a guy when I lived up north. He played pro football. I sold him his condo, and we started dating, and, gosh, I don't know why I'm telling you all that because that part isn't really important."

Knox reached for her hand. "It's okay. Just tell me what you want to tell me."

"Okay." She gripped his fingers tight. "We dated for a couple of years. He rose up through the ranks and became their starting quarterback. I hated the limelight, but he couldn't get enough of it. Things finally came to a head when they went twelve–zero in the regular season. I ended it. Told him I couldn't take it anymore. He was more concerned about how he looked on his social media accounts than he was about spending time with me."

"Asshole," Knox muttered under his breath.

If she heard him, she didn't acknowledge it. Instead, she kept going, like if she didn't get it all out, she wouldn't be able to. "He blew it in the second round of playoffs. Told the press the reason he couldn't come through for the team was because he was so emotionally distraught over our breakup."

"Full-level douchebag," Knox said. He tightened his grip on her hand. "I'm sorry, Claudia. Guys can be major dicks."

"That's not all." Her gaze flicked to his, then away. "The press ran with it. I guess they needed someone to blame, and I became the scapegoat."

The more she talked, the more a sense that he'd heard that story pricked the edges of his memory. "King Campbell. You're the real estate agent, aren't you?"

Tears filled her eyes. "I had to shut down my real estate business. Fans trashed me on social media. They parked outside my house. Slashed my tires. Called my sellers and threatened them until they canceled their contracts with me." She lifted her head and met his gaze straight on. "They sent me death threats."

"Baby, I'm so, so sorry." He pulled her into his arms and cradled her against his chest. Rage filled him. Every fiber of his being wanted to lash out at the people who'd treated her like that. "What the fuck is wrong with people?"

"It was King. He could have stopped it. His fame was more important to him than my safety. I had to leave. Had to disappear. I rented a car and drove it as far as I could. When I hit the coast, I turned it in and took the ferry to Paradise."

"And you found Chick?" Knox guessed.

She nodded. "I was there the night his bartender walked out. By that time, I'd used up most of my savings and had no idea where to go. I thought if I stayed away long enough, it would blow over, but the media kept resurrecting the story. So I stepped behind the bar and started making drinks. Four years later, here we are."

Four years she'd been hiding away on Paradise. Hiding because her dickwad boyfriend hadn't had the balls to own up to his own mistakes. Her famous dickwad boyfriend.

The realization of what that meant for them leveled him like a ton of bricks crashing down on his head. He couldn't tell her who he was. If she found out he'd been the top country artist for the past two years, she'd shut things down between them before they even had a chance to get started.

She let out a huge sigh. "It feels good to finally tell someone the truth."

The truth.

"What did you want to tell me?" she asked.

He smoothed his hand over her hair and inhaled the scent of her shampoo. "It's not important, baby."

He'd have to find a way to tell her. But not tonight. The

connection between them was too new, too fragile. He'd tell her. He promised himself he had to before he headed back to Nashville to record his new album. She'd understand. With enough time, he'd show her how good things could be between them. He just needed the chance to make her fall in love with him as deeply as he'd already fallen for her.

Then he'd tell her.

22

❀

Claudia

The day after they came back from the lighthouse, everything had changed. The sun shone brighter. The birds sang louder. The sky was bluer. Claudia was sure of it. She wasn't the only one who thought so, either. Nolan smiled more. Tripod had a little extra hop in his step, and even Chick seemed to be in better spirits.

"How's the work on the bungalows going?" Chick settled onto a barstool and reached for the cup of coffee she set down in front of him.

"Good. It's still too wet outside to work on the patio, so Nolan's framing out the interior of the biggest one. We're adding a separate bedroom." She planned on heading over there after the lunch rush to test out the new bedroom area with him. They needed to make sure there was enough space for two grown adults to be able to roll around on a king-size bed in there before they finalized the design.

"When am I going to get to see a complete 'bungalow' so we can start taking pictures and get them listed for rent?" Chick made air quotes around the word "bungalow." He'd always referred to them as beach huts. Claudia couldn't wait to blow his mind.

"They're already listed. I posted the floor plan, and you're booked through the summer."

"Well, aren't you a peach?"

"I am feeling rather peachy today." Claudia didn't bother to try to hide her grin.

Chick lifted his mug to clink against hers. "You and Nolan enjoy the lighthouse yesterday?"

Her cheeks burned, and she almost spit out the sip of coffee she'd just taken. "Um, yeah, I think we did."

"Good. I don't know what they're going to do with that place." If Chick suspected anything was off with her, he didn't show it.

"What do you mean?"

"No one wants to raise the funds to fix it up and they're bringing in an engineer to see if it's still structurally sound. If not, we either have to make repairs or tear it down."

Claudia's gut churned. "They can't tear it down."

"Actually, they can. It's an important piece of Paradise Island history, but unless we can save it, we might not have another choice."

"What about a special concert? We could bring in a big band during spring break and donate a portion of the proceeds to fix it up. She'd just finalized the spring break entertainment a few weeks ago. There were a few bands scheduled to play that would bring in a decent crowd.

"You might be onto something. Let me see what comes back from the engineer." Chick pointed toward the carafe of coffee. "Mind topping me off before I head up to the office?"

Claudia poured a little more coffee into his mug, her mind already spinning with ideas on ways to save the lighthouse. If they tore it down, some big developer would probably try to scoop up that piece of prime real estate and build a huge hotel. They'd been after Chick to sell ever since she started working with him. If they got ahold of that strip of land, the laid-back way of life on the island could come to an end, not to mention what it would do to the wild horse sanctuary and Lovers' Falls.

She thought about it while she mixed drinks for the few folks on vacation and served trays of burgers, salads, and sandwiches to the locals, who stopped in for lunch. The non-profit group had already tried a fundraising campaign last year to save the lighthouse. They'd raised a few thousand dollars, but it was going to take hundreds of thousands to reach their goal.

She was still thinking about it when she stopped by the bungalow to check on Nolan's progress.

"Knock knock." She would have actually knocked if there had been a door. Instead, Nolan must have taken the front door off the hinges.

"I'm in here." Nolan's voice carried through the empty structure.

She followed it to the back, where he was digging a perimeter around the patio area so he could lay down edging pavers. He'd taken off his shirt and his muscles bulged as he hoisted a shovel full of dirt over his shoulder. Seeing him like that, all rolling muscles and naked from the waist up, she forgot what she wanted to tell him.

Nolan stuck the shovel into the ground and rested a work boot on the edge. "Damn, you're a sight for sore eyes."

"You're not looking too bad yourself." Since she'd given in to the desire that had been pulling her toward him for weeks, the pressure had eased. She didn't feel nervous or on edge around him any longer. All she felt was horny. Horny, like a teenager who'd just had her first kiss and finally realized what everyone else had been talking about. And what had happened between her and Nolan went way beyond a great first kiss.

He lifted his arm and swiped the sweat away from his brow. "I'm a mess. Covered in sweat and dirt and . . . wait a sec. Are you trying to tell me you like it dirty?"

Heat sparked low in her belly. "Maybe."

His deep laugh sent that spark of heat sizzling through her veins. "You look too pretty to get dirty right now, baby."

"Oh, yeah?" She reached down and swiped her finger through the mud. Then she slowly touched her finger to her throat and trailed it down to her collarbone. "What about now?"

Nolan's smile widened. "Not quite there yet."

She held his gaze while she dipped her finger in the mud again. This time she ran it up her bare leg to where the hem of her shorts met her thigh. "Now?"

His tongue darted out and swept along his lower lip. "Come here."

He abandoned the shovel, leaving it sticking out of the ground, and covered the short distance between them in just a few steps. His hand went to the back of her head. His mouth slanted over hers. His hips nudged against her pelvis. The smell of sun and sweat mingled together—a potent aphrodisiac.

She tangled her fingers in the hair at the nape of his neck and surrendered to his kiss. If she'd been thinking the night before was a fluke —just a culmination of too many sexless years—what Nolan was doing with his hips wiped that thought out of her brain. She wanted him just as much this afternoon as she had yesterday. Maybe even more, since she already knew what kind of magic was in store.

"Should we make sure the bedroom's going to be big enough?" he mumbled into her ear.

She barely had a chance to nod before he swept her up in

his arms and carried her through the living room and into the bedroom. There wasn't a bed yet, but at least there was a door.

He kicked the door closed and flipped the lock with his fingers. Then he pressed her back into the freshly primed wall. One hand went under her ass. The other started working on his waistband.

Claudia closed her eyes against the bright sun filtering through the temporary window shade. Her hands gripped his shoulders, her legs wrapped around his waist. Within moments, he'd rolled on a condom and was inside her. Their mouths collided in a mix of hot, wet kisses. With her back wedged against the wall, he was in total control. She held on while he took the lead.

The first waves of her release swept over her before she even realized she was close. The intensity of her orgasm rolled through her in surges, each one more powerful than the one before, until she couldn't hold back any longer.

Nolan sensed it coming and joined her, his deep thrusts slowing until the two of them stood motionless.

Her limbs became wet spaghetti noodles, unable to support her. Nolan eased her down the wall until her feet touched the floor, then held her against him while he pressed kisses to her forehead, her hair, her eyelids.

"Is your back okay?" He rubbed a big palm over the spot on her back that had been pressed against the wall.

"Yeah." She nestled her cheek against his chest, the steady beat of his heart bringing her back to reality. "There's only one problem."

He pulled back enough to meet her gaze. Tipping her head up with a finger under her chin, he whispered, "What's that, Claudia?"

"Now we're both dirty. Want to come over to my place for a shower and to get cleaned up?" She had no intention of letting him anywhere near her shower until they'd spent at least an hour in her bed. Now that she'd rediscovered what it felt like to have something that didn't require batteries between her legs, she was eager to experience it as often as possible. At least, that's what she wanted to tell herself.

The truth was, it had very little to do with how good the sex was and everything to do with how he made her feel. The orgasms were good, but the companionship, the feeling of not being alone anymore, the way he made her feel special, were addictive.

"Are you going to let me scrub your back?" He dipped down and trailed kisses along her neck.

She arched into him, ready for another round. "Only if you scrub my front first."

"You've got a deal."

23

❧

Knox

Knox couldn't remember a time when the words had flown so easily. Over the past five days, he'd been able to write half the songs for his new album. He was still messing with the melody for a couple of them, but the bones were there. He'd even sent two of them on to his manager to share with the label. They were a bit of a departure from the pop-country tone they'd insisted on for his last few albums, but they were truer to his roots than anything he'd submitted before.

And he had Claudia to thank.

It had been tricky trying to find time to work on his music between spending his days revamping the bungalows and his nights in Claudia's arms. Usually she closed down the bar, so he'd stop by the restaurant for dinner, then have a few hours to fiddle around with his guitar before she came back. Then they'd stay awake long enough to satisfy each other's insatiable needs before waking up the next morning and doing it all over again.

He knew it was too good to be true. Knew he needed to tell her the truth about who he was and why he'd really escaped to the island. But he didn't want to ruin the magic.

Being with her felt so good, so incredibly right. As soon as he told her the truth, he risked breaking the spell they'd been caught up in.

She'd talked about what it was like when the world turned against her. It was almost like once she'd decided not to keep it to herself anymore the floodgates opened. All Knox could do was hold her close and listen while she relayed one terrifying story after another.

Now that he knew what she'd been through, he was absolutely convinced that she'd end things between them as soon as she found out who he was. He just needed time to figure out a way to gently ease her into the knowledge. It would take time and trust, but a future without Claudia by his side wasn't an option.

She'd left him with the old-style boom box, since his phone didn't get great reception on Paradise. He'd been working on installing the new luxury vinyl flooring for the past hour and still had a few hundred square feet to go. A new release from one of the country music artists who'd opened for him on his last tour played on the radio.

Knox hummed along, remembering the night the guy worked on the tune. They'd been sitting around the kitchenette on his tour bus and messing around with a few different chords.

His phone rang, and he thought about letting it go to voice mail. But when he saw his manager's number, he reached for it. Maybe Tripp already had some feedback on the songs he'd sent over. Anticipation and excitement swirled around in his stomach, twisting together like one of those blended frozen fruity drinks Claudia served at the bar.

"Hey, Tripp. What's up?"

"I had a chance to listen to the files you sent over." Tripp's voice lacked the enthusiasm Knox had been hoping for.

A knot formed in his gut, but he tried to stay positive. "Oh yeah? What did you think?"

"I think you've lost your goddamn mind. The stuff you sent over doesn't fit your brand, it—"

"Maybe I'm tired of being their pop-star cowboy. When I signed on with you, you knew what kind of music I wanted to play." Knox put his hand to his temple. He'd been afraid of this.

"And I told you once you got established with a label, we'd be able to explore that. Do you have any idea how many artists would kill to be in your position? You just wrapped up a worldwide tour a few months ago, you've got a label who's putting everything they've got behind you, and you sold over two hundred thousand copies of your album last year." Tripp let out a dramatic sigh. "Why don't you want to get on board the Knox Shepler gravy train, man?"

Knox knew the answer, but it wasn't the one his manager wanted to hear, so he watered it down. "When I first started, I was thrilled to get a deal. I figured it didn't matter so much that the label tweaked the songs I'd written. Like you said, once I had an album or two under my belt, I'd have more say."

"That's exactly right," Tripp agreed.

"But I've been doing it their way for a few years now. The further I get from my roots, from the music my granddad used to play for me, the music I want to play, the less I want to play at all." Fuck, admitting that felt like ripping out a piece of his soul. Not because Tripp didn't already know his feelings, but because Knox was realizing the time would probably never come when he'd be in charge of his own career.

"Hey, I know it's been rough. We're not talking about changing who you are as an artist, they just want—"

"They want a modern-day pop-star cowboy is what they want." Tripp could try to disguise it, but that was the honest-to-god-truth.

The silence stretched.

Then Tripp let out a huff. "Hell, we both know you're right. Give them one more album, and I'll talk to them about taking the next one in a different direction. You don't want to shift sounds right away, anyway. We'll want to ease your fans into the idea. Blend a little old country in with the new, so it doesn't come as such a shock. What do you say to that?"

Feeling like he'd pushed as far as he could, Knox backed off. "Yeah, you know best."

"I feel your frustration. Let me handle the label. You just come up with something more in line with what they're expecting. We'll get you where you want to go. It just takes time."

"You got it." Even as he said the words, a hollow ache pulsed against the walls of his chest. Tripp's loyalties swayed depending on which way the dollars fell. As long as he could keep Knox in line, the label would be happy and the money would follow. Knox just wasn't sure he had the patience to wait as long as it might take.

"I'll let them know they can expect something in the next couple of days. Sound good?"

"Sure." Knox tucked his phone into his pocket and tossed his head back. He didn't have much time left.

Maybe he could add a little more pop to one of the songs he'd been working on. His shoulders bunched with tension even thinking about it. The songs he'd been writing lately came from deep down inside. Taking them in a different direction would ruin them.

He'd have to start over. He wasn't willing to give up one of the songs he'd written while thinking about Claudia. Hoping the radio might provide some inspiration, he switched the station to one that played current hits and refocused his efforts on installing the vinyl.

With his body occupied by the repetitive task, his mind wandered. The beat from the song on the radio meshed with a few lines he'd been tossing around in his head. He might be able to make something out of it. While he clicked the next few planks into place, he started to hum the melody he had in mind.

"Hey, how's it going?" Claudia stepped into the bungalow, holding a basket in her hands.

Knox got up from where he'd been kneeling on the floor and held out his arms. "Better now that you're here."

"You're making good progress." She wrapped one arm around him while she looked at the floor. "It's amazing what a difference that vinyl makes."

"I hope so. Tearing out the tile was a pain in the ass." As satisfying as it felt to smash up the ugly tile, hauling it out had taken a toll on him. He thought he'd been in shape before, but his body had been teaching him he had a ways to go.

"Aw, poor baby. Do you need a back rub?" She set the basket down on the floor and reached her arms around his waist. Her fingers dug into the muscles of his back while she rose onto her tiptoes to kiss him.

"Mmm, yeah, a little lower, please," he mumbled against her lips.

She moved her hands around, kneading the muscles of his lower back.

"Can you go a little lower?"

Her hands rubbed the top of his glutes. "Are you trying to get me to feel you up?"

"Is it that obvious?" She smelled so good. And her hands on his ass felt amazing. He nudged his nose into her hair and nibbled on her earlobe.

She moved her hands lower and gripped his butt cheeks. "All you have to do is ask, you know."

"Okay then. I'm asking." He picked her up, carried her into the bathroom, and set her ass down on the counter.

Within minutes, he'd buried himself inside her—his new favorite place to be. She wrapped her legs around his waist and gripped his shoulders as he pumped into her. He couldn't keep his hands off her, and she seemed to feel the same way. He'd learned to read her body language and knew when she shifted her hips and relaxed her shoulders that she was on the verge.

He adjusted the angle slightly, losing himself as she climaxed around him.

No matter what he had going on, being with Claudia distracted him. She took his mind off of the crap with Tripp and the label. With her he could be himself, at least the Nolan version of himself, which was a hell of a lot more real than the country superstar who performed to sold out arenas.

He needed to tell her the truth, especially now that she'd shared the deepest parts of herself. Every day that went by without telling her his real name was like falling another foot into a dark hole he'd have to dig himself out of.

"Well, that was . . . quick." Claudia looked up at him, her hair sliding out of the clip she'd used to pull it back and her lipstick smeared across her mouth.

"Do you want to register a complaint?" He chuckled.

"Not officially." She pulled out her clip, and he held it for her while she redid her hair. "But maybe if we eat the lunch I brought real quick, we'll have time for another back rub before I have to head to the bar."

He hadn't even pulled out yet, and she was already working on when he could be inside her again. That was his kind of lovin', his kind of woman, his kind of just right.

"I think that can be arranged."

"Good. Now let's eat. You're going to need your energy for what I've got planned for later this afternoon."

Claudia

Nolan sucked the grape she held out to him into his mouth, his lips tickling her fingers. She loved watching him eat. Loved watching him do anything. Claudia hadn't seen it coming and would have avoided it like the plague if she had, but even she had to admit she was falling head over heels for Nolan.

It was irrational . . . absolutely bananaramas . . . but it was the truth. She never thought she'd ever be able to have feelings for anyone again, but somehow he'd worked his way into her heart. Not only her heart, but her head, too. She couldn't keep thoughts of him from taking over. From the moment she woke up in the morning with the scruff of his beard rubbing against her cheek until the seconds before sleep claimed her, thoughts of him filled her head.

She couldn't help it, and she didn't want to. She'd been alone for so long, so vigilant in trying to protect herself. With Nolan, she didn't have to worry about that anymore. He knew her secrets and accepted her for who she was. She didn't want what they had together to end.

"Did you get enough to eat?" She crumpled up the paper she'd used to wrap their sandwiches.

"Sure did." Nolan leaned in for a kiss. "But I always save room for dessert."

Claudia rummaged through the basket. "Good. I made you cookies this morning."

"Seriously?" His eyes lit up like a little kid who'd just been told Santa was coming.

"Don't get too excited. They're just chocolate chip." She pulled out a plastic baggie full of chocolate chip cookies.

"I can't remember the last time somebody made me cookies." His lips spread into a smile that sent butterflies racing through her stomach. "My mom used to whip up a batch from time to time, but it's been years."

"Are you and your mom still close?" He didn't strike her as a mama's boy, but the way his eyes softened when he talked about her made Claudia hopeful that he had a good relationship with at least one of his parents.

"Yeah. She's an amazing woman. I don't get to see her nearly as much as I'd like since I'm on the road, I mean, away on jobs so much. Now give me all the cookies, baby."

He was so easy to please, so unlike her last relationship, where no matter how hard she tried, she always fell short. She'd never been with someone who made it so easy to love him. Nolan asked so little of her, but gave her so much. Doing things for him, even something so small as making a batch of chocolate chip cookies, made her grin like she'd just won the lottery. In some ways, she supposed she had.

She held out one of the cookies, and he snatched it from her hand.

"Chocolate chip is my favorite," he said, already sinking his teeth into his first cookie.

"Are you sure?"

His forehead bunched. "Yeah. They're the best."

"Have you ever had a Paradise Island cookie?"

He swallowed a big bite of the cookie and licked a smudge of chocolate from his lip. "You mean from the bakery by the ferry dock?"

"They sell them, but it's a certain kind of cookie, just like chocolate chip or snickerdoodle." Her mouth watered at the thought of sinking her teeth into one of the chewy, thick cookies full of coconut and white chocolate.

His eyebrows shot up. "You've been holding out on me? What's in them?"

"Nothing good." She wrinkled her nose. He was too fun to tease.

"You sure about that?" He didn't believe her. Over the past few weeks, she'd let down her guard, and he'd figured out how to tell when she was joking.

"Not unless you like coconut, white chocolate chunks, and big macadamia nuts." She lifted her shoulder, knowing he wouldn't be able to resist that kind of combination. Who would?

"That's it. We're going on a dessert date. I need to find out what other Paradise Island delicacies you've been keeping from me." The serious set of his jaw dared her to challenge him.

"Well, there's the piña colada fudge at the candy store. You'd probably like the margarita cheesecake they serve at the coffee shop, too."

"Yes." He took another cookie out of the bag. "I need to try everything. How is it I've been here for this long and we haven't made it to any of those places?"

"I didn't know you had such a sweet tooth." She took a bite out of the cookie he held out for her.

"Now you know. When are we doing this? I need a firm date on my calendar because these are going to be gone in about five minutes."

"How can you eat like that and still look like you do?" It wasn't fair. She just had to look at a cookie and could gain an inch on her hips.

"I burn it off as fast as I take it in. Want me to show you how?" His eyebrows waggled.

She breathed in the scent of cookies and ocean air. Two months ago she never would have believed someone if they'd told her she'd be sitting in one of Chick's bungalows with a hot-as-hell construction worker who made her heart feel like it had wings.

She wrapped her arms around his neck and pulled his mouth close. "Yes, please."

He leaned in to kiss her and she jumped back.

"Oooh, I remembered what I wanted to talk to you about."

"Right now?" His breath still brushed her cheek. "Does it have to do with me and you working off the cookies I just inhaled? Because if not, can you hold that thought for about fifteen minutes?"

The fact that he couldn't seem to get enough of her did wonders for her confidence, but she didn't want to risk getting distracted again. "Give me two minutes to tell you. Otherwise I'm afraid I'll forget."

"How about you start talking while I start working on my cardio?" His nose brushed against her cheek.

She didn't care that he'd been working on flooring all morning. No matter what he looked like or what he'd been doing, she wanted him. Assuming her silence meant she agreed with his proposal, he sucked her earlobe into his mouth and she tried to remember what had been so important.

The lighthouse. That's right.

"I want to plan a benefit concert during spring break to raise money for the lighthouse. Chick said if they can't fix it up, they might have to tear it down."

Nolan tensed. "Our lighthouse?"

"Yes, *our* lighthouse." Hearing him refer to it as theirs sent shivers racing up and down her arms.

He pulled back enough to meet her gaze. "I thought it was a piece of Paradise Island history?"

"It is. But it's more of a liability if they're worried about it falling down on someone." She loved that he felt such ownership of the place where they'd first made love.

"We'll have to do something about that. A concert? You really think you can pull in enough cash with just a concert?"

This was the part she wasn't sure about. She hadn't paid attention to music for years and preferred to listen to her ancient CDs or playlists she'd curated from old favorites. "We can get local cover bands to come, but I was thinking if it's not too big of an ask . . ."

His eyes narrowed. "What's on your mind?"

"That friend you mentioned who might be able to help Gabe . . . do you think he might have some connections?"

24

Knox

Knox's heart skipped a handful of beats. The friend she was talking about didn't exist. He needed to tell her who he was before it was too late.

"Look, Claudia—"

The custom ringtone she'd assigned to her sister interrupted. She pulled her phone out of her pocket. "Hold on one sec. It might be baby news."

He nodded. Even though the baby wasn't due for another month, Claudia had been on high alert. She said it was something about proteins being off that might cause the baby to come early. Knowing she had a niece and nephew she'd never met in person with one more on the way made his heart ache for her. He could imagine how hard it would be for her to go back to Minnesota and return to the place where she'd experienced so much hate, but her sister was the only family she had left.

He'd learned a long time ago how important it was to surround himself with people who only wanted the best for him. While she got up to pace the small living room, he pulled out his own phone. His friend Decker had sent a text.

Decker: Hey, how are the coconuts hanging? Wondering if you're still up for helping me propose?

Knox: Are you sure she'll say yes? Who wants to wake up to your ugly mug every day for the rest of her life?

Decker: LMFAO. Not funny.

Knox: Of course I'll help. When? Where?

Decker: On the yacht. Pick you up Friday at 5?

Knox: Ok

Decker fell in and out of love multiple times a year, and had even proposed years ago, without success. Hell, with Justin and Emmeline tying the knot recently and now Decker popping the question again, it made Knox think about what kind of future he wanted for himself.

While he'd been texting with Deck, Claudia had gone out to the patio and stood in the shade of the pergola he'd added. She had her back to him, and he let his gaze roam over the curve of her shoulders, then lower. Yes, she was attractive. A twelve on a scale of one to ten. But it wasn't just her looks that had captured his heart. It was everything about her: the way she looked out for Chick and Tripod, how she took care of everyone at the bar, and how she made him feel like he could do absolutely fucking anything he set his mind to.

She might not know his real name, but she knew the real him . . . the one so very few people had access to.

Yeah, he needed to tell her. If he knew her as well as he thought he did, she'd be pissed, but she'd understand on some level. But if he kept up the lie, it was going to keep getting harder and harder. Looking at her now, he knew he couldn't lose her. He'd have to risk telling her and then figure out how to make it up to her. Because keeping the lie going would only lead to a dead end.

Claudia slid her phone into her pocket and stepped back into the bungalow. Even with the faint smile she gave him, he knew something was wrong.

"Everything okay?" He'd barely taken two steps toward her when she rushed to him and buried her cheek against his chest. "What happened, sweetheart?"

"They're worried about the baby. Andrea needs to go on bed rest. Derek has to go to a huge board meeting in Sydney in two weeks, and she's not sure what she's going to do."

Instinctively, he smoothed his hand over her back. "Do we need to go up there to help?"

"We?" Her voice sounded weak, so different from the confidence he'd heard in her tone over the past few weeks. "You'd go with me? You'd do that for me?"

Without any regard to the consequences, he nodded. "Of course. I'll need to rearrange my schedule a little bit, but family comes first. If you want me to go with you, I'll be there."

"What about the job you've got coming up?"

Damn. The job. That was the lie that started the whole thing. He couldn't risk making her even more upset. He'd have to keep up his ruse for just a little while longer. Once she calmed down about her sister and the baby, he'd tell her.

"The job can wait. You're more important." He clasped his hands behind her back and rested his chin on top of her head. Holding her in his arms, her heart beating against his, he realized it was the truth. Somewhere in the middle of renovating a bunch of run-down bungalows and trying to come up with new songs to please the people who held his career in their greedy hands, she'd become more important than all of it combined.

The knowledge settled into his gut. Nothing else mattered. Not while the woman he cared about had to deal with literal matters of life and death.

Scratch that. He didn't just care about Claudia, he loved her. Loved her with a certainty he'd never known before. Loved her with every bit of his being. They were soulmates, two strangers who'd been destined to meet, two halves who'd joined to become whole. Every single cheesy iteration of being in love played through his head, and instead of laughing, he embraced them.

He was all of those things: whupped, head over heels, and madly in love. And he couldn't wait to tell her.

Only one thing was stopping him. How could he tell a woman he loved her when she didn't even know his real name?

25

❦

Claudia

With Andrea promising to take it easy and keep that baby in until she could get there, Claudia started making arrangements to head to Minneapolis. The only reason she even entertained the idea was because of Nolan's willingness to go with her. She was probably strong enough to do it on her own, but was also grateful she wouldn't have to.

There was so much to do before she could leave, especially with the spring break crowd ready to descend. Thankfully, she'd be back in time for the biggest rush. The kids in the northern states tended to head south at the beginning of March and the kids in Texas, where most of the crowds came from, tended to have their breaks a little later.

She'd promised Chick she'd be back in time for the busiest two weeks, though he kept telling her he'd done fine before she got there and that while it would be difficult, if he had to, he could manage without her.

Between making sure the bar was in good shape and the bungalow project wrapped up before she left, Claudia had very little time to follow up on the idea she'd had to start her own design business. After going on the home tour with Nolan, she'd realized how much she missed staging houses and been inspired to find a way to take on a few clients. That afternoon, she had a meeting scheduled with a new store that planned on opening on the main shopping route on the island. The owner wanted to sell a mixture of high-end western beachwear and interior decor. She'd described it as a boho chic boutique.

Claudia had been excited about the prospect of getting her name out there, especially with a commercial business that might lead to other clients, but with everything else going on, she'd been tempted to cancel. Nolan made her promise she'd go, even told her he'd meet up with her after for their dessert date. He'd seemed so excited about it. She didn't want to let him down.

"So I'll meet you there around six?" he asked.

"Are you sure you want to do this? I've still got to check the supply order for when we'll be gone and come up with the final list of who's going to play at that benefit concert for the lighthouse. Did you ask your friend if he had any connections?" She leaned closer to the mirror and swept a neutral shade of lip gloss over her lips.

Nolan came up behind her and wrapped his arms around her waist. "Let me take care of that for you. You've got so many other things going on, I've got that piece, okay?"

Her eyes met his in the reflection of the bathroom mirror. "You're going to plan the benefit concert?"

"Yeah."

She searched his gaze for a crack in the confidence he projected. "It's a lot of work, especially if we're trying to get someone who has an actual fan base. You've got to get their list of requirements, make arrangements with their manager, talk to their publicist—"

"I've got it, baby. Let me do this for you."

Her plate wasn't just full, it was running over. Letting

Nolan take the lead on the concert would give her some breathing room. It wasn't like she wouldn't be back in time to handle the details as the date got closer. He'd just be making the preliminary arrangements. Even thinking about handing it over made her nerves relax a teeny tiny bit. "Yes. That would be great if you're sure you don't mind."

"I don't mind at all." He brushed her hair away from her neck and trailed kisses from her collarbone to behind her ear.

Her heart swelled with love for this man who'd come out of nowhere and saved her from a future of loneliness. "Did you have a chance to check with your boss about pushing your start date back?"

His forehead wrinkled, then he nodded. "Oh, yeah. It's not a problem. I was actually thinking maybe I could stick around Paradise for a little while longer, I might need to travel for a few days to clear things up, but what would you think about that?"

"About staying? With me?" She whirled around in his embrace and threw her arms around his neck. "Yes!"

His lips found hers and he kissed all of her carefully applied lip gloss away. She didn't care about that. Didn't care about anything except for the fact that he wanted to stay. She'd been afraid to ask, nervous that he didn't harbor the same kind of bone-deep feelings for her as she did for him. Now she knew.

"I love you, Nolan," she whispered against his lips.

His hand paused on the small of her back. Her heart stuttered. Had she read him wrong?

"I love you, too, Claudia." His breath brushed her cheek, and then his mouth was on hers again, hot, demanding, intense.

The alarm on her phone chimed. She had to go if she wanted to make it to her appointment on time. It took every ounce of willpower she possessed to break their kiss.

"I've got to go. I'll see you at six?"

"I'll be standing outside." He pulled her close for another kiss, sliding his tongue against hers.

All she wanted was to wrap herself in his arms and bask in the warmth of knowing he loved her. Tempted to cancel her appointment, she pulled away. "What if I reschedule?"

"You need to go, baby." He tapped his forehead against hers. "We've got the rest of the night to pick up where we left off."

He was right. She took in a deep breath, trying to inhale enough of his scent, his very essence, to carry her through the rest of the afternoon. "Until later."

"Until later." He kissed the tip of her nose and released his grip.

She snagged a tissue and rubbed the smeared lip gloss off her mouth. Not wanting to make herself any later, she'd have to reapply after she made it through the front door.

Nolan patted her butt as she passed, and she resisted the urge to turn around and do the same to him. The fun and games would have to wait.

The sun seemed to shine a little bit brighter as she stepped out onto the sidewalk. She usually made the walk to the busy shopping district a couple of times a week, but today the colors seemed more intense. The scent of fresh cut grass hung sweet and heavy in the air. Maybe it was true what they said about love heightening the senses. If so, she was in trouble, since she also had to pass the dock where the boats pulled in and prepped their catches.

Based on her time with Nolan, not even the overwhelming smell of fish could bring down her mood.

A mile or so later, she stopped in front of one of the oldest buildings on the block. Over the years, it had housed a general store, a consignment shop, and, most recently, a candle store. Claudia had always thought it would make a great location for a storefront. Leaving the salty breeze and bright sun behind, she stepped through the doorway.

A life-size cutout of a man who looked uncomfortably familiar greeted her just inside the door. Thinking it might be a prank Nolan was playing on her, she waited for him to jump out and yell, "Surprise!"

"Claudia?" A tall woman with turquoise jewelry dripping from her neck, her wrists, and her earlobes came out from the back. "Hi, I'm Nina Blouchet. It's so nice to meet you."

Still expecting someone to jump out and explain what a life-size cutout of Nolan was doing at the entry of a home decor store, she eyed the woman with hesitation. "Hi."

"Oh, I see you've met our cowboy greeter. Isn't he yummy?" Nina grinned like they were both in on some delicious secret and gestured for her to head to the back of the space.

"Who is that?" she asked. The man had the same brown hair as Nolan. Even the lopsided, sexy smile was an identical match to the man she'd just been kissing not even a half hour before. The cutout man had a guitar over his shoulder and wore a cowboy hat that looked like it weighed fifty pounds, thanks to all the bling. It wasn't Nolan, but the resemblance was so weird.

"Oh"—a giant crease bisected Nina's forehead—"well, that's Knox Shepler. Country music's sexiest man alive for the past two years?" Her voice lifted at the end, making it sound like she was asking Claudia instead of telling her.

"Knox who?" Claudia asked.

"He's a country music star. Our shop in Austin sells a lot of those. I guess women who'd never have an ice cube's shot in hell of getting a date with him figure they can have him all to themselves if they get the cardboard version. Come on in. Can I get you a glass of water? Maybe some lemonade or tea?"

Claudia followed the woman to the counter area, her gaze still tracking back to the cardboard man. Did Nolan know he had a celebrity doppelgänger? Wouldn't it be funny if someone mistook him for a famous singer sometime?

"A glass of water would be wonderful." She took a seat at one of the tall stools and pulled out her notebook. It was turning into quite a day. Her first meeting with a potential client plus hearing the three words she'd never thought she'd hear coming from a man's mouth again? This would be one for the record books.

Claudia took the frosted teal glass full of ice water Nina handed her. "Thank you."

"No, thank you. I really appreciate you meeting with me, especially on such short notice. I got your name from a friend of mine who recently moved to Austin from Minnesota. She said you were the reason her store back in Minneapolis did so well. Do you think you can help me come up with some ideas on how to set up a flexible design for this space?"

Eager to get back to doing something she loved—something she was good at—Claudia nodded. "Of course. Let me ask you a few questions and we'll see what we can come up with."

By six o'clock, she'd sketched out a few ideas that Nina couldn't stop gushing over.

"I don't know how I'm going to be able to decide."

Claudia stuck her pen back in her bag and closed her notebook. "Whichever choice you go with, you'll still have a lot of options."

"That's what I love about it. I can change things around and give the space a whole new look without having to invest in new displays. You're a genius."

"I don't know about that." Claudia's cheeks burned at the

praise. It had been too long since someone had complimented her on something she actually cared about. Sure, she received compliments at the bar all the time, but how hard was it to follow a recipe for a margarita? When she was designing something, she started from scratch. It was only by blending her ideas with the clients' needs that she could come up with an optimal solution.

Based on the huge smile on Nina's face, Claudia had nailed it.

"Do you do residential designs as well? My husband and I just downsized to a condo."

"I do. I'd love to have the chance to work with you on your new place." Though she'd been hesitant to start her design business again, all the stars were aligning. "I'll be out of town for a couple of weeks, but I can call you when I get back so we can set up a time to meet."

"That would be wonderful," Nina said.

Claudia tried to hold her excitement in while she packed up her things to leave. Nolan stood outside, his phone pressed to his ear. She wanted to have him take a look at the cutout, but the way his shoulders hunched forward and his mouth turned down at the corners made her think it wouldn't be a good time. Instead, she paused by the cutout and snapped a quick selfie. They'd probably both get a kick out of it when she showed it to him later.

Knox

"How did it go?" Knox shoved his phone into his pocket and wished he could forget about the conversation he'd just had with Tripp. The label still wasn't happy, despite him sending over some of the best songs he'd ever written. He had one more shot to come through before they assigned a songwriter to work with him. None of that mattered at the moment. Not when Claudia stepped toward him, her lips spread into a smile so bright it could light up the entire state of Texas.

"Better than I could have expected." She reached for him, wrapped her arms around his neck, and rose onto her tiptoes to kiss him.

He hated the fact that having the meeting go so well surprised her. She was talented, smart, and creative. The combination ought to guarantee her success. She just needed that extra boost of confidence, and he wanted to be the one to help her see how amazing she really was.

"I told you so." He tapped the tip of her nose with his finger. "Do you think you'll listen to me next time?"

"Probably not, but I love you for being so encouraging and supportive." She wrapped her fingers around his and kissed him again. "She wants to meet and talk about working on her new condo, too."

Knox rolled his eyes while he slowly shook his head. "And you were nervous nothing would come from it."

"It's been a while since I put myself out there like that." Her voice came out softer as all the false bravado she'd conjured for her meeting started to fade away.

"I know it doesn't mean shit, but I'm so proud of you, baby." He shifted to her side and slung an arm around her shoulder.

"Why wouldn't that mean anything to me?"

"Because you're the one who needs to be proud of yourself. Shouldn't matter what anyone else thinks." He held her hand and spun her away from him in an impromptu dance move.

Claudia laughed. "I suppose I am proud of myself, at least a little. It's been so long since I've been willing to share my ideas with anyone. Well, except for you and Chick. I guess I've been afraid of what could happen."

Knox's heart clenched at the idea of anyone making her think less of herself. If he could fly up to Minneapolis and knock that sorry sonofabitch's teeth out for making her take the heat for his failure, he would.

"The world deserves to be blessed with your creativity." He tugged her back to his side. That's where he wanted her—right next to him forever.

"It's all because of you." Her arm went behind his back and she slipped her hand into the pocket of his jeans.

Things between them had evolved to a place where he couldn't imagine a future without her, and he suspected she felt the same. If only he could tell her the truth, he could get rid of the five-thousand-pound weight sitting on his chest. The longer he waited, the worse her reaction would be. He knew that, but still, he couldn't summon the courage to tell her.

"Are you sure you don't want to eat dinner before we go on our big treat tour of Paradise Island?" Claudia tilted her head and glanced up at him.

"Nope. Bring on the sweets." After tonight, he'd tell her. They'd both been working so hard lately, they hadn't had much time to spend together. He wanted their time tonight to be perfect. She deserved a night away from the bar, the bungalows, and from worrying about her sister.

"Okay. The candy store is right up here on the corner." She pointed to a pink-and-white-striped awning.

As they moved closer, the sweet smell of sugar drifted through the air. "I think I might get a sugar high just from walking by."

"It's the fudge. They make it fresh every day. See?" She stopped in front of a huge window.

A woman wearing a pink-and-white-striped apron stood behind the glass, her attention focused on the slab of marble in front of her. She used a giant paddle with a long handle to scoop up some oozy brown liquid and move it around.

"That's fudge?" Looked more like brown slime to him.

"Yep. I've watched them do demos a few times. Right now she's mixing in air to make it creamier."

"Mmm, I like things that are creamy." He nudged his shoulder into hers.

She nudged him back. "Why do you always make things sound so dirty?"

"Me?" He loved the fact that she could appreciate his sometimes raunchy sense of humor. "Do they ever mix nuts into the cream?"

"You're hopeless." Claudia bumped his shoulder again before heading into the candy store. "Come on. If you want to get your first course of our sweets-only dinner, you'd better come inside."

"Oh, I'm coming, all right." He held the door open for her, then followed her inside. The shop looked how he'd imagine an old-fashioned soda fountain would. Shelves lined one wall holding huge glass containers with every color and kind of candy imaginable. His mouth watered as the smell of sugar and chocolate filled his nose.

Claudia walked all the way to the back, where a huge glass display case featured dozens of slabs of fudge. Knox read over the fancy printed labels. Rocky road sat next to classic flavors like chocolate pecan and peanut butter chocolate. Or there were their special varieties. The piña colada fudge held specks of lime and coconut. Maybe he'd try that. Then his eye caught on the pink and white swirls of strawberry cheesecake fudge.

"How the hell do you decide what kind to get?" He leaned over to look at the flavors on the bottom shelf. There were too many to choose from.

"When I come here, I always pick something I know I'll love and then make myself try a new flavor." She tapped her finger on the glass. "They have a whole boozy fudge section, too. If you've ever wanted to try Irish stout fudge, now's your chance."

Knox glanced over the boozy options. "I'll be damned. We should have stopped by here for St. Patrick's Day."

"They do an amazing rainbow fudge for that. I tried some the first year I was here."

"And?"

"Delicious." Her eyes closed, and she ran her tongue over her lip.

"Can't be any more delicious than you." He leaned over and kissed her on the lips. The way he felt about her made him do the kind of sugary-sweet things that gave him a stomachache when he saw other couples do the same. He didn't care. She brought out a side of him he'd never seen before.

"You're so cheesy sometimes." She opened her eyes and smiled against his mouth.

"It's your fault. You bring out my cheesy side."

"Is that supposed to be a compliment?"

"Take it however you want, it's the truth."

"The truth, huh?" Her arms went around his waist and she leaned into him. "You have no idea how good it feels to know I'm with someone who always tells me the truth."

His gut pitched and rolled. He should take that opening she'd given him. The longer he waited, the worse it would be, especially now. "Claudia, I—"

"Can I help you?" A teenage girl in one of the striped aprons stepped behind the counter.

Claudia let go of him and turned to face her. "Yes, we'd like to get some fudge. What flavor do you want to try, Nolan?"

He should tell her he needed to talk to her. He should take her hand and tug her outside. He should find a quiet spot to come clean with her. Instead, he sucked in a breath and looked over the choices. "I can't decide. Get whatever you'd like, because it all looks good to me."

"Okay, let's go with a quarter pound each of the piña colada, the whiskey walnut, the cookies and cream, and the strawberry cheesecake. Sound good?" She looked up at him, such love in her eyes.

"Sounds great."

As the girl wrapped their fudge in paper and packed it in a box, Knox warred with himself. He needed to come clean with Claudia. She'd be pissed, but she'd understand. She'd been hiding out and knew what it was like to crave being out of the spotlight for a bit. He'd needed a place to catch his breath. If he'd been up-front about who he was, he never would have had that chance.

He was 99 percent sure she'd understand why he hadn't given anyone his real name. But after she found out who he really was, would she stay with him? She'd been traumatized by the time she spent in the public eye, and he usually had people watching his every step. His life unfolded on the pages of tabloids and celebrity gossip shows. Having been burned once by the public and the press, would Claudia be willing to take another chance?

That's the question that kept him awake every night, long after she'd fallen asleep in his arms. She trusted him, especially since she'd shared such a painful part of her life with him. How could he expect her to put herself in a similar position? Even though he'd never sacrifice her to save face, would she ever be willing to trust him after she found out he'd been lying to her for over a month?

26

◦─◦♡◦─◦

Claudia

Claudia bit into a square of the piña colada fudge. "You've got to try this one. It's the perfect blend of coconut and pineapple."

Knox took the bite she offered. "Oh, that's good. It tastes like you."

"Yeah, right." She bumped him with her hip. His compliments sent warm fuzzies racing through her. She'd never get tired of hearing his praise, even if she didn't always believe him. He was everything she'd wanted in a man, everything she dreamed of in a lifelong partner.

"Should we find a spot to sit down and enjoy our fudge?"

They'd just left the candy store, and Claudia had a few other stops planned on the tasty treats tour he'd requested. She glanced at her watch. "It's already six thirty. Most places close around seven or eight this time of year. Next week, with the influx of spring breakers, they'll be open until midnight, but if you want to get to the other stops on our tour, we'd better keep going."

"You're in charge." He tucked the box of fudge back in the bag. "Lead the way."

"Do you want to try the cheesecake next or stop by the ice cream shop?"

"Either is fine with me."

"Why do you have to be so accommodating?" she joked. It was a nice change from dating someone who had to be in charge and in control every moment of the relationship. She was still getting used to it, though. Nolan was so flexible, so easygoing, often she still felt like he was way too good to be true.

"When you're happy, I'm happy." He twined his fingers with hers.

Her heart expanded. Every time he said something nice to her, every time he did something to show her affection, her heart swelled a tiny bit. It made her think of the way the Grinch's heart multiplied in size when he finally realized the true meaning of Christmas—though her life was a lot more complicated than a holiday cartoon. Still, it felt . . . nice. *Nice* seemed like such a waste of a word, but it was true. Being with Nolan was comforting, peaceful, safe.

She didn't have to worry about him springing some huge surprise on her. He always took her feelings into consideration, even when they were talking about something that seemed insignificant and small. She'd already admitted she loved him. The more in love with him she fell, the more she wanted to think about the future. She wasn't ready for a lifelong commitment, not by a long shot, but she was ready to talk about next steps. Knowing he was rethinking the job he'd lined up and might stay with her instead was moving them in the right direction.

Happiness bubbled up inside her and she tugged him toward the next stop on their tour, a shop on the same block that sold the best ice cream she'd ever tasted in her life.

"Next up, ice cream." She stepped up to the photo op display sitting outside. Someone had painted two giant waffle cones holding hands. There were holes cut out where people could stick their faces and take a picture of them posing as the two ice cream cones, "We need someone to take our picture."

"You want me to pretend to be a waffle cone?" Nolan's brows arched.

"Is that a problem? You can pick first. Looks like Nutty Peanut Butter Chocolate or Silky Sweet Cream."

"Well, you're definitely Silky Sweet Cream. I'll be the one with nuts." He pulled out his phone.

Claudia laughed. "You're so predictable."

A family of four came out of the shop. The dad held a little girl on his hip who couldn't be more than two or three years old. She took big bites of the cone he held in his hand, her face already covered in chocolate.

"Hey, would you mind taking a picture of us?" Nolan asked.

"Of course not." The wife handed her cone to the little boy at her side and took the phone.

Claudia met him behind the display and reached for his hand as they both stuck their faces through the cutouts.

"On the count of three. One, two, three." The woman pressed the button for the shutter and a series of clicks sounded. "There, I think I got a couple of good ones."

"Thank you so much." Nolan took the phone back. "I appreciate it. Y'all have a good night."

"You, too." She studied Nolan like she wanted to ask him something, but then shook her head and took her ice cream back from her son. The family moved on, and Claudia stepped to his side.

"Let's see the pictures. I need to know what you look like as a cone full of nuts." She gripped his arm while she waited for him to pull up the photos.

The photos caught the two of them smiling into the camera, the early-evening sun casting a reddish glow on the building behind them.

"You need to send that to me." She wanted to remember this day forever, tuck it away in her thin file folder of memories she never wanted to forget. Unfortunately, it was a small folder. So many bad things had happened in her life to prevent her from having an overflowing cache of happy moments to capture. But now, with Nolan, she planned on filling it up with too many magic moments to count.

"You need to get a better phone," he commented. It wasn't the first time he'd dogged her early-generation smartphone. "It would be nice to have the option to video chat when we have to spend time apart."

"Maybe I will." She'd never cared about that kind of thing before. When she left Minneapolis, she'd wanted to disappear and go off the grid. If it had been up to her, she wouldn't have had a cell phone at all, but she had to have some way to keep in touch with her sister. "Wait a minute. What do you mean about spending time apart?"

His lips curved up in a slight smile. "It could happen."

"Not if I have any say in it." She gripped his hand and moved toward the door of the ice cream store. Saying it out loud didn't bring on the wave of panic she'd expected. She didn't want to spend time away from him. The idea of spending every waking moment with him didn't make her feel claustrophobic. It made her feel calm, secure, and, most important of all, loved.

"I like your train of thought."

"Good. Now let's get some ice cream."

They passed into the tiny shop and the smell of freshly baked waffle cones hung in the air. Chick was a sucker for butter pecan, so he'd talked her into visiting the ice cream shop numerous times since she'd been on Paradise Island.

Nolan looked around, then moved closer to the glass cases holding the dozen or so flavors of handmade ice cream.

"Welcome to Paradise Cones." A man Claudia recognized

as one of Chick's poker buddies greeted them. "We make everything fresh right here and use all organic and locally sourced ingredients. If you'd like to try a sample, just let me know."

"I already know what I want. One scoop of cherries jubilee in a dish, please." Claudia tightened her grip on Nolan's hand. "What are you going to get?"

"What's in the Texas Trash?" Nolan asked.

The man behind the counter handed Claudia her cup of ice cream. "That's our tribute to Texas. It's got a butter pecan base with pieces of homemade churros and lots of cinnamon. One of our most popular flavors."

"I'll try that in a cone." Nolan turned to her. "How's your cherries jubilee?"

"Delicious." She held out her spoon so he could try a taste.

"Mmm. You're right. Best ice cream I think I've ever tried."

"Here you go." The man handed over Nolan's ice cream in one of their giant chocolate-dipped waffle cones.

"I hope you're planning on helping me finish this," he said to Claudia as he reached for it.

She shook her head. "You're on your own with that. Just make sure you save room for the cheesecake."

He paid for the ice cream and they left the shop. "I might need to rethink this idea. How many more places do you have in mind?"

"Only a couple more. A lot of places don't even open until next week. The last two weeks of March and the first week of April are the busiest. Then things slow down again until Memorial Day. At least in the summer, the tourists are a little more spaced out. You're lucky you'll miss most of spring break. It gets pretty crowded."

And this year she'd get a bit of a break when she flew out to stay with her sister. She should feel as anxious as a cat in a room full of rocking chairs, but knowing Nolan would be with her the first time she traveled back to Minnesota gave her an unshakable sense of comfort.

"About the trip to Minnesota . . ." he started.

Her heart thumped, pumping extra hard for a few beats. "What about it?"

"I can't wait." He held his waffle cone out to her. "Want to try some Texas Trash?"

"Sure." She bit into it, her nerves soothed. She couldn't wait, either.

Knox

Knox smoothed the hair away from Claudia's cheek. Last night had been a good night. A fucking fantastic night. She'd been so high from her meeting with the boutique owner, he'd decided not to ruin the evening by telling her his secret. It was selfish, but also, she deserved to bask in her win for a day before he brought her world crashing down around her.

Now it was time. Time to tell Claudia about who he really was. Time to come clean and explain the reasoning behind why he'd kept it from her for so long. Satisfied he'd be getting his lie off his chest soon, he kissed her temple, then got out of bed to make coffee. He never thought he'd be the kind of man who enjoyed doing mundane things like making a pot of coffee in the morning. But doing little things for Claudia—especially the type of things she could do for herself—brought him joy.

He looked out over the back patio of the bungalow they'd been sharing for the past week. The vines they'd planted had started to twine their way around the posts on the pergola. Though the sun hadn't fully ascended, there was enough light outside to see they had a visitor.

While the coffee brewed, Knox grabbed a bunch of lettuce from the vegetable drawer and headed out back. Tripod greeted him by rubbing the top of his head against Knox's cotton pajama pants.

"Good morning. What's got you up and moving around so early?" Knox asked the giant tortoise.

Tripod answered by sniffing the air between them, his beady eyes focused on the lettuce in Knox's hands.

"Want some breakfast?" He ripped off a piece of lettuce and held it out to Tripod, who took off a chunk at the end.

Knox sat there, hand-feeding Tripod while he watched the sunrise over the east side of the island. He could be content here. Not just content, but really, truly happy.

He patted Tripod on the head and ripped up the rest of the lettuce to leave it for the big tortoise.

When he went back inside, he washed his hands, then poured two mugs of coffee. He was about to pick them up and head into the bedroom to finally tell Claudia the truth when his phone rang. A picture of Decker lit up the screen. He wasn't supposed to be coming until later on in the week. Figuring he'd no longer need his help, Knox set down the coffee and answered the call.

"Hey, man, to what do I owe the, ahem, pleasure, of this early-morning call?"

"I'm sitting off the southern tip of Paradise Island on the business yacht. I need you to come today. Do the whole proposal thing. Are you in?" Decker's voice held a trace of panic, making him sound desperate.

"What's going on? I didn't think you'd be here until Friday."

"Dad needs the yacht to entertain some oil guys at the end of the week, so I had to move up my trip. Can you help me out, bro?"

Knox's plan of telling Claudia the truth fell by the wayside. Decker needed him. Plus, he'd promised he'd help out. He tried to tamp down the relief he felt at buying himself more time.

"Yeah, sure. What time do you want me to be there?" They didn't have big plans today. Claudia would be working at the bar, and he'd planned on finishing painting the bungalow closest to the beach. They just had a few more little touches to make before everything was done.

Decker let out a sigh. "Thanks. I'll send the dinghy out for you at what time? Ten? Eleven?"

"How's this supposed to go down?" He'd need more info if Decker wanted him to play an active role in his big ask.

"I'll have you come out while she's on the island shopping or something. Then we'll sit down for drinks on the deck and you can start singing. I was thinking you could do the one about being my only baby."

"Got it. Let me get cleaned up and I'll be ready by eleven." That would let him spend as much time as he could with Claudia before she had to head to work and still give him time to shower and practice on his guitar. He'd messed around with it since he'd been on Paradise, but hadn't played any of his older stuff in ages.

"Thanks, man. I'll owe you one."

"Don't worry, I won't let you forget." Knox let out a soft laugh, but he meant it. With his relationship with Claudia progressing, there might come a time when he'd need a place to get away from the public eye. Decker's dad owned houses, chalets, and condos around the world.

"I can't wait to see you. Later." Decker ended the call.

Knox set his phone down and picked up the two mugs. He'd planned on telling Claudia this morning, but he couldn't drop that kind of info and then disappear for a few hours. She'd proven she was a runner, and he didn't want to risk her taking off on him when he told her. Tonight, he promised himself. When he got back from helping Decker and she got back from the bar. He'd wait up and they could have the conversation before bed.

His heart clenched as he wondered how she'd react. He didn't have a choice, though. He'd let it go on long enough. It was time to put an end to the secrets. Knowing it might be a little while before things would feel right between them, he set her coffee down on the nightstand and crawled back into bed.

He pulled her close to him and, half-asleep, she nestled her cheek onto his chest.

She had to understand. Losing her wouldn't be an option. Not now. Not ever. Knowing that gave him some resolve. She'd be upset, but he could handle it. The relationship they'd built over the past couple of weeks would be able to withstand the truth. It would bring them closer, make them stronger.

"Have you been up for a while?" Her eyelids cracked open, and she gazed up at him.

"Not too long. Just enough to make coffee and spend a few minutes with Tripod on the patio." He'd never get tired of seeing her first thing in the morning. This was where she belonged: in his arms.

"You're going to spoil him and then he's going to keep coming back here looking for treats. He'll probably scare the crap out of whoever rents this place." She rolled over and reached for the coffee he'd made.

"You'll just have to add that to the website. Warning: expect visits from a hungry, overly friendly giant tortoise. Don't you think people would get a kick out of feeding him?"

She sat up in the bed, pulling the sheet over her naked breasts. "I suppose."

"Hey, about today." He sat up next to her. "I've got an errand I have to run later."

"Do you want me to go with you? I've got time before I need to be at the bar this morning." With her hair piled on top of her head and sleep still lingering in the corners of her eyes, she'd never looked more gorgeous.

"That's okay. I can think of a lot of other things I'd rather do with the time we have left before you have to go to work."

"Oh, yeah?" She arched a brow. "What kind of things might those be?"

He gently eased the mug from her grip and set both cups on the table next to him. "I'd rather show you than tell you."

Heat sparked in her eyes. "Well, then get to the showing."

Knowing it might be the last time she looked at him with the same level of love and trust in her eyes for a little while, he felt guilty for taking advantage of the moment. But he wanted to show her how much she meant to him. Love her up before he let her down. He tugged at the sheet covering her breasts. Damn, she was gorgeous.

He bent to capture one of her nipples in his mouth while he dragged his finger down her side and slipped his hand between her legs.

She was already wet. He loved that about her. No matter how much or little time they spent kissing and touching and stroking each other, she was always ready for him.

"I like this part." She scooted down to lie flat and rubbed her palm against his cock through the front of the pants he'd pulled on when he got out of bed.

He couldn't kick them off fast enough. While he circled her clit with his finger, she wrapped her hand around his dick and applied the perfect amount of pressure.

They'd gotten to know each other so well over the short time they'd spent together. She knew what turned him on—everything—and what turned him off—hardly anything—and he'd learned the same about her. How she melted when he rimmed the shell of her ear with his tongue. How she writhed underneath him when he hooked his finger just right and touched her G-spot. But his favorite thing he'd learned was what she looked like when she stared deep into his eyes while she fell apart around him.

That was the look he was going for when he shifted to hover over her and nudged her thighs apart with his knees.

She gripped his shoulders and angled her hips. He slid into her, every fraction of an inch feeling the walls of her sex grip him tighter.

This was what he wanted. This was what he needed. This was what he'd fight like hell for.

He pumped into her, basking in the way her breath hitched and her fingernails dug into his shoulders

"Love you, Claudia."

"Love you more."

Damn, he hoped so.

27

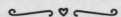

Claudia

The smile Nolan put on her face that morning stuck with her, even after she got to work. It stayed with her through the lunch crowd and even during the time she'd set aside to chat with Gabe before his shift started.

"Did you get good news today or something?" Gabe asked when they finally sat down together.

"What makes you think that?" she asked.

He shrugged. "I've just never seen you smile so much."

Nolan was responsible for the good mood that seemed to constantly flip her lips into a goofy grin. Gabe wasn't the only one to notice, either. A few of the regulars from the bar had said something similar over the past couple of days. Their comments made her wonder what she usually looked like.

"I guess I'm happier than I've been in a long time."

"Good. You deserve to be happy." He said it like he meant it.

She nodded. Knowing what kind of hardships his family had gone through, she wished the same for him. "We all do. Now, what did you want to ask me about?"

"Chick said you're planning that fundraising concert to

raise money for the lighthouse." Gabe fidgeted with the edge of the napkin sitting under his soda.

"That's right. It's going to be all hands-on-deck. You'll be around then, right?" Hopefully, he wasn't asking for time off. They couldn't afford to lose any of the staff during the busiest weeks of the year.

"Of course. I just wondered if"—he shifted his gaze to stare at what was left of his napkin—"maybe I could perform a song or something before the real musicians take the stage."

Her heart went out to him. "Real musicians? Gabe, you've taken the stage during a couple open mics now. I'd say you're definitely a real musician."

His shoulders rose and fell as he took in a deep breath and lifted his head to meet her gaze. The hope in his dark brown eyes made her stomach clench. "Do you think I could sing one song?"

She didn't want to discourage him from following his dreams of becoming a singer, no matter how out of reach they might seem. And with Nolan encouraging him, promising to connect him with his famous friend, Gabe's sights were set on the stars.

"Of course you can perform a song. I'll make sure we leave room in the lineup for you, okay?"

His lips split into a wide smile. "Thanks, Claudia. You won't regret it, I promise."

"What song are you planning on performing?"

"Oh, I don't know for sure yet, but I'm thinking of singing an older one by Knox Shepler. My dad has an early CD from when he first heard him perform."

There was that name again. Something tugged at the back of Claudia's mind. The cardboard cutout she'd seen yesterday . . . that's where she'd heard it. "I guess he's a pretty popular artist now."

"He is." Gabe's eyes lit up. "Thanks again. I've got to clock in for my shift, but I'll start practicing."

"You're so welcome. I can't wait to watch you sing up on that stage."

"Thanks." Gabe got up and headed toward the door to the kitchen.

Claudia turned to slide off her stool and carry the dirty glasses to the kitchen when two people she'd never seen before walked into the restaurant. The lunch crowd had died down, and it was too early for the regular happy hour customers to roll in. She left the glasses where they were and headed toward the hostess stand.

"Welcome to A Cowboy in Paradise. Would you like a table inside or out on the patio?" She reached for two menus.

"Neither. We're looking for someone." The man had on a black cowboy hat, dark-wash jeans, and a pair of shiny alligator boots. The woman next to him tightened her grip on the bag at her side.

"Do you want to talk to Chick? He's the owner." Though she hadn't seen him yet. He'd been up late with his poker buddies the night before and might not make it in before the dinner crowd.

"No. We're looking for my client. I understand he's been staying in one of the bungalows on-site."

"Oh, Nolan. He had some errands to run but should be back by this evening." Even as she said the words, she wondered what kind of business Nolan would have with a man who looked like he'd never set foot inside a construction zone.

"Nolan?" the man asked. "No, my client is Knox Shepler, the musician. I'd appreciate it if you could tell me where I can find him."

Claudia started to shake her head but stopped. Knox Shepler. The man whose face she'd seen on the cardboard cutout last night. The man who looked like Nolan. She tried to picture Nolan without the scruffy beard and with a cowboy hat on his head instead of the baseball cap he always seemed to favor.

"Would you like to come in and take a seat? I might know where you can find him, or at least where you might be able to find him in a few hours." Her hand shook, but she forced her lungs to take in a deep breath. This wasn't happening. Nolan and Knox couldn't be the same person. It was impossible. She'd know if Nolan had been lying to her. Wouldn't she?

The two of them followed her to a table at the back. She set down the menus she'd grabbed and went to the bar to get them some water.

"I'm going to call Chick to come in, and we'll figure this out. Can I give him your names so he knows who's waiting for him?"

"Of course." The man held out his hand. "I'm Tripp Sanchez, Knox's manager."

Claudia took it even though she couldn't feel a thing. Her body had gone numb. "Nice to meet you."

Tripp released his grip and turned to the woman next to him. "This is Morgan Yancy, this year's songwriter of the year."

What would Nolan need with a songwriter? Claudia blinked, trying to wish away what was happening. Her brain shifted the pieces of the puzzle around. Nolan was Knox. The signs were all there: the guitar he kept in his bungalow and the notebooks he said were full of ideas for new designs. And the first time they met, Chick had introduced him as Knox, then said something about it being a nickname because he used to like knock-knock jokes.

The need to get out of there as soon as possible washed over her. "I'll call Chick. He'll be here in just a few minutes."

"Great. We'll have a look at the menu while we wait."
Tripp gave her a reassuring smile and reached for one of the
menus.

Claudia couldn't breathe. She needed to know the truth.
Had the man she'd fallen in love with been lying to her all
along? Her fingers fumbled with her phone as she tried to
dial Chick's number. It rang a few times before he answered.

"Yeah?" His voice came through groggy, like she'd woken
him from a deep sleep even though it was after two in the
afternoon.

"There's a man here looking for Knox." She gripped her
phone tighter, hoping Chick would be just as confused as she
was. Still hoping it was all a mistake.

Chick sighed. "I suppose you know, then."

"Know what? Tell me what's going on." Her voice cracked
as panic edged its way up her throat.

"He'll have to fill you in, hon. It's not my story to tell.
Where is he?"

It was true. Ice water seeped into her veins, making her
entire body freeze. "I don't know. He said he had to run a few
errands and would be back later."

Chick let out a low groan. "I'll be there in a few minutes.
It's not what you think, Claudia."

She didn't have the bandwidth to hear any more. The
phone fell from her hand, bounced off the bar, and landed
facedown on the floor. She didn't bend down to pick it
up, just left it lying there. Then she grabbed her purse from
where she'd stashed it under the bar and walked toward the
patio.

The need to flee pulsed through her. She could change her
flight to Minnesota and leave a few days early. How ironic
was it that in order to protect herself, she'd be running from
a place she thought she'd been safe, back to a town where
she'd sworn she'd never go again?

In the moment, none of that mattered. The only thing she wanted to do was get away.

She entered the bungalow where she and Nolan had been staying together. Even though all signs pointed to the fact that Nolan was actually Knox and he'd been lying to her since day one, she still needed to know for sure.

The guitar case wasn't where he usually left it. But she'd seen him with the guitar. It wasn't anything special, definitely not the kind of instrument she'd expect to see an international star playing onstage in front of thousands of people. Maybe they were wrong. There was a resemblance between her Nolan and the country singer, but they could be two different people. It could still be a mistake.

Then she pulled the notebook he was always scribbling in off the shelf. Page after page of his handwriting filled the lines. Song lyrics. The last shred of hope she'd held out faded away.

He'd lied to her.

Knox

Knox climbed on board the giant Wayne Holdings yacht.

"There you are!" Decker greeted him with a tight hug, then immediately released him. "Thanks so much for making this happen. I really appreciate it."

"You know I'd do anything for you." He took the guitar case the guy who'd driven him from the dock to the yacht handed him. "Fill me in. What do you need me to do?"

Decker gestured for him to head up a few steps to the deck. "Let's get you something cold to drink, and I'll tell you what I have in mind."

The day couldn't be more perfect. A light breeze carried the scent of sea salt, but the bright sun ensured the temperature hovered in the low seventies. Knox hadn't been on the yacht before, so he tried to soak it all in.

"Sun or shade?" Decker asked.

The open-air deck provided both options. Knox nodded toward a table in the sun. May as well enjoy the gorgeous weather. He'd be heading to Minneapolis with Claudia next week, and the forecast predicted a spring snowstorm.

An attendant set glasses of water on the table when they sat down. "Will there be anything else?"

"Two Coronas, please." Decker reached for his glass.

"This is the life, huh?" Knox looked around, taking in the 360-degree view of the vast expanse of the Gulf of Mexico and the curve of the Texas coastline. "How long will you be boating around the gulf?"

Decker rested his arm along the back of the sofa. "Just a couple of days. Dad needs the yacht at the end of the week. It's nice to be able to take a break, though. Speaking of breaks, how's your time on Paradise been going? You said you were able to start writing again?"

"Yeah, there's something about the island. The words are flowing and I actually met someone." Knox wasn't sure how much he wanted to share about his budding relationship with Claudia, but Decker was one of his closest friends, so he wanted to say something.

"You?" Decker's eyebrows shot up. "Tell me about her."

"She's amazing." He struggled to find the words to describe Claudia. None of them came close to conveying her spirit, her resilience, her incredible drive.

"That's it? I mean, 'amazing' is good, but what's she like? How did you meet?"

"She works at the bar Chick owns, but she's started to get back into interior design. We've been working on getting those bungalows renovated and being around her just kind of opened up something inside me. The words have been flowing ever since."

"Congratulations. I'm happy for you." Decker took the bottle of beer the server handed him and held it out for a toast. "To our women."

Knox clinked his bottle against Decker's. His friend had always had a flair for the dramatic.

"If anyone deserves to find happiness again, it's you. What does she think about you being a superstar?" Decker squeezed the lime slice and shoved it into the neck of his beer bottle while he waited for Knox to respond.

"She, uh, doesn't quite know about that yet."

"You're fucking with me." Decker's lips curled into a half smile.

Knox shook his head. "I wish I was. When I came down here, I told everyone my name was Nolan. I didn't want to get hounded by fans or the press."

"So she thinks your name is Nolan." Decker nodded. "You have to head into the studio soon, right? Nothing wrong with keeping it to an island fling. Gets you back in the saddle—"

"It's not just a vacation hookup. I love her." Saying it out loud made it real. Made it impossible to deny. He clenched his jaw and took in a breath through his nose to try to calm his thundering heart.

"Oh-kay." The smile faded from Decker's face. "You know you've got to tell her the truth, then. Once word gets out you're seeing somebody, they're going to find her. It's not fair to her if she's not ready for that."

"I know." Knox leaned forward, ripped off his baseball cap, and funneled his hand through his hair.

"When are you heading home?"

"Something's come up. Claudia's sister is on bedrest and

her husband has to travel to a conference next week, so the two of us are flying up to Minneapolis to help out."

"You're supposed to go into the studio in two weeks, aren't you?" Decker leaned forward.

"Yeah. I left a message for Tripp to call me. It's complicated."

"Damn, bro. You really know how to twist the shit out of your downtime, don't you?"

He was right. The getaway to Paradise was supposed to give him some breathing room to make things better, not open him up to crap that would make his life even more complicated.

"I've tried to tell her, but she had a bad experience dating a celebrity in the past. I don't want to ruin what we've got going. If I tell her, I'm pretty sure she'll end things."

"If you don't tell her, she's going to find out on her own and end things anyway." Decker shrugged.

Dammit, he was right about that, too. "I'm going to tell her when I get back tonight."

"Good. Now, about this proposal. Cherice is down below. She just finished her online yoga class and is getting cleaned up. When she comes up on deck, I'll hit my knee and propose."

"Where do you want me?" Knox asked.

"Over there." Decker nudged his chin toward the front of the boat. "If you can just play something sweet in the background until she says yes, that would be great. Once she accepts, I need you to play 'Baby, I'm Yours.'"

"That's what you decided to go with?"

Decker shrugged. "Cherice likes it."

Knox bit back a laugh. He'd written that song as a sweet, slow ballad. The label had turned it into a fast-paced pop song with a hint of country twang.

"Don't start with me," Decker warned.

"I'm happy to play it for you, but I didn't bring my cowbell." The tune wasn't bad, it just wasn't him.

"Play it the way you wrote it, will ya? I don't need all that extra shit. You and your guitar. That's how country music ought to be."

"You got it. I'll go get set up. Any idea how long she'll be?" Knox stood and grabbed his guitar case.

Decker checked his watch. "Probably another ten minutes. There's nobody out here but us, but she won't come up on deck until she's all made up."

"Can I ask you something?" Knox paused and looked at Decker.

"Of course."

"How many times have you proposed to a woman?"

Decker glanced at the deck and pursed his lips. "Three. But Cherice is the one."

"How do you know?" Decker's dating history was as long as the list of songs Knox had written. Both of them had been rejected by people they loved. While Knox had hardened his heart, Decker had opened his up wide, always searching for that one person who'd make him feel loved. Knox had his doubts about Cherice being the one, but he'd never discourage Decker from following his heart.

"You trying to convince me not to pop the question?" Decker's mouth set in a straight line.

"No. Just trying to figure out my own shit."

His jaw softened. "I'm not an easy guy to get along with. I am bullheaded, can be pretty dense, and like to be in charge. Cherice puts up with me. She loves me for who I am, the good and the bad. Why wouldn't I want to be with someone like that for the rest of my life?"

"I'm glad you found her." Decker deserved to be happy. Hell, they all did. Knox was glad Decker had found someone. He might look like he had it all together on the outside with the expensive toys, the designer suits, and a net worth that had so many zeroes behind it, his hand would cramp if he tried to write them all down. But Knox knew the guy behind the facade. The one who'd been passed off from one step-mom to the next, who'd been shuffled from camp to camp in the summers and didn't have any kind of relationship with his dad until he reached legal drinking age. Everyone had a backstory, but Decker's was lonelier than most.

"I'm going to go check on Cherice and see how much more time we have. Need anything else?" Decker wiped his brow with a handkerchief.

"You nervous?"

"A little."

"It'll be fine. Just speak from your heart."

Decker rolled his eyes. "That's what I'm nervous about. I can read an hour-long speech from a teleprompter with no problem, but saying something off the cuff has me sweating like a sinner in church."

"You'll do fine." Knox turned his attention to tuning his guitar while Decker disappeared down below. Maybe some-day he could take Claudia on a boat like this. Maybe some-day he'd sweat bullets with a ring in his pocket while he tried to search for the right words to pop the question. The idea didn't make him feel like he wanted to pass out. He actually liked the thought of the two of them reaching a place in their relationship where they'd both be ready for a permanent commitment.

Of course, all of that hinged on how she'd react when he told her the truth.

Decker came up the steps and barely had time to signal before Cherice appeared. She was gorgeous. Tall and thin, with bronzed skin and the kind of figure that often appeared in the centerfold of a men's magazine, she had on a sundress that hugged her hips and she was made up from head to toe.

Knox strummed the opening chords of his song and Cherice turned her head to see where the music was coming from. Her eyes widened before she turned to look at Decker.

He got down on a knee and pulled a small box out of his pocket. "Cherice, we haven't known each other that long, but I feel like the only reason I was put on this earth was to love you."

She clasped her hands together. A high-pitched squeal came from somewhere, but it sure didn't sound human.

Decker opened the box. "Will you make me the happiest man in the world? Will you marry me?"

She took the ring out of the box and slid it onto her finger. Twisting her hand one way, then the other, she caught the sunlight and sent sparkles racing over the shaded section of the yacht.

"Cherice?" Decker reached for her other hand. "What do you say, sweetheart?"

"Oh, um, sure. YOLO, right?" She let out a loud laugh and hopped up and down. "We're getting married!"

Decker got to his feet and pulled her in for a hug.

Knox started to sing the slow version of "Baby, I'm Yours." He would have played whatever Decker wanted, but was relieved not to be singing the song he'd written for his ex. He'd been dumb and horny and convinced his eighteen-year-old self she was his forever. When he'd found her in bed with his dad, he left town and didn't look back. As Decker twirled his fiancée around the deck, Knox thanked his lucky stars he'd been shown her true character before he'd popped the question and saddled himself with the wrong woman for life. Hopefully, Decker knew what he was getting himself into.

When the song ended, Decker brought Cherice over so Knox could meet her.

"I can't believe he brought you all this way just to sing for me." She put a hand to her heart.

"You're worth it, baby." Decker put his arm around her. "Do you want to head to the mainland for a celebration dinner, or would you rather stay here?"

"I want to show off my ring." She held her hand out again, admiring the largest diamond Knox had ever seen outside a museum.

"Why don't we head to the island to drop off Knox and meet his new girlfriend?" Decker suggested.

"Oh, no, she has to work tonight. Y'all probably want a private celebration. We'll catch up with you another time." The last thing he needed was to try to explain Decker and Cherice to Claudia. Once he'd told her the truth, they'd probably share plenty of evenings together. But not yet. Not while she still thought of him as Nolan the construction worker.

"I'll have someone run you back to the island. Thanks so much for helping me propose." Decker pulled him in for a quick hug.

"Congratulations to both of you." Knox packed up his guitar and headed back to the boat he'd arrived on. He'd expected nothing less from a Decker Wayne proposal. Deck was so desperate for someone to love. Knox just hoped he hadn't rushed things, though it was becoming obvious to him that when a man found the woman he was supposed to spend the rest of his life with, he just knew.

Eager to get back to the woman he intended to propose to someday in the not-too-distant future, Knox left the newly engaged couple behind.

28

◦~♡~◦

Claudia

She couldn't believe she'd left her phone at the bar, but there was no way she was going back to get it. Claudia struggled to lift her giant suitcase onto the scale at the check-in counter. When Chick had confirmed Nolan wasn't who she thought he was, all she'd wanted to do was to get the hell off of Paradise as soon as she could. So she'd grabbed handfuls of clothes from her drawers and closet and shoved them into her suitcase, then stuck out her thumb and caught a ride on a golf cart to the ferry.

Changing her flight to Minnesota would take a huge chunk out of her savings account, but it would be worth it. She couldn't stay. Not even Texas was big enough to put adequate distance between her and Nolan. Ugh. Her and Knox.

She took the boarding pass and baggage claim ticket the woman behind the counter handed her and turned to look for the line for security. Holding back the waterfall of tears that threatened made her eyes burn, but she wasn't about to give in. This wasn't the first time a man had taken advantage of her, but it damn sure would be the last.

How had she missed it? Obviously, Chick had been in on it. Screw him. He could figure out how to rent out the bungalows on his own.

She'd thought she and Nolan had built something worthwhile. He knew she'd been hurt before and still he'd lied to her. Her fingers curled into fists, fueled by her rage. The only problem was that there wasn't anything to punch. She'd let down her guard and trusted him. She was the one who'd given him the power to hurt her, because she'd let him in. Not only that, she'd given him her heart.

The flight finally boarded, and she slid into her seat by the window. How sad was it that between staying on Paradise or going back to Minneapolis, she chose Minneapolis? She pressed her head against the seat and gazed out the window. The plane barreled down the runway and lifted into the air.

Claudia watched as the lights of Paradise Island grew smaller and smaller. When they disappeared for good, she closed her eyes and didn't open them again until the wheels touched down at the Minneapolis–Saint Paul International Airport. With no phone to arrange for a ride share, she had no choice but to take a cab to her sister's address in one of the south Minneapolis suburbs.

Though it was almost ten at night, the front porch light burned bright when the cab stopped in front of the remodeled bungalow. Thankfully, Andrea had always been a night owl. Claudia paid the driver and tugged her suitcase behind her as she made her way to the front door.

She didn't want to ring the doorbell, since the kids were probably sound asleep, so she knocked instead. Derek opened the door. His eyes lit up when he saw her.

"Claudia, what are you doing here? We weren't expecting you until next week." Her brother-in-law pulled her into a hug and called back over his shoulder. "Andrea, you're never going to believe who's here."

Claudia managed to hold it together while Derek lifted her bag off the stoop and set it just inside the door. She didn't let a single tear slip as he invited her into the front living room. Didn't let the dam break until he led her back to the bedroom and she saw her sister propped up with a few pillows behind her.

"What happened?" Andrea opened her arms wide.

Claudia leaned into her hug, being careful not to squash the huge baby bump between them. "He lied to me."

"Can I do anything?" Derek asked.

"We're going to need some tea and probably something a little stronger," Andrea said. Then she squeezed Claudia even tighter. "Let it all out, girl. I've got you."

The tears poured out of her—an embarrassing deluge of emotion. Like one of the spring thunderstorms she'd experienced in Texas, they fell fast and furious and within a few minutes it was over. Her eyes felt raw. Snot ran from her nose, and her chest heaved as she tried to catch her breath.

"Feel better?" Her sister pulled back and smoothed Claudia's hair away from her face. "Need a tissue?"

Claudia nodded as she reached for a tissue on the nightstand. "I'm sorry."

"For what, sweetie?"

"For showing up on your doorstep with no warning and drenching you with tears and snot." Wet spots dotted the front of her sister's pajama top.

"I've got two kids and a third on the way. You can't imagine what kind of body fluids I've been doused with. Tears and snot are nothing." Andrea patted the empty space next to her. "Sit down and tell me what's going on."

Derek came into the bedroom carrying a tray. Silent communication passed between husband and wife in a series of nods and raised eyebrows.

"Here you go. Tea should be ready in a few minutes, and

I brought you a little something extra." He set the tray hold-ing their mom's favorite teapot and a small bottle of Tennes-see whiskey down on the bed. "If you don't need me for anything . . ."

"Thanks, love." Andrea gave his hand a squeeze and tilted her head back for his kiss.

"It's good to see you, Claudia." Derek gave her a sympa-thetic smile before disappearing down the hall.

"Ugh." Claudia closed her eyes. "Your poor husband. I'm sorry for surprising you. I would have called, but I left my phone at the bar, and all I wanted to do was get the hell out of there as fast as I could."

"Do you want to talk about it?"

She opened her eyes and studied her sister's expression. After their parents died, Andrea took on a mothering role. She'd always been the first person Claudia reached out to when she needed something . . . the only person Claudia trusted to give her rock-solid advice. After the tide turned against her and she moved away, Claudia hadn't had anyone to share with.

"Nolan lied to me. I mean, Knox. Whoever the hell he is." She waved her hand in the air.

"What level of lie are we talking about here?"

"He lied about everything. Who he is, what he does for a living . . . he probably even lied about his feelings for me. I have no idea who he really is."

Andrea shifted closer. "Did he say why?"

"What? No. I didn't stick around long enough to confront him about it. He knows what happened to me with King. I told him everything. If he cared about me at all, he would have told me the truth." She still couldn't wrap her head around the fact that Nolan was Knox Shepler.

"Let's start with his name. It's not Nolan. You said his name is really Knox?"

Claudia turned to face her sister. "He's Knox Shepler, the country singer."

Andrea's forehead creased, and a wrinkle formed between her eyebrows. "The guy I hear on the radio sometimes?"

"The guy who's been on top lists of most beautiful people. The guy who's won enough music awards to fill an entire bookshelf. Yes, that's him."

"Oh, shit. I thought he was a construction worker."

"So did I. He actually did a really good job on the bungalow renovations."

"How did you find out? Did he tell you?" Andrea nudged her chin toward the tray.

Claudia poured two cups of tea, then added a shot of whiskey into her own before handing the other to Andrea. "Hell no. A guy walked into the bar today and said he needed to see his client. Turns out he's Knox's manager and he had some songwriter with him. I had no idea who he was talking about, so I called Chick. I guess my boss was in on it, too. I can't believe he didn't tell me."

"Where was Nolan? I mean, Knox?"

"He had some errands to run. I have no idea where he was."

"Honey"—Andrea reached for Claudia's hand—"he must have had a good reason for not telling you who he really is. I think you need to give him a chance to explain."

Claudia pulled her hand back. "Whose side are you on?"

"I'm not on anyone's side. I just think you need to talk to him. Let him share his side. You stayed down there because you wanted to hide. Maybe he was doing the same thing."

Claudia wanted to be outraged. It was easier to channel her anger than to think Knox might have a legitimate reason to keep his identity a secret. Especially after she'd shared the most painful part of her life with him. He knew how important it was to her that they didn't have lies between them. She'd made that perfectly clear.

"I don't know. I'm not ready to talk to him yet, and I don't know when I will be."

"So what's your plan? Are you going to move back to Minnesota?"

"No." She'd been so numb when she landed, the fact that she was back in the state where the worst moments of her life had taken place hadn't registered yet. "I came to help with the kids while Derek is out of town, like I said I would. Once he gets back, I'll have to figure out where to go, but I know I won't stay here. Not while King is still playing for the Tigers."

"You know you're welcome to stay here as long as you want," Andrea said. "We've got a guest room set up in the basement, so you can have a little privacy. I know it sounds selfish, but I'm really glad you're here."

Claudia shook her head. "It's good to be here. I can't wait to see the kids. And the baby." She held out her hand. "Is it weird if I ask to feel your belly?"

"Of course not. You're my sister." Andrea put Claudia's hand on her stomach. "Squirt's been pretty active tonight. Put your hand right here, and you might feel a kick."

Claudia let her sister move her hand around her firm, round belly. All of a sudden, something pushed on her palm. "Was that it?"

"Yep. This one's been a real acrobat."

The movement pressed on her hand again. "That's amazing."

"It really is, isn't it?"

Regret washed over her. She hadn't been there when her sister was pregnant with either of the other kids. She'd missed so much. Let her experience with King steal so much from her over the years.

"I like what you've done with your hair." Andrea smiled. "You look a lot like Mom."

"I know. I can't help but see her face every time I look in a mirror." Claudia kept her hand on her sister's belly and leaned her head down to rest on her shoulder.

"She would have been so proud of you. Both of them would have."

"I don't know. Mom and Dad always fought for what they believed in." Claudia had grown up hearing stories about how they'd risked everything to stand up to their parents and elope. They wouldn't have let something like King's stunt get to them or run away from Paradise without forcing the truth out of Knox.

"Look at you, back in Minnesota when you swore you'd never step foot in this state again. And it sounds like you're getting your design business off the ground. I think you don't give yourself enough credit."

Claudia let her sister's words sink in. Once upon a time, she hadn't been afraid to put herself out there and go for what she wanted. She'd built her real estate business from the ground up and had a reputation for being a tough negotiator. Where had that woman gone? Over the past month with Knox, she felt like she'd found the tiny sliver of that woman that was left inside her. He'd encouraged her to let her out, to take more chances, to stop limiting herself.

"I don't know. My brain hurts right now."

"You need a good night's sleep. Come on, I'll show you to the basement. We've got room-darkening shades down there, and it's the best mattress in the house. You'll feel like you're sleeping on a cloud."

Sleep of any kind seemed like a good idea. "You're on bed rest. That's why I'm here, remember? I'm sure I can find my way to the basement by myself."

"Are you sure? I bet Derek carried your bag down already. Will you let me know if you need anything?" Andrea held out her arms again.

"I won't need a thing." Claudia gripped her sister in a tight hug, then drained her teacup and carried the tray out to the kitchen before making her way down the stairs to the finished lower level. Though she missed the sound of the waves crashing on the sand right outside her window, the nip of whiskey she'd poured into her tea had the intended effect of making her sleepy.

Tomorrow would be soon enough to make sense of things. She changed into her pajamas and pulled the down comforter up to her chin. Just as she was about to doze off to sleep, a shrill noise rang out.

29

❧

Knox

Knox couldn't wait to see Claudia when he got back to the island. Watching Decker and Cherice bask in the glow of being newly engaged made him realize that's what he wanted for himself. He wanted that with Claudia.

Determined to tell her the truth, no matter what obstacles might pop up, he pulled his phone out of his pocket. He'd left it on silent while he'd been on the yacht. The last thing Decker needed was to have his proposal interrupted by a phone call.

His stomach clenched when he saw the missed calls from Tripp. Something must have happened with the label. He flipped to his texts to see if he could figure out what was going on. Messages from Chick, Tripp, and even Gabe filled the screen.

With an uneasiness settling in his gut, he opened up the first text.

Chick: Jig's up. Your manager is here looking for you.

Wait, Tripp was at the bar? He flipped to Tripp's text to confirm.

Tripp: Where are you? We need to talk.

The one person he wanted to hear from hadn't reached out. He pulled up the last text from Claudia just to make sure.

Claudia: Can't wait to see you tonight! Love you!

She'd sent it this morning, hours ago. He pulled up her number and tried to connect. The phone rang several times, then went to voice mail. Something was wrong. It wasn't unusual for her not to pick up during a busy shift, but she ought to be between lunch and dinner. He closed his eyes against the bright sun. With Tripp in town, she had to have found out. Dammit. He wanted to be the one to tell her. He *had* to be the one to tell her. With his heart rumbling louder than the engine on the boat he was riding on, he called Chick.

"Where the hell are you?" The older man didn't waste his breath with a useless greeting.

"I'm on my way back now. I had to do a favor for a friend." Knox clenched his jaw. "She knows, doesn't she?"

Chick let a few moments go by before he answered. "Yeah."

"How bad is it?" Knox could take her anger. He'd let her rail against him as long as she needed. As long as she was still there. Please, please, please let her still be there.

"She's gone."

The two words dropped like a twenty-ton weight, landing with a heavy thud in the pit of his stomach. "Gone where?"

"Wish I knew, son." Chick took in a deep breath. "Packed a bag and took off. She didn't tell anyone where she was headed."

"I need to call her, I'll—"

"Won't do any good. She left her phone."

Fuck. How was he supposed to reach her? She'd be pissed, and knowing her like he did, he expected she'd want to get as far away from him as quickly as possible. "Do you think she left the island?"

"I'm not sure, but you've got other issues to worry about.

Your manager's been sitting in my bar for the past two hours, and it sounds like he's extremely eager to talk to you."

"Yeah, okay I'll be there in fifteen minutes. Can you let him know?" It would be easier to talk to Tripp in person.

"Sure. Can I offer you a piece of advice?" Chick asked.

Knox would have given his best guitar for a recommendation on how to get himself out of the situation he'd wedged himself into with the least amount of damage. "Of course."

"Know what you want." Chick clucked his tongue. "Not only that, but know what you're willing to give up in your pursuit of it. You got that?"

"I got it. See you in a few." He hung up as the boat slowed to approach the dock. Chick had always struck him as a straight shooter and someone who didn't waste a lot of words. Knox mulled over the advice. He knew what he wanted, always had. He wanted to make a living by playing music. But now there was a wrinkle in his plan. Claudia.

He had to make things right with her. She was the one who'd unlocked his muse, who'd inspired him to start making music again.

He walked into A Cowboy in Paradise with his mind made up. No matter what Tripp tossed his way, he had to find Claudia first.

"Here he is." Chick got up from his seat as Knox approached the table. "I told them you were on your way."

"Thanks." Knox reached for the hand Tripp held out. "Tripp, you should have told me you were coming."

Tripp squeezed his hand in a firm grip. "It was a last-minute decision. Have you met Morgan before?"

Knox released his grip and turned to the woman. "I don't believe I have, though I'm familiar with your work."

"Nice to meet you." The smile she gave him was genuine.

"Join us." Tripp gestured toward the empty chair between them.

Knox sat down, a sense of apprehension prickling his gut. He didn't have time to entertain Tripp. Claudia was out there somewhere, probably confused, most likely pissed as hell. He needed to talk to her before she jumped to all kinds of conclusions.

"What's going on, Tripp? I don't mean to be rude, but there are a few things I need to take care of tonight. What do y'all need?" He didn't want to piss off his manager, and he had a good guess as to why Tripp had shown up with the songwriter of the year in tow, but he wanted to hear it from him.

Tripp slowly shook his head as he reached for his glass of whiskey. "The label's done waiting. They're giving you the option to continue to work on the new album down here with Morgan or head home and work on it with her there."

"Doesn't sound like much of a choice to me." Knox figured this day would come. He'd done his best and hadn't been able to find the sweet spot between what the label wanted and what he was willing to put out under his name.

"Can you excuse us for a few minutes, Morgan?" Tripp gave her an easy smile that stuck to his lips until she'd gotten up from the table and headed out to the beach.

"Talk to me, Tripp." Knox braced himself.

"If you refuse to work with Morgan, you're through. The label's tired of the runaround. They're willing to shift a little more your way, but you've got to give them something they can work with." Tripp swirled the amber liquid around in his glass. "It's up to you."

"Let me make sure I'm hearing you right. Either I let Morgan write all the songs for my new album or I'm out? Just like that?" His throat constricted at the thought of his career coming to an abrupt end.

"Not all the songs, Knox. The two of you can collaborate. Work as a team. She's already agreed to give you top billing."

"How long has this been in the works?" If he had to bet

on it, Knox would wager Tripp had been planning this coup for quite a while.

Tripp avoided eye contact. "Are you in or out? That's the only thing that matters at this point."

"How long do I have to decide?"

"I've got a room booked at a hotel on the mainland. Flight takes off at eleven tomorrow morning. I'll need you to let me know by nine if Morgan should stay here, if you'll be returning with us, or if you'll be staying here alone."

There was so much more Knox wanted to say, but really, what was the point? It all boiled down to that decision. Did he want to stick with the label and let them continue to dictate the music he played, or did he want to strike out on his own?

"Did you hear me?" Tripp got to his feet. "Nine o'clock tomorrow. Got it?"

Knox waved a hand. "I heard you loud and clear."

"Morgan's a fantastic songwriter. I think the two of you could work very well together." Tripp put his hand on Knox's shoulder. "Another album or two their way. Three at the most. Your goals aren't nearly as far away as you think."

Easy for him to say. He wasn't the one selling out. "Thanks. You'll hear from me by nine."

Tripp left and Knox immediately got to his feet to look for Chick. He found him mixing drinks behind the outside bar. Chick poured a few shots for a couple on the opposite side of the bar, then headed his way.

"What happened here tonight?" He couldn't deal with Tripp's ultimatum until he knew Claudia was okay.

"You should have told her sooner," Chick said.

"I couldn't agree more. Do you have any idea where she would go?"

Chick lifted a scrawny shoulder. "The only family she has is her sister up in Minnesota. My guess is she went there."

Knox shook his head. She'd never go back to Minnesota, not without him. They'd already bought their tickets for next week. "I don't think she'd go back alone."

"She told you what happened to her up there?" Chick asked.

Knox nodded.

"I might have her sister's number listed somewhere in one of my files. You want me to try to find it?"

"It can't hurt. Maybe she's checked in. At least then I'd know she's safe."

Chick called one of the part-time bartenders over to take his spot, then motioned for Knox to follow him to his office. "It's time like these I wish I'd listened to Claudia and let her come up with a better filing system."

Knox tried to stay calm while he climbed the stairs. "We'll find it."

"It's here somewhere." Chick pushed open the door and Knox's gaze drifted over the cardboard boxes stacked high against the wall.

"Let me guess, it's on a piece of paper in one of those boxes?" Knox clenched his jaw. He didn't have time for this, not with Claudia hurting somewhere out there.

"Come on, son. It can't be any harder than finding a needle in a haystack." Chick grabbed a box from the top of the stack and set it on the ground between them.

With the hope of getting to Claudia before she shut him out completely, Knox sat down and pulled off the lid.

Claudia

"What should I tell him?" Andrea held her hand over her phone and looked up as Claudia entered the bedroom.

It had only been ten minutes since she'd left her sister to

head downstairs, but it felt like hours had passed. Rubbing the sleep out of her eyes, Claudia glanced at her brother-in-law. He'd been the one to trek downstairs and let her know Knox was on the phone.

"Tell him I don't want to talk right now."

Andrea relayed the message, then said something Claudia couldn't hear before disconnecting the call.

"What did he say?" Just because she didn't want to talk to him didn't mean that she didn't want to know what he wanted to say.

"He said he needs to clear things up."

"I bet he does. How did he even get your number?" As mad as she was at Knox, a tiny piece of her heart lit up when her sister said he was on the phone. He might not have cared enough to tell her the truth, but at least he wanted to make sure she was safe.

"He apologized for that and said Chick gave it to him. For what it's worth, he sounded really sorry." Andrea shrugged.

Claudia tightened her grip on the doorframe. "It's pretty ballsy of him to call a stranger this late at night."

"Not if he's checking on someone he really cares about," Andrea countered.

"Why do I keep getting the feeling you're on his side?" Jaw clenched, Claudia glared at her sister.

"I'm not on a side. Clearly, the two of you need to communicate. It doesn't have to be tonight. In fact, it's probably better if it's not. Give yourself some time to cool off and see how you feel tomorrow."

A quick twist of guilt cut Claudia's midsection in two. "Thank you so much for letting me crash here. I really appreciate you. I'm supposed to be the one helping you, but you always seem to find a way to turn it around and take care of me instead."

"It's not like I'm keeping score."

Claudia moved toward the bed to give her sister another hug. "I love you."

"Love you, too. Now rest up. The kids are still on spring break, so you're going to have your hands full tomorrow."

Even though her heart had split into shards, Claudia managed a smile. She couldn't wait to cuddle her niece and nephew. It had been too long since she'd been home. She'd forgotten what it felt like to snuggle up under a down comforter. She'd forgotten what it felt like to be pulled into her big sister's arms. She'd forgotten what it meant to have a family. Her time in Paradise had provided a much needed break, but no one understood her like her sister did.

Maybe, just maybe, it was time to come home.

She woke to something wet pressing against her mouth. Cracking one eye open, she tried to remember where she was. Darkness engulfed the room. Her hand felt around for something on the bed that might trigger her memory. No ocean waves. No calling seagulls. It all came back to her in an instant. Knox's lies. The flight. Hugging her sister. The room in the basement.

"Open up, Aunt Claudia." Her nephew sat next to her on the bed, his legs pulled up tight. He held a plastic baby spoon to her mouth. Smelled like something sweet. Peaches or apricots, maybe.

She opened her mouth to say something, and he slid the spoon inside. Bleh. She didn't know whether to swallow or spit it out, so she tried to tuck it into her cheek and talk around the blob of goop instead. "Whaf waf thaf?"

Her nephew keeled over laughing. "You ate the baby food."

"There you are." Andrea swept into the room and grabbed her son off the bed. "I told you not to wake up Aunt Claudia."

"It's okay. I'm awake." She swallowed the goop and sat up. "What time is it?"

"Almost one."

"Oh my gosh." Claudia tossed the blankets off. "How did it get to be so late? And what are you doing downstairs? You're supposed to be in bed."

"You had a pretty long day yesterday. Go easy on yourself. I'm on limited bed rest, so I don't need you to baby me until Derek leaves on Sunday."

"Speaking of, put him down." Claudia pointed to her nephew. "You're not supposed to be doing any heavy lifting, right? Besides, I need to get even with him for feeding me baby food."

She took her nephew from her sister and flopped him down on the bed, her fingers already reaching to tickle him under the armpits.

"You know what happens to little boys who trick their aunt, don't you?" she teased.

"Tickles?" he asked.

"You got it." She bent over, aiming for his ticklish points. He squealed and kicked out, his four-year-old giggles taking the edge off of her broken heart.

"Knox called again," Andrea said. "Four times, maybe five? I think you need to talk to him. He probably won't give up until you do."

"I'm sorry. I'll call him back and tell him to leave you alone. You shouldn't have to put up with this on top of everything else you've got going on."

"Hey, you're what we've got going on. Whatever you need, just say so, okay?"

Claudia reluctantly nodded, not used to being on the receiving end of someone's caretaking.

"Here's the phone for whenever you're ready. I'm going to take this one upstairs for some quiet time." Andrea left the phone on the bed and tugged her son through the doorway behind her.

Claudia took a quick shower, made a fresh pot of coffee, and stared at the cordless phone she'd left sitting on the counter. She couldn't avoid him forever. The sooner she talked to him, the faster it would be over with. He'd lied to her. He didn't deserve a second chance. Nothing he could say would change her mind.

With a heaviness in her heart, she dialed his number. At the sound of his deep tone coming through on his voice mail message, she almost hung up. The beep sounded, and she sucked in a gulp of air.

"Hey, I know you've been trying to track me down. I don't think we have anything to say to each other. Please stop calling my sister's number." She paused, her pulse beating so loud in her ears that she was sure he could hear it through the phone. "Just leave me alone. Please."

Then she hung up. Whatever pieces of her heart hadn't already broken now shattered inside her chest.

30

Knox

The message Claudia left him cut to the bone. Despite her request to leave her alone, he'd called multiple times a day for the past week, even though her sister had stopped answering. He was tempted to buy a ticket and fly up to Minnesota to beg her to hear him out, but he hadn't had more than a few minutes to himself since she left Paradise Island.

He'd been unsure of what to do about Tripp's ultimatum and reached out to his mom for advice. After a long heart-to-heart, she told him he needed to think about the big picture and do what was best for him. He went back and forth so many times he made himself dizzy, but he finally decided to follow Tripp back to Austin and start working with Morgan on the songs for the album.

His heart wasn't in it, but he didn't want to leave the security of the label. They'd promised he could still have complete control over one of the singles. When he convinced Claudia to take him back, he wanted to be able to provide for her. That's the only reason he'd agreed to give working with Morgan a shot.

"You ready to dive back in?" Morgan asked. She set one

of those fizzy flavored waters she liked down on the table and resumed her spot on the sofa. They'd been working out of a suite Tripp had booked at a hotel in downtown Austin. Knox figured his manager wanted to keep him close so he had the ability to check on him multiple times a day and make sure he stayed on task.

"Yeah, let's do it." Knox checked his watch. Two more hours and they'd call it a day. He'd try to hold on that long, though he wasn't nearly as inspired without the sound of the ocean in the background. He even missed the sand that found its way into everything he owned. He'd just grabbed his guitar when his phone rang.

Chick's number popped up on the screen. "Do you mind if I take this real quick?"

Knox didn't wait for Morgan to shake her head before he reached for his phone and headed to the balcony so he could talk in privacy.

"Hey, Chick. Have you heard from Claudia?" His heart stopped while he waited for a reply.

"She'll be back on Monday. She's been staying with her sister while her brother-in-law is out of town."

Knox nodded. They were supposed to take that trip together. Hopefully she hadn't had too difficult of a time being back in Minnesota. He should have been with her for that. Just one more way he'd failed her.

"Is she okay?"

"I suppose she's as okay as she can be under the circumstances. She's pissed at me, too. Figures, since I knew the truth. I shouldn't have kept it from her for so long." Chick sighed into the phone. "That woman's been my right hand for so long, I'm not sure I know how to run the place without her."

"I need to talk to her. I'll come down." Knox tried to remember the schedule Tripp had given him. There had to be time in the next week or two that he could head down to Paradise for a night.

"You come down here and corner her, all you'll do is scare her away," Chick said.

"I need to tell her how sorry I am. Damn, I can't help but think if I'd been up front with her earlier, none of this would have happened."

"No use crying over spilled beer," Chick said. "You want to get her attention, you'll need to do something she doesn't expect. If she sees you coming, she's not going to stick around."

"You're right." He needed a big move. Something like what Decker had orchestrated. It's not like he had a yacht at his disposal, though. Then it hit him. "The concert for the lighthouse. I want to be on that stage."

"We already booked that act."

"Yeah, I know. I'm the one who made the arrangements." He hadn't wanted to tell Claudia the "friend" he knew in Nashville was himself, so he'd called in a favor and booked the opening act from when he'd been on the road. By the time the concert rolled around, he'd planned on her knowing the truth. "Don't tell Claudia I'm coming, okay?"

Pieces of a plan started to take shape. The lighthouse was important to her. Hell, it was important to both of them. If he showed up to play for the fundraiser, she'd at least have to interact with him. That was the best way to get her attention. Maybe even the only way.

"I won't tell her you're coming, but you're only going to get one shot at this. Better make it count."

"That's exactly what I plan to do." He hung up with Chick and found Morgan sitting on the overstuffed leather sectional where he'd left her.

"Ready to go?" she asked.

"I need to take the rest of the afternoon off."

She frowned. "Did you talk to Tripp about that? We've only got a few more days before we head into the studio."

"Tell you what. Write whatever you want. I'll sing it. You can take full credit on the lyrics. I need a couple of hours to work on something." He didn't mean to put Morgan in a tough spot, but he had to figure out a way to get to Claudia. Without her, nothing else mattered. She'd become his muse, his inspiration, his heart.

Morgan packed up her guitar. "I'll be in my room if you need me. I don't have any idea what's going on with you, Knox, but I hope you know what you're doing."

"For the first time in my life, I think I do." He shut the door to the suite behind her and moved back to the couch where he'd left his notebook and guitar. A song had started to take shape in his head right after he'd found out Claudia left. The need to finish it urged him to pick up his guitar.

He played a few chords, stopped to scribble something down in his notebook, then started over again. As the afternoon faded into early evening and then into the deepest, darkest part of the night, he lost track of time. He could try to tell her how he felt, but it was so much easier to do it in a song.

The clock on the living room wall showed it was just after three when he finally set down his guitar, convinced he'd done the best he could. Now all he needed to do was make sure he was standing on that stage with Claudia in the audience. She might not be willing to talk to him on the phone, but she wouldn't have a choice but to listen to him as he poured out his heart in front of thousands.

He just hoped it wasn't too late.

31

Claudia

She'd only been gone two weeks, but everything had changed. Claudia had been avoiding Chick since she got back to Paradise Island yesterday, but she knew it wouldn't be long before they'd need to have it out. When she'd called to let him know she was in Minnesota, he'd sounded hesitant to ask about her plans. She wasn't the kind of woman to leave a friend in a lurch, no matter how angry she was, so she told him she'd be back to finish up the bungalows and help him get through the spring break crowd. After that, she didn't know what she wanted to do.

A few weeks ago, her future looked clear. Knox had hinted at sticking around Paradise, and her business had been poised to take off. As she took clean glasses from the plastic rack and put them on the shelf under the bar, she couldn't help but wonder where she'd be this time next year.

There was no way she could stay on Paradise Island. Not knowing that Chick had lied to her. No way she was moving back to Minnesota, either. Seeing Andrea and the kids had been wonderful and Claudia promised she'd return once the baby was born, but the Twin Cities didn't feel like home anymore.

She picked up the empty plastic rack to carry it back to the kitchen, and Chick entered the bar. Her stomach clenched. The fundraising concert was happening that night, and she didn't have time to get into things with her boss right now.

"Claudia, darlin', we need to talk." Chick stopped in front of her, blocking her path to the kitchen.

"Do we have to do this now? I've got a to-do list half a mile long and all those people coming tonight . . ."

He took the rack and gestured to the closest table. "Yes, we need to do this now."

"Fine." Feeling like a little kid who was about to get grounded, she sank into the closest chair.

Chick set down the rack and clasped his hands in front of him. "I'm sorry I didn't tell you about Knox. I figured it wasn't my tale to tell."

"Maybe not, but you could have said something. I feel like a fool for walking around with no idea the man I was . . . with no idea of who he was." Her cheeks flamed with embarrassment.

"How were you supposed to know? You shut yourself away from the outside world. When's the last time you watched TV or listened to the news?"

She lifted her head and met his gaze. "You should have told me."

"Maybe so." Chick leaned back and scrubbed a hand over the scruff on his chin. "Would it have changed anything?"

"Of course it would have changed things."

"How?"

"I would have avoided him. The last thing I needed was to have some famous singer holing up here and drawing attention to the bar."

"Exactly." One of his bushy gray brows lifted. "If you

knew, odds were someone else would find out, too. Knox came here looking for the same thing you did. Privacy. A chance to catch his breath and take a break."

Her back straightened. "You think I would have told someone he was here?"

"No, but word travels. When he asked if he could come down here, he insisted I keep his real identity a secret. The man's been dealing with a lot of crap. I figured the least I could do was give him a chance to get his head on straight again without a ton of people following his every move."

Claudia didn't want to give Knox the benefit of the doubt, but Chick's words made sense.

"His request sounded a lot like what someone else asked me a few years before that." Chick held her gaze, making sure she caught on to the meaning behind his words.

"I'd received death threats. I don't see how you can compare letting me hide out here to him covering up his entire identity." She crossed her arms over her chest. He wouldn't make her feel guilty about this. No way, no how.

"I'm just saying, we don't always know the reason behind why someone does the things they do. Maybe you should hear him out." Chick matched his body language to hers.

She didn't have time to think about it today. Maybe tomorrow, after the concert was over, she'd let herself revisit her time with Knox. At the moment, it was still too painful. If she opened the lid on that treasure chest of memories, she'd lose herself.

"Is that all you wanted to talk about?" she asked.

"Damn, you remind me of my second wife. So smart and so stubborn that she couldn't help but get in her own way." Chick put his palm on the table as he got to his feet. "You don't have to be so goddamn independent. You've got a man who loves you out there trying to set things right. The least you could do is give him a chance to explain."

A wave of emotion swelled in her chest, but she wouldn't give in. Chick didn't know what he was talking about. Loving someone meant telling the truth, even when it was hard. Knox had had plenty of time to set things straight and had instead opted to keep lying every chance he got.

"I need to get with Gabe and make sure the stage is ready to go for tonight." Jaw clenched, she waited for him to respond.

"Thanks for coming back. I wouldn't be able to get through the next few weeks without you." Chick set a gnarled hand on her shoulder.

Her heart dipped. He might be a grizzled old cowboy with misplaced priorities, but he'd become the family she didn't have here on the island.

She shrugged off his hand and wrapped her arms around him instead. "We're good. I know you were just doing what you thought was best. Don't push me, though, okay?"

·   He held her tight against his chest for a long moment. "Thanks for coming back."

"Thanks for picking up the slack on the concert. Have you seen the band yet? What time did they say they'd be here?" She let go, happy that she and Chick had made peace.

"You just worry about the food and beverage stuff. I've got the performers taken care of." Chick pulled out his phone. "Looks like they ought to be here in the next hour or so."

Claudia felt bad that Chick had been forced to take over the concert plans since she'd bailed to head to Minnesota. At least Knox had come through on booking his friend's band. They'd already raised a bundle in advance VIP ticket sales and a few other businesses on the island had volunteered to donate a percentage of their weekend sales to the cause.

"I'm going to check some people into the bungalows, then will be back to get the staff assigned for tonight." She picked up the crate and carried it back to the kitchen, grabbing the keys to the two bungalows that were ready for guests. Chick had hired Antonio to wrap up the work on two of the bigger bungalows, in hopes they'd be able to have them ready for spring break.

Claudia walked the path from the bar to the bungalows, the keys jangling in her hands. She hadn't had the heart to clean out the studio where Knox had stayed while he'd been on Paradise. He might have let her down in all the ways that mattered, but she couldn't turn off her feelings so easily.

Once they got through tonight, she'd have a chance to pull herself together and figure out where she wanted to go next.

Knox

Knox stood in the wings while on the stage Gabe sang his heart out to one of Knox's old songs. His chest swelled with pride. The kid was going to make it big someday, and Knox would make sure no one tried to take advantage of him or force him into a position where he didn't have a say in his own future.

The crowd roared as Gabe held on to the last note a few seconds longer than should have been humanly possible. The music ended, applause thundered, and Gabe took an awkward bow.

"That was fantastic." Knox clapped the kid on the back when he arrived backstage. "You killed it out there."

"You really think so?" Gabe asked. He was the only one who hadn't wanted to strangle Knox when he found out his real identity.

"I know so. Find me later on. I want to introduce you to a couple of the guys in the band, okay?" Knox slipped the strap of his guitar over his head.

"Thank you, Mr. Shepler," Gabe said.

"It's Knox. Got it?"

Gabe nodded, his smile so bright it rivaled the spotlights the crew had set up on the stage. Knox grinned back as Gabe's family swarmed him, surrounding him with hugs and congratulations.

"Showtime." Chick came toward him, giving the growing crowd of people around Gabe a wide berth. "You ready for this?"

Knox had played sold out stadiums and arenas across the world, but he'd never been as nervous as he was tonight. His performance on this stage would determine his future. If Claudia could forgive him, he planned on using the second chance she'd give him to make her the happiest woman on earth. If she still wouldn't talk to him, hell, he didn't know what he'd do.

Chick went out onto the stage and waited for the crowd to settle before he spoke into the mic. "This next performer wasn't listed on the program, but I don't think y'all will mind listening to him play one of his new songs. This one's not even out on the radio yet. He'll be debuting it right here on this stage. Please put your hands together and give a big welcome to Knox Shepler."

Knox swallowed, feeling like he was trying to choke down a prickly pear cactus instead of getting ready to sing. He stepped up to the mic, the baseball cap he'd worn during his time on Paradise replaced by his favorite cowboy hat.

"Hey, y'all. Thanks for letting me crash the party. How about another hand for Gabe Gonzalez? You heard him here first. Keep an eye on that kid. He's going places."

The crowd clapped and a few high-pitched whistles sounded.

Knox strummed his guitar. Not the fancy blinged-out one Tripp had arranged for him to take on tour, but the one he'd started on. The one his dad had given to him before their relationship had gone to shit. He kept it low and soft so he could talk over the music.

"Most of y'all probably don't know this, but I spent some time on the island recently while working on the songs for my next album. There's a lot to love about this little slice of paradise." He searched the crowd, looking for the one person he hoped would be in the crowd. "While I was here, I did some tourist stuff. I visited the lighthouse we're all here to support. Got stranded overnight in the bay when I ran over a fishing net."

Soft laughter rumbled through the crowd.

"I did something else, too." He strummed a few more chords while desperately looking for Claudia. Chick said he'd make sure she was watching. All Knox could do was give it his best shot and hope she'd hear him.

Leaning toward the mic, he spotted her at the back. His heart jumped into his throat and he almost lost his grip on his guitar. Focusing on Claudia—the only person in the sea of faces that mattered—he touched his lips to the microphone. "I also fell in love."

She was too far away for him to get a read on her expression, but he caught the way she wrapped her arms around her middle. Afraid she'd leave before she heard him out, he continued.

"Things were amazing for a little while, but then I messed up. I wrote this song for the woman who stole my heart, in hopes that she'll forgive me and let me spend the rest of our lives trying to make it up to her."

He stepped back and started to play the song he'd written just a few days before.

You're the whisper in my ear while I'm walking on the sand.
You're the tow rope I get tossed when I need a helping hand.

His voice became stronger as the words poured out of him.

> *You're the smile on my lips and the sunshine on my face,*
> *You're the angel sent to save me from this never-ending race.*

She still stood at the back, but her arms had fallen to her sides. He kept going, sharing his feelings through the lyrics of the song he'd written just for her.

> *You're the light I want beside me when the nights are*
> *dark and long.*
> *You're the answer that I need every time I get things wrong.*

Knox held her gaze as he sang the next two lines, hoping it was enough.

> *You're the owner of my heart and the reason I can sing.*
> *You're the only one that matters. You're my*
> *beautiful everything.*

The last notes faded away, and a thick silence fell over the crowd. Knox stood there, his gaze locked on the woman he loved, willing her to come toward the stage. Someone clapped, breaking the quietness. The crowd erupted in applause. Hoots, hollers, and loud whistles sounded around him.

Chick appeared next to Claudia. He seemed to be nudging her toward the stage, but she sidestepped him and disappeared into the bar. Knox's lungs squeezed, making it almost impossible to breathe. While the crowd continued to show their appreciation, he leaned toward the mic.

"Thanks for your support. Y'all enjoy the rest of the show." Then he left the stage. He'd done what he could, but it looked like it wasn't enough.

32

❧

Claudia

Seeing Knox onstage had sent her into a tailspin. She couldn't believe he'd written her a song and then performed it in front of thousands of people. The man sure knew how to orchestrate a grand apology. She'd been avoiding his calls because it would have been too hard to hear his voice. Too painful to listen to him try to justify his actions, especially since he knew the lies in her past had nearly destroyed her.

But Chick was right. Knox deserved the chance to explain himself. Rather than fight the crowd to try to reach the backstage area, she sent a message through Gabe, asking Knox to meet her at her bungalow after the concert was over. She still had a few hours of work to do and couldn't afford to let herself get distracted.

She mixed drinks, kept tabs on employees, and shuttled cash back to the safe in Chick's office for the next several hours. Even though she kept moving, her mind was preoccupied with what she wanted to say to Knox. By the time she shut down the bar, she still didn't have any idea how to start the conversation or what kind of outcome she expected. She just wished they could go back to how it had been between them.

Every muscle in her body ached as she walked to her bungalow. Maybe she should have asked Knox to meet her for coffee in the morning instead. She wasn't sure she had the mental or emotional capacity to handle the conversation that needed to take place between them.

She opened the door to her bungalow and sucked in a breath. White votive candles covered every surface. There had to be thousands of them. The flames flickered, casting a soft, romantic glow around the room.

Knox stood as she entered. "Hey, I hope you don't mind, but Chick let me in. I figured you'd be exhausted after a day like today. There's a warm bath waiting for you with a glass of wine on the edge of the tub, if you want it."

"You did this?" Obviously he had, but her brain had stopped firing a couple of hours ago.

He shrugged. "I wanted to do something nice for you. We don't have to talk tonight. Chick's letting me stay over in my old bungalow, so I'll be here tomorrow if you want to wait until then."

"It already is tomorrow." Claudia glanced at the clock on the wall where the small hand edged closer and closer to the three. She'd been up for almost twenty-four hours.

"I know it might not matter anymore, but I'm sorry, Claudia." His shoulders slumped forward and a deep wrinkle bisected his brows. "You don't know how many times I tried to tell you the truth."

She didn't want to get into it now, but she also didn't want to get into it later. If she could avoid the entire conversation, she would pick that option. But it had to be done.

"Where's that wine?" She slipped off her shoes and headed toward the living room.

"I'll get it." Knox passed her and returned with a glass of red wine.

She settled into the corner of the couch and tucked her feet up underneath her. "You may as well pour yourself a glass and sit down."

"If you want to wait—"

"Wait for what? Let's talk." She'd rather walk barefoot over broken shells than talk to him, but she wouldn't be able to sleep knowing he was so close by when there was still so much unsaid between them.

Knox sat in the chair perpendicular to the couch, close enough that she could reach out and touch him if she wanted to. Seeing him tonight had brought back so many emotions and so many memories. He looked good. Too good. He'd trimmed his beard and had his hair cut. The tight Cowboy in Paradise T-shirt he had on clung to his chest, and she ached to snuggle against him and bury her head in the crook of his neck.

But he'd lied.

"I'm sorry, Claudia. When I came to Paradise Island, all I wanted was a chance to catch my breath. My manager was on my case, the record label was giving me ultimatums . . . I needed a place to pull myself together and see if I could find my way back to the music deep inside." He looked up at her, his eyes full of pain. "I had a couple months to write the songs I needed before we went into the studio. Chick let me work on the bungalows in exchange for a place to stay, and—"

"Why here? You could have gone anywhere: rented out a private island, holed up in some remote resort, or even bought your own hotel somewhere. Why did you have to come here?" She didn't mean to sound so accusing, but it was his fault her life had been tossed upside down. If he'd gone somewhere else, maybe she wouldn't feel so awful right now.

"When I was in high school and college, I worked construction in the summers. Keeping my hands busy freed my mind, and I wrote most of the songs I've recorded up until now during that time. I thought if I could do something similar, I might reconnect with my muse."

She took a sip of her wine and set it on the table. Hearing the heartache in his voice chipped away at her anger. Still, he could have told her the truth. "I get why you didn't want anyone to know who you were at first, but why did you keep it up? Why did you keep it from me?"

"I didn't reconnect with my muse." He leaned forward, resting his arms on his thighs. "I found a new one. Being around you, seeing the island through your eyes, you opened up that part of my heart I'd had on lockdown. I was about to tell you, then we went to the lighthouse."

Her heart skipped a few beats as she remembered that first time they made love. She'd been so happy then.

"You told me what happened to you in Minneapolis. By that time, I was already falling in love with you." He looked up at her, his eyes full of truth. "I knew you'd never want to be with me if I told you who I was and what I do for a living. It was selfish of me, but I didn't want things between us to end."

Her fingers itched to smooth over his beard and tell him she wouldn't have run away, but that would have made her a liar as well.

He sat up straight and sighed. "After we'd been together, hell, I didn't want to give that up. I kept looking for a way to tell you the truth. Then you asked me to go to Minnesota with you. I was so damn proud of you for being so strong. You were ready to face your fears, and the last thing I wanted to do was pull you back. I was so stupid."

Claudia couldn't stand to hear him be so hard on himself. "You weren't stupid. You were scared."

His eyes met hers. "Terrified. I didn't want to lose you."

Maybe it was the long day she'd had or the two sips of wine, but something loosened inside her chest. She'd been terrified, too. "I think when I found out you'd lied to me about who you were, I was almost relieved."

"What?" He put his hand on the armrest of the couch, just a few inches from hers. "Why would you feel like that?"

"Because things between us seemed too good to be true." Admitting it felt like she'd just opened up the dam holding back all of her emotions. Tears pooled in her eyes and started to stream down her cheeks.

"Oh, baby. Come here." Knox moved to the cushion next to her and gently tugged her into his arms.

She let him hold her while the tears fell and soaked through the front of his shirt. Not being able to keep control of her emotions wasn't just embarrassing; it pissed her off. She hadn't felt this out of control since . . . since never.

Knox kept one arm around her while he reached for the box of tissues. "Hey, don't cry. I can't stand to see you hurt."

She took the tissue he handed her and wiped at her eyes. "Sorry."

"You've got nothing to be sorry about. I'm the one who let you down. If I could go back and change the way I handled everything, I would." He smoothed his hand over her hair. "You deserve to be loved in a way that seems too good to be true. I want to be the man to love you like that, Claudia. Will you let me?"

She gulped in a deep breath. "The only thing I can think of that would be scarier than saying yes to you right now would be to say no. I understand why you lied, but that can't ever happen again."

"It won't." He tightened his arm around her and pressed a kiss to her forehead. "I promise there won't ever be another lie between us."

Hope filled her heart at the possibility of being with Knox again. She could forgive him for keeping his identity a secret. Though her reasons were different, she'd wanted to hide and forget who she was when she first moved to Paradise, too.

"Does that mean you'll give me a second chance?" he asked.

"I don't know." There was one more major issue now that she knew he was a famous country western superstar. An issue so big that she couldn't see a way around it. "I'm not sure I can survive being with someone who lives in the public eye again. What if we get in a fight and your fans start trolling me?"

Knox shifted, pulling back enough so he could make eye contact. "If anyone hurts you for any reason, they'll have to answer to me. You might have called me by a different name, but you know my heart. I'm the man you fell in love with, and I would never put you in that kind of position. No matter what. You can call the shots on whether you want to claim me in public or keep things just between us."

She wanted to believe him, was desperate to be able to put her trust in someone again.

"I don't know how to prove it to you, but I'm willing to give it all up for you, Claudia. Nothing means anything without you by my side. I'm scared to trust again, too, sweetheart, but I believe we've found something with each other that's worth fighting for."

Tears started again. She was surprised she had any left. He was right, though. They'd both been hurt in the past. He was putting just as much faith in her as she would be in him. They both had a lot to lose, but they had everything to gain.

"Can we live somewhere out in the country, far away from everyone?" she asked.

"We can live anywhere you want. Hell, I'll see if Chick will sell me your bungalow if you want to stay on Paradise Island."

"Okay."

"You mean it? You want to give things between us a shot for real?"

Her heart gave a final lurch as she nodded. It wouldn't be easy to squash her fears, but Knox was right. She knew his heart. There wasn't a mean bone in his body. She'd never known such certainty about anyone or anything before. If she didn't take a chance with him, she'd never be able to live with herself.

"Yes. Let's do it. I was miserable without you."

"Baby, you've got me. However you want me, for as long as you'll have me. I'm yours."

"At the risk of being super cheesy, can I tell you something?"

"Of course."

"That song you wrote for me . . . I could have written the same words about you, Knox Shepler."

She would have said more, but he cut off her words with a kiss. A kiss that led to more kisses. More kisses that led to him shedding the shirt she'd dampened with her tears.

Claudia didn't need to say anything more after that. She showed him with her heart, soul, and body just how much he meant to her.

He was her beautiful everything, too.

Epilogue

~ ♡ ~

Knox

Knox stood at the front of the small group of family and friends as Claudia held up the giant pair of fake scissors. He couldn't be any prouder of the woman he loved. It had been six months since they moved from Paradise Island to their ranch outside of Austin, and Claudia was already opening her own interior design business.

"Get up here with me." She motioned for him to join her. "You're just as much a part of this as I am."

She didn't like being in the spotlight, especially by herself, so he tucked his phone into his pocket and ducked underneath the thick ribbon to stand by her side.

"Thank you," she whispered.

"Whatever you need, baby. I'm your guy." He wrapped his arm around her waist as she sliced through the ribbon.

The photographer from the local paper snapped a few pictures, then Claudia invited everyone inside for the small grand opening reception she'd planned with the help of Justin's sister, Jenny.

Knox couldn't believe what Claudia had done with the space. When they'd wandered through less than a month ago, it had been one giant room. She'd divided it into an area where she could meet with clients and a bigger section where she could display different vignettes and the decor and furniture she'd use for staging.

"Congratulations, Claudia." His mom reached out and pulled her into a hug. Knox had known they'd get along, but he hadn't predicted how much they'd actually like each other.

Claudia hugged back. "Thank you. It means so much that you're here."

"I wouldn't miss it." His mom shot him a knowing glance. "I'll let the two of you get back to greeting your guests."

"I hope we'll have time to chat when the party winds down," Claudia said.

"Don't worry, I'll stick around to the end." She nodded toward the back of the space. "I'm going to go see if they need any more ice. Have fun, you two."

Claudia turned toward him. "I sure do like your mom."

"Good, she likes you, too. Probably even more than she likes me." He was only half joking. Still, it made his heart so happy to see the two women he cared about most enjoy spending time together.

A reporter from one of the local design magazines stopped next to Claudia to see if she'd be willing to answer a few questions.

"I'm going to go say hi to Decker. I'll be back in a few minutes." He kissed her cheek and headed toward his friend.

"Hey, sorry I'm late. There was traffic heading into the city." Decker reached out to shake his hand.

"I'm just glad you could make it. Where's Cherice?" Knox asked. Decker and his fiancée had been inseparable since they got engaged. She had to be close by.

Decker glanced toward the back of the room. "Is that a bar back there?"

Knox's stomach clenched. "What happened?"

"She broke it off. The wedding's in six weeks, and she fucking broke it off." Decker tried to smile, but it didn't reach his eyes. "She's moving in with a guy twice her age who owns a chain of hotels. What the hell's wrong with me?"

"Nothing, man." Knox had had his suspicions about Cherice from the start. She hadn't struck him as someone who was with his friend for the right reasons.

"There you are." Justin met them by the bar, with Emmeline by his side. "This place looks great. Jenny told me it was special. Now that we've seen it in person, I can understand why."

Em hugged Decker first. "Hey, it's so good to see you. Where's Cherice?"

"She had a family thing she couldn't get out of." Decker glanced toward Knox and shook his head slightly.

"And you"—Em wrapped her arms around Knox next—"you've been back for months and we've barely seen you and Claudia."

Knox squeezed her tight. He'd missed getting together with the three of them, but there had been so much to do between reimagining his career and getting settled, he hadn't had much free time. "Sorry about that. Now that things have slowed down a little, we should have a lot more availability."

"Slowed down?" Claudia came up behind him. "Did he tell you he's heading out on tour for the new album after the first of the year?"

Knox let go of Em and draped his arm over Claudia's shoulder. "It's not a big tour."

"Not yet," she said. "But if the fans show up, and we know they will, you're going to have to add more dates."

Knox pulled her closer. She'd been the one who'd convinced him to stop selling out and hiding behind the label and to follow his own dreams. Tripp had been pissed, but Knox had to be true to himself and the music he wanted to play Within a few weeks of reaching an agreement with the label, Knox had hired a manager who encouraged him to find his own sound and cut a new album full of songs he could be proud of. Songs inspired by the woman next to him.

"Sounds like y'all have it all figured out." Justin tipped the brim of his cowboy hat toward Knox and Claudia. "Em and I are real happy for you."

"Thanks. We're pretty damn happy for us, too." Knox pressed a kiss to Claudia's temple. He couldn't remember a time when his heart had been so full. The woman he loved stood by his side. He was surrounded by his closest friends and his mom, and he still had one more surprise to share that would ensure this day went down in history as one of the happiest in the life they were building together.

Jenny signaled to him from halfway across the room

"Can y'all excuse me for a minute? I need to take care of something." He left the four of them standing near the back of the space and met Jenny by the front door.

"They should be pulling up any minute," Jenny said. "I just got an alert from the driver. It's too bad we couldn't have held off on the ribbon cutting."

"It's okay. Decker said traffic was bad. I'm just happy we were able to keep it a surprise." With the move, getting settled in their new place, and Claudia starting her business, they hadn't had the chance to get up to Minnesota to meet her new nephew. Knowing how important her relationship with her sister was, Knox had made arrangements for Andrea and her family to come to Texas for a few days. It had been hell trying to keep it from Claudia, but he couldn't wait to see the look on her face when she saw them.

"I think this is them." Jenny nodded at a black SUV that stopped at the curb. "I'll go greet them. Do you want to get Claudia to come out front?"

"I'm on it." Knox headed to the back of the room and

slipped his arm around Claudia's waist. "Can I borrow you for a minute?"

"We'll be right back." She turned toward him. "Is everything okay?"

"Everything's fine. There's a delivery for you up front that you need to see for yourself." He caught his mom's eye and nudged his chin toward the front. She knew what he had planned and he wanted her to be a part of it.

"A delivery from who?" Claudia's brow furrowed.

"You'll see." He put his hand on the small of her back and guided her through the crowd. They stepped through the front door onto the sidewalk and she spun around to grab his arm.

"What did you do?" Her eyes went wide, and she didn't wait for an answer before she pulled a woman who could have been her twin into a tight hug.

Knox shook hands with Derek and introduced himself and his mom to the kids while the two women clung to each other.

"I can't believe you're here." Claudia finally pulled away from her sister. Her eyes shone with happy tears.

"Knox invited us. I'm sorry we missed the ribbon cutting. The highway was backed up, and—"

"But you're here!" Claudia hugged the kids and her brother-in-law, then kissed the baby's forehead and turned toward Knox. "I can't believe you pulled this off."

"Anything for you." His own heart expanded from seeing the happiness on her face. "There's just one more thing I need to do today."

"Besides help me open my business and surprise me with a visit from my family?" She let out a laugh. "Don't you think that's enough for one day?"

Knox got down on one knee. "One more tiny thing."

She covered her mouth with her hands. "What are you doing?"

"Claudia, I love you with everything I am. Will you let me spend the rest of my life with you? Marry me?"

Her hands shook as she reached for his. "Yes. Of course, yes."

He stood and pulled a ring box out of his pocket. "Your sister helped me with this."

A marquis-cut solitaire with smaller diamonds on the side was set into a platinum band.

"Some of the stones are from Mom's wedding ring," Andrea said.

Claudia looked up at him, her eyes as big as the sand dollars they'd picked up on Paradise Island. "How did you do all of this?"

"Love, baby." He slid the ring onto her finger.

"It's beautiful."

"Not as gorgeous as you."

She shook her head. "You're incredible. Do you know that?"

"You're incredibler." His nose wrinkled. Was that even a word? "More incredible? Hell, you know what I mean. Now come here and kiss me so we can go inside and I can tell everyone I somehow convinced the most amazing woman in the world to settle for a guy like me."

Claudia wrapped her arms around his neck and tilted her head. "Make me yours, cowboy."

He dipped her backward, then claimed her mouth with his. Making her his was exactly what he planned to do. For now, for always, and forever.

Acknowledgments

Putting a book together takes a whole team, and I'd be lost without mine! Thanks to my editors, Kristine Swartz and Mary Baker, and everyone else at Berkley for your efforts and support! And to Jessica Watterson, my agent, I wouldn't be able to do this without you!

To Mr. Crush, HoneyBee, GlitterBec, and BuzzleBee . . . you'll always be my why.

And huge thanks to YOU—whether you've read everything I've ever written or are taking a chance on one of my books for the very first time. Without readers, there would be no one to appreciate the books I write. Thank you for loving words as much as I do!

If you'd like to stay in touch, please sign up for my newsletter at www.dylanncrush.com/signup. Thank you!

Keep reading for an excerpt from the first book in
the Cowboys in Paradise series . . .

KISS ME NOW, COWBOY

Available now from Berkley Romance!

Justin

"Forzas aren't quitters."

Justin Forza took in a deep breath through his nose and met his dad's hard glare with a softer version of his own. "I know, Dad. You've drilled that into me my entire life. I'm not saying I want to quit. I just need a little more time for my shoulder to heal."

Grabbing hold of his right shoulder with his left hand, Justin rolled it forward. Pain radiated through the socket, but he didn't flinch.

His dad picked up a saddle from the tack room, and Justin followed him to the last stall in the barn. They didn't have time for this conversation. Not again, and especially not now. He was supposed to be on his way to pick up his best friend, Em. If they didn't hit the road soon, they'd never get to Dallas in time for the concert tonight.

"I've got to go get Emmeline. Can we table this for now?" Justin sighed, not looking forward to the inevitable continuation of the same conversation. Whether his dad picked it up again tomorrow or the next day, it was bound to happen. Monty Forza had never been accused of letting a sleeping dog lie, not even when it appeared to be as dead as the arguments the two of them had been flinging back and forth for weeks.

"The two of you going to that concert in Dallas tonight?" Monty's mood lightened at the mention of Emmeline's name. She had that effect on people. Em had a way of bringing out the best in folks, even someone as hardheaded and cold-hearted as his father.

"Yes, sir. Knox is playing, and Decker invited us to watch from his dad's suite." Justin had been friends with Knox and Decker since the three of them could ride a horse. Seeing as how they'd learned how to ride before they could even walk, Justin couldn't remember a time in his life without them.

"I can't believe a good woman like Emmeline's still available." Monty's eyes narrowed. "Won't be long before some good-looking, smart-talking cowboy scoops her up."

Justin gritted his teeth. He and Emmeline were friends. Had been since second grade, when she'd shown up at school with two long braids and a smile as wide and open as the Great Plains of Texas. She'd fit right in with the tight trio of him, Knox, and Decker. Over the years, the four of them had done just about everything together.

Then Emmeline started changing, and Justin couldn't help but take notice. Her lanky limbs gave way to curves that wouldn't quit. The hair she used to pull up and out of the way fell in soft waves around her shoulders. Green eyes, the color of the fields surrounding his family's ranch in the springtime, took on a new shine.

He wouldn't admit it to anyone, especially Emmeline Porter, but he'd fallen hard for her their junior year at Blewit High and had been pining for her ever since. Knox and Decker had figured it out, but his secret had been safe from Emmeline for the past twelve years.

"You need anything else before I head out?" Justin fingered the key to his F-350—the one luxury he'd allowed himself to indulge in with the winnings he'd earned over the years as a pro bull rider. The rest had gone into savings, waiting for a time when he could retire from the circuit and invest in a place of his own.

"Nah. Y'all have a good time tonight. We'll pick this conversation up again tomorrow. Just remember, the longer you wait to get back in the game, the harder it's going to be, son." Monty tossed the saddle over the back of his favorite ranch horse.

"I know." Justin let out a long exhale. He didn't want to sit out from the bull-riding circuit any longer than necessary. Securing the world championship was the only thing standing in the way of what he really wanted out of life . . . Emmeline.

This year should have been his. He'd started off the year in the top ten and, after winning a few events in February and March, had earned enough points to put him in the top five. Once he secured the title and the cash prize that went with it, he'd planned on announcing his retirement on the spot and finally telling Emmeline how he felt.

But things never seemed to go as planned. Instead of being the one to catch, he'd been bucked off a ranker bull on the last night of a three-day event in Nashville with half a second to go. He'd healed from his surgery and a severe concussion, but his shoulder still wasn't quite where he needed it to be.

His dad was right, though. If he didn't commit to an upcoming event, he'd lose out on the entire year and have to start over again in January. That would mean waiting at least another eighteen months to come clean with Emmeline. He had no idea if she felt the same, but he knew one thing . . . it wasn't worth the breath he'd waste telling her how he felt about her if he still planned on riding bulls.

She'd made one thing perfectly clear over the years . . . she'd never date a rodeo cowboy.

The sooner he got back to riding, the sooner he could snag the title his dad expected, and the sooner he could finally admit his feelings.

He just hoped it wouldn't be too late.

Emmeline

"Here you go, Daddy." Emmeline held the fork out to her father. It had clattered to the table when one of his tremors started.

"Dammit." He closed his fingers around it. "Pretty soon I won't even be able to feed my damn self."

Emmeline swallowed hard. She hated seeing him struggle. "Some days are just more difficult than others."

He glanced at her across the solid oak table—the one he'd built with his own hands before he got injured—and frowned. "I don't know how y'all put up with me."

"It's because you're so lovable." She got up from her chair to kiss his cheek. "I've got to get ready to go. Justin's going to be here soon. You need anything else?"

A spasm ran through her dad, making his hand twitch again. "Nah. I'll be fine. Your mama will be home soon, anyway."

Emmeline put a hand on her dad's shoulder and squeezed. She'd volunteered to come sit with him while he ate dinner tonight since her mom had a garden club meeting. It's not that he couldn't be left alone, but dinnertime always proved to be extra frustrating, and sometimes his temper got the best of him.

"You want me to cut that up smaller for you?"

"I'm fine, baby girl. You go have a good time. Tell the boys I said hello and to come around and visit once in a while when they're in town, will you?"

"Will do." Wouldn't do any good to remind her dad "the boys" weren't boys anymore. That's how he'd always referred to them, ever since Em started hanging out with the trio of troublemakers in second grade. They were grown-ass men now, at least on the outside. Even though she hadn't seen Knox in a couple of years, and didn't spend much one-on-one time with Decker, she couldn't help but notice how much Justin had changed the last few times she'd seen him.

Em picked up her purse and slung the strap over her shoulder messenger bag–style. Before she had a chance to peek through the front window, the door leading to the garage opened, and Justin walked in.

"Speak of the devil." Her dad pushed back from the table.

"Don't get up on my account." Justin reached out to shake her dad's hand. "I didn't mean to interrupt your meal."

Emmeline's breath caught at the sight of him. He'd been gone more than he'd been home over the past several years, traveling from one rodeo to the next, and fitting in other events along the way. Justin had what her mama liked to call "presence" and he always seemed to fill a room with it, whether it was her mama and daddy's eat-in kitchen or a venue the size of Madison Square Garden. It wasn't something he did on purpose. Either a man had it or he didn't.

And Justin Forza had it in spades.

"You want to join me for a quick bite?" her dad offered. "Homemade chicken-fried steak, mashed potatoes, zucchini bread, and creamed corn. We can fix you up a plate right quick."

Justin rubbed a hand over his washboard abs. "That sounds wonderful, but we'd better get a move on if we're going to make it in time."

"Y'all have fun tonight." Her dad picked up his fork again. Emmeline held her breath, hoping he wouldn't drop it in front of Justin. Her daddy didn't like to appear weak, even though he had no control over the brain injury that had saddled him with challenges he'd face for the rest of his life.

"You ready, Em?" Justin turned toward her, the full force of his bright blue gaze hitting her smack-dab in the center of her chest.

"Yeah. You want a water bottle for the road?" It would take them about an hour and a half to make the drive from their tiny hometown of Blewit about ninety miles southeast of Dallas into the city—just a hop, skip, and a jump away when considering a place as big as Texas.

"Got one in the truck already. Mr. Porter, it was nice to see you, sir."

"Don't forget that bag of zucchini your mom set aside for him." Her dad nodded toward a plastic grocery bag of summer squash her mom had picked that afternoon.

Em handed the bag to Justin. "Don't even think about trying to leave it here."

His grin widened so much the dimple on his left cheek popped.

"Come back when you have more time, son. I want to hear all about how you're recovering. That was a wild ride you took back in March." Her dad lived for stories of Justin's time on the road, though Emmeline could do without them.

There was something crazy about a man who'd risk life and limb to seat himself on the back of a two-thousand-pound animal whose sole purpose in life was to buck him off as quickly as possible. She'd known enough bull riders in her life to reach that conclusion. Seeing how her dad's love for the sport had ruined his life, she'd never understand why a man would do that to himself once, let alone hundreds of times over the course of a career.

"Shoulder's doing okay and my concussion's better. I just need a little more time to heal, and I'll get back out there again." Justin shifted the bag from one hand to the other, and Em bit her tongue.

The last ride he'd taken almost killed him. If he were ever going to stop putting his life on the line, he would have done it then. She'd hoped the last concussion would change his mind about pursuing such a dangerous career. Their friend Decker had even mentioned the possibility of getting Justin a job with his dad's oil business.

But Justin wasn't a suit-and-tie kind of guy. He'd lived his whole life in jeans and a pair of well-worn cowboy boots. No matter how much Emmeline wished things would change, he'd never give up his chase for a world championship. How could he when his dad and brother reminded him of his failure to do just that about twenty times a day?

"See you later this week, Daddy." Emmeline pressed a kiss to her dad's temple. If Justin wanted to see what the future had in store for him, he ought to take a good, long, hard look at her father. His dogged pursuit of the perfect ride had almost ruined his marriage and nearly taken his life.

Justin held the door for her, and she brushed past him. He must have just showered, because she caught a whiff of the fresh, clean scent of that bar soap he loved. Some guys she knew dabbed on enough cologne or aftershave, it smelled like they'd gone swimming in it. Not Justin. He always smelled like soap, leather, and the great outdoors.

The late afternoon sun beat down on her as soon as they stepped outside, and she was grateful he'd left his truck running. He pulled open the passenger side door before she reached it. As she climbed into his truck, the blast of the air conditioner chased the heat away.

"You don't have to race around opening doors for me," she teased.

"And risk word getting back to my mom that I've lost my manners?" He shook his head, the smirk stretching across his lips telling her he wasn't taking her seriously. "No, thank you."

If his mama would give him a tongue-lashing for not opening a woman's door, no telling what she'd do if she found out about some of the stunts he, Decker, and Knox had pulled over the years. It wasn't Em's place to rat out her friends, especially when she'd tagged along with them most of the time.

Emmeline snapped her seatbelt into place while he walked around the front of the truck and climbed in the other side. Tonight would be the first time the four of them had been together in ages. She'd been looking forward to it for weeks. It wasn't every day a gal got to watch one of her friends sing his heart out in front of thousands of adoring fans. The last time she'd seen Knox play in person, it had been at a side stage at the Texas state fair. He'd come a long way since then and was now headlining his own shows.

"I was hoping to say hi to your mom. How's she been doing lately?" Justin asked.

"Good. She's at a garden club meeting. They're hoping to raise enough money to sand down the statue and put a fresh coat of paint on Queenie the giant zucchini this summer. I guess they're tired of everyone thinking she's a cucumber."

Justin pointed out the window as they passed the eyesore of a landmark that had been sitting on the edge of town for decades. "Have they considered tearing the damn thing down?"

"And take away Blewit's one claim to fame as the zucchini capital of the US?"

"I suppose it's better to have people think they're coming to visit the world's largest cucumber than to not have anyone come visit at all."

Em wasn't sure she agreed with that, but her mom had to have something to focus on besides taking care of her dad. Time for a change of subject.

"Are you excited to see Knox perform?" She twisted to

face Justin, studying him through the dark shades she'd slid over her eyes. They hadn't spent too much time together since he got injured. He'd been in a lot of pain since then, a shell of the guy whose smile used to make her light up inside like the Fourth of July.

"Hell, yeah. It's been too long since we've all been together." His fingers drummed along with the beat of the song on the radio. "How was the last day of kindergarten this year?"

She settled her hands over her belly, trying to tamp down the mixture of relief and regret that always hit her hard on the last day of school. "Good. I got four bouquets of dandelions, three loaves of zucchini bread, and two proposals."

"Two proposals? Anyone I need to check out for you?"

His faux concern made her laugh. "Not unless you're in the habit of shaking up five-year-olds."

"I don't remember ever having a crush on a teacher. Even if I did, I never would have had the balls to make a move." Justin fiddled with the radio dial. "Kids these days have got some big cojones."

"I even got a ring." She held her left hand out, showing off the bread tie one of her students had presented her with that afternoon.

"Let me see that." Justin reached for her hand and held it up, his gaze bouncing back and forth from the road to studying the paper-wrapped wire. "Man, he really went all out, didn't he?"

Emmeline pulled her hand back with a laugh. "I don't think he had a very big budget to start with."

"The kid's definitely got big balls. To propose with a ring like that . . ."

"It's not about the ring, it's about the intention behind it, right? He's a sweet kid. I'm going to miss him next year." The end of the school year was always bittersweet. She started off every August with an unruly passel of kids and by the time June rolled around, not only had they learned how to read, they'd also learned how to treat each other with kindness and respect. At least most of them.

"Don't go getting all sappy on me, Em. I know how you get when you have to say goodbye. It's not like they're going far, though. Just a few classrooms over to first grade." Justin shot her a knowing grin. "Cheer up. Tonight's about letting loose and having a good time, right?"

"Who says I'm not going to have a good time?" she challenged. "My summer vacation starts tonight. I'm not the one who has to get up early tomorrow morning for a workout with my personal trainer."

"Good point. Maybe I should have rescheduled."

Emmeline reached over to snag his cowboy hat off his head, then settled it on her own. "That just means that you'll have to keep it low-key and keep track of the rest of us tonight."

"Seeing as how Knox has an entire management team to keep tabs on him, and Decker's bringing his new girlfriend, I guess that means you'll have my full attention."

Emmeline smiled in response, as a hint of something she didn't recognize fluttered against the walls of her belly. She was just excited. It had been a while since she'd spent an evening out with the guys. Had been too long since she'd spent much time with anyone over three feet tall. Nothing to get too worked up over. Justin was right. Tonight was about cutting loose and having fun, and all of them could use a night like that.

Ready to find
your next great read?

Let us help.

Visit prh.com/nextread